FEB 2014

CH

By C. L. Parker

A Million Guilty Pleasures
A Million Dirty Secrets

a million guilty pleasures

a million

guilty pleasures

million dollar duet

c. l. parker

Bantam Books
Trade Paperbacks
New York

A Bantam Books Trade Paperback Original

Copyright © 2014 by C. L. Parker

Published in the United States by Bantam Books,
an imprint of Random House,
a division of Random House LLC, a Penguin Random
House Company, New York.

BANTAM BOOKS and the HOUSE colophon are registered
trademarks of Random House LLC.

Library of Congress Cataloging-in-Publication Data
Parker, C. L.
A million guilty pleasures: million dollar duet/
C. L. Parker.
    pages cm
ISBN 978-0-345-54878-8
eBook ISBN 978-0-345-54879-5
1. Prostitution—Fiction.   I. Title.
  PS3616.A74424M55 2014
  813'.6—dc23
  2013020133

Printed in the United States of America on acid-free
paper

www.bantamdell.com

9 8 7 6 5 4 3 2 1

Book design by Elizabeth A. D. Eno

This book is dedicated to my baby sister, Brittnie Day, who possesses an extraordinary talent of her own. Some days, I think she forgets that. Britt, it's impossible to be in anybody's shadow when you're casting a light of your own. The world is yours. All you have to do is take it by storm.

a million guilty pleasures

I am a man who paid for sex. Not that I needed to, mind you, but it was the only way to be sure I wouldn't get fucked. Well, getting fucked was kind of the point, just not the one I was trying to make. Bottom line: I paid an insane amount of money, two million dollars to be exact, to own a woman for two years. She was a virgin, and well worth the trade, but then I did the unthinkable.

I fell in love with her.

To make matters worse, I found out the truth behind why she put her body up for sale in the first place. She did it to save a life. I had purchased her to get laid. Clearly, I was the ass in the equation, but I was going to make it up to her or die trying.

My name is Noah Crawford, and this is the continuation of my story.

1

jinx

Noah

Walking away from Delaine Talbot was the hardest thing I'd ever had to do in my life. And that was saying a lot considering I'd been responsible for the death of my parents and had subsequently inherited a multibillion-dollar corporation, Scarlet Lotus, which I ran alongside my mortal enemy, David Stone.

David had once been my best friend until I'd come home from a business trip to find him fucking my girl, Julie, in my bathtub. Needless to say, Julie was no longer my girl. A pariah, yes, but my girl, no. All of those events had inadvertently led me to Lanie. I still wasn't sure if I should be bitter or happy about that fact.

I'd heard about an underground organization that procured women to auction off to the highest bidder. It was all very illegal, of course, as human trafficking—voluntary or not—should be. However, these women agreed to become the property of the winner in whatever manner they required. I might not have trusted women after the Julie/David debacle, but I was a man, and I had needs like every other man. So when I'd heard about the auction, it seemed the best route to take.

Scott Christopher was the proprietor of Foreplay, a club that on its face catered to the shenanigans of college students, while hosting the auction underground. I didn't like Christopher in the least, but I hadn't gone there to make friends. I'd had a single purpose in mind, and I'd always gotten what I wanted.

Delaine Talbot was a twenty-four-year-old virgin. Unsullied, untamed. Perfect. The two million dollars I paid to own her for two years was a very fine investment indeed. Two years for me to have my wicked way with her whenever and however I wanted. And I did. Although I hadn't expected her to have zero experience with sex, I was pleased that I was the one who got to teach her. She was a star pupil, accelerating in her lessons to the point that I thought she might actually be the death of me. An added bonus, she came equipped with an attitude. You'd think that would be a turnoff. Quite the opposite, it had only made my cock even harder for her.

We went round and round, butted heads like nobody's business, but in the end, it always landed with my cock buried deep inside her exquisite pussy while she moaned my name. I was a sex god and she was every bit the goddess—until I found out she was actually an angel and I was the devil in disguise.

Had I been half as smart as I'd thought I was, I would've hired someone to do a background check on her in the beginning. But no. I was a horny fucker without morals, hence the purchase of a human being in the first goddamn place.

It turned out Lanie Talbot had made the ultimate sacrifice. She'd sold herself to save her dying mother's life.

Faye Talbot was in need of a heart transplant. The problem was that the Talbot family couldn't afford the transplant, nor did they have health insurance. Mack, Lanie's father, had lost his job after having missed so much work tending to his wife. Corporate America could be a cold bastard at times, caring more about the bottom line than about the people who were the reason for their success in the first place. But what was done was done. All they could do was trudge forward and hold out hope.

That hope came in the two million dollars that I'd paid for Lanie.

How very altruistic of me. I don't think that had been what my dearly departed mother, Elizabeth, had in mind when she'd first started the charity campaign at Scarlet Lotus. Noah senior would've disapproved greatly as well.

Once I'd found out what I'd done to Lanie, I knew I couldn't do it to her anymore. I'd fallen for her. Big-time. And although it nearly killed me to admit it, I knew I had to let her go. She belonged at her mother's side, not in my bed.

I'll admit I hadn't thought I could actually follow through on it, so I'd hedged. It was the night of the annual Scarlet Lotus Ball that the dam had finally broken. First of all, Julie had shown up and shown out. She had been all over me like a second skin, and there wasn't a damn thing I could do about it at the time because of the board members and potential clients who were in attendance. Add to that the fact that Lanie had been openly flirting with David Stone, and you have a catastrophe in the making. So I'd been forced to drag Lanie out of there before I lost all composure and made a horrific scene from which I'd never be able to recover. It was what David had been hoping for, I was sure.

Lanie and I had argued on the ride home. Well, she had

argued. I'd ignored her. Which had only pissed her off more. She wanted me to fuck her, expected it, because that was what we'd always done. Only I hadn't wanted to fuck her anymore. I couldn't. Not after everything I'd learned. Don't get me wrong; I wanted her. Goddamn, did I ever. But I couldn't do that to her anymore.

She wouldn't leave well enough alone, though. Nope. Not Lanie. When I'd spurned her advances, she'd bolted from the limousine and into the rain toward the house. I'd followed after her, of course, but she was crazed, spewing anything at all to get a rise out of me.

She hit the proverbial jackpot when she told me if I wouldn't fuck her, someone else back at the ball would, and one person in particular sprang to mind. David Stone.

My possessive nature kicked in. Admittedly, I was angry, but it was no excuse for what I'd done. None too gently, I'd grabbed her and fucked her right there on the staircase. I hadn't cared if it felt good to her. I hadn't cared if she was uncomfortable. I hadn't cared about anything other than claiming what I'd considered mine.

Only she wasn't mine. Sure, maybe I owned her body, but I didn't own her soul or her heart, and those were the parts I'd wanted the most. Those were the parts of me I'd given her without even realizing it. And they hadn't cost her one red penny.

After fucking her like a goddamn animal, I'd finally forced myself to confess everything I'd been keeping from her. I told her that I knew about her mother, about why she had to auction herself off to the highest bidder. And as fucked up as I knew it was, I told her that I'd fallen in love with her. And then I left her there without another word.

To my utter amazement, Lanie had come to find me in the shower. Imagine my surprise when instead of cutting my balls off, she asked me to make love to her, to let her know what it felt like to be loved by me. Just once. That was all she'd wanted. And I would've given her anything she asked for, so of course I gave her my heart on a silver platter. Cliché, but true.

I'd known while I was making love to her, while I was baring my fucking soul to her, that it was the last time. I'd known it, and still I managed to push all of that to the side and revere her the way she should've been from day one. I loved her freely and completely, with all of my might and all of my being. There had been no room to doubt how I had felt about her, how I still felt about her.

I loved her. God help me, I fucking loved her.

Afterward, she made a point to state the obvious, that we needed to talk. But I'd known everything she was going to say already, so I claimed the night and just held her. I knew it would be the last time I'd ever be able to do so.

The next morning, it had taken every ounce of strength I had to leave the measured serenity of that bed. It had to be done. So I'd nuzzled her neck and softly kissed the bare skin of her shoulder before whispering one last "I love you" into her ear. She'd stirred and smiled in her sleep, which made it even harder to leave her side, but somehow I did.

The shower was quick, my dressing time even quicker. And when I'd come out, there she was, my million-dollar baby, looking even more beautiful than I'd ever thought her to be before. She'd wanted to talk, but again, I knew the score, and I just didn't think I could handle hearing her say the words. So I did the right thing.

I ripped up the contract and told her to go be with her family. And then I willed my shaky legs to take me away from her. She didn't follow or try to stop me, which was just as it should've been. The fantasy I'd tried to buy was over, and it was time for me to get back to the real world.

As the limousine pulled away, I refused to let myself look back at the front door. I didn't want to see that she wasn't there. It was hard enough knowing she wouldn't be when I got home. Maybe the day would eventually come that she'd think about me and not hate my guts. Maybe she'd even smile warmly. Maybe, but I wasn't counting on it. As long as she was happy, that was all that mattered to me.

And so I found myself in my limousine, alone and fucking dying on the inside. I'd turn to the only thing that had gotten me through every other tragedy in my life: Scarlet Lotus.

Lanie

As I watched the limousine disappear from sight, something came over me. I expected it to be defeat, agony, betrayal, or heartache, but it wasn't.

Rage. Rage and more rage.

How dare he? Stupid man with his stupid big house, his stupid big ego, and his stupid big head, thinking he knew what was best for me. He said it wouldn't work, but I didn't believe he meant it. I saw that look in his eyes. It was killing him. So why do it? Why go through all he had the night before to prove how he felt for me, only to turn me loose the second he had a chance to make a clean getaway? Because he had control issues—that was the reason. Well, he couldn't tell me what to do. I wasn't one of his employees anymore. The shredded piece of paper he had discarded on the bed was the end of that contract.

Discarded . . . just like me.

I was going to tell him I loved him, too, to put an end to his ridiculousness, but no such luck. Before letting me get out of my mouth the words that were sure to prove him wrong, the control freak told me to get lost.

How was it fair that he got to say all he wanted when I didn't? I mean, sure, I could've echoed his declaration while in the throes of passion, but that passion had been pretty epic and I'd had a hard enough time remembering to breathe, let alone being able to say anything that would have sounded in the least bit coherent or endearing. Besides, I really thought I had all kinds of time to tell him how I felt. I mean, hello? I'd told him to call me Lanie, for Christ's sake. Plus I didn't want him to think I was saying those three little words just because he had. I wanted a separate moment to do the whole shout-it-from-the-highest-mountaintop-for-the-whole-world-to-hear thing so that there'd be no doubting my sincerity, because a declaration of that magnitude was a pretty serious thing. But I was all kinds of prepared to make that leap. For him, for me . . . for us.

And then he just had to go and ruin it with his caveman crap.

Men are jackasses.

But at least I could do something about my jackass, because I really had nothing to lose by confronting him. I was going to make him listen to me, whether he wanted to or not. He was going to know that I loved him, and he was going to feel like a total jerk for dismissing me the way he had. Because I was going down to that posh little office of his to demand his attention. He was going to see how wrong he was to make the assumptions he had, and he would never jump to conclusions again. I was a woman who had given up everything to save her dying mother's life, and I had a voice that was screaming to be heard. I'd be damned if everything I'd been through since I entered Noah Crawford's world was going to be for nothing.

Resigned to that plan, I turned on my heel and stalked back into the house with my shoulders back and my head held high. After a quick shower and a tour through Polly's wonderland of inappropriate clothing, I dressed and grabbed my cell phone from the table before leaving.

I was really quite impressed with myself as I scurried down the stairs, again avoiding a neck-breaking, skull-crushing fall. When I reached the first floor, I heard a car pull up. It had to be Samuel returning from dropping Noah off, and I gave myself a healthy dose of see-this-was-meant-to-be because how perfect was that timing?

And then there was an insistent pounding on the door, followed by "Lanie Marie Talbot, I know you're in there! Get your fat ass out of bed and open the door!"

That was my bestie, Dez.

I sprinted for the door and yanked it open just as Dez was about to pound her fist against it again. For a girl, she was pretty strong, and I was lucky that she narrowly missed cold-cocking me in the forehead. Like I needed to look like a unicorn when I went to confront Noah.

"Dez!" I shrieked as I ducked her fist. We both took a step back and looked each other over.

"What the hell are you wearing?" we asked simultaneously.

"Jinx! You owe me a Coke!" I yelled at the same time Dez yelled, "Jinx! You owe me a cock!"

Every time we played this game, I never got my Coke. Dez, however, always got her cock—without my help.

Dez was dressed head to toe in black on black. Well, mostly. Black skinny jeans, black turtleneck, black snakeskin boots. A skull belt buckle adorned the center of her low-slung hip huggers, and she was wearing a black cap embroidered with yet another skull just over her perfectly sculpted eyebrows.

I tackled my best friend, wrapping my arms around her torso and pinning her arms to her sides. "Oh my God! I've missed you so much!" It wasn't until she was right in front of me that I realized just how badly.

"Get off me, Hulkette! Damn, what are they feeding you here, steroids?" she asked, trying to wriggle out of my hold.

I turned her loose, realizing my hug was probably borderline bone-shattering, and stepped aside to invite her in. "What's with the *Mission: Impossible* getup?"

"I'm breaking you out." She turned to look me over once again with an approving smile. "Boyfriend sure did trick you out, huh? Look at you with the little red minidress, Slutty McSlutterson." Then she suddenly gasped, her eyes going wide. "You have been thoroughly scrogged! Spill!"

I felt my face go red. "What? No!"

"Yes, you were, Lanie Talbot! Don't forget who you're talking to. I think I know that just-been-fucked look."

I wanted nothing more than to gush to my best friend, but I needed to catch up to Noah, and Dez's arrival was keeping me from doing that. Speaking of . . . "Wait, what do you mean you're breaking me out?"

"I mean get your shit and let's go. I'm on a covert mission to bail your ass out of sex-slave prison," she said, and then looked around in awe. "Although I don't really see how you could exactly call these digs a prison. This is a freakin' palace!"

"Okay, seriously. Why are you here, and how did you know where I was?"

Dez rolled her eyes. "You said Noah Crawford bought you, and it didn't dawn on me at first, but then it hit me like a whore getting bitch-slapped by her pimp in a dark alley: Noah Crawford of Scarlet Lotus. Right? I mean, how many Noah Crawfords can there be in the world, much less in this corner of the country, with enough money to pay two million little cha-chings for his own personal little *oh-yes-daddy-milk-me-papi*?" she asked with all the great acting skills of a porn star destined for the not so silver screen.

"Yes, but that still doesn't explain why you're here, insisting on breaking me out. I'm fine, and really, it's not exactly like I'm a prisoner. Noah treats me very good."

My best friend took a deep breath and sighed. "I have something to tell you, sweetie," she started. She never called me *sweetie* unless she was about to lay something heavy on me. My heart jumped into my throat and tried to claw its way out.

"Faye has taken a turn for the worse. She's been admitted to University Hospital, and they've called in the family. I promised Mack I'd get you there. It doesn't look good, babe."

Just then the front door opened and Polly bounced over the threshold. "Good morning, Lanie!" she greeted me in her usual bubbly voice as if my whole world hadn't been turned upside down mere seconds before. The smile immediately dropped from her face once she saw my expression. "Oh, God. What's wrong?"

My chest constricted like an anaconda was squeezing the life out of it in preparation for swallowing it whole. "Noah was right. My parents do need me more than he does."

David

My head hurt. Hurt like I'd been sucker-punched by an I beam that had fallen from twenty stories up. Or maybe it was more like one of those chandeliers on the *Titanic*—or, hell, even the *Titanic* itself.

And my mouth tasted like ass.

I cracked one eyelid open and surveyed the damages. Usually when I woke up like this, there was always one or two, maybe even three whores that I needed to get rid of fast before they got too clingy.

Thank God I was in my office at Scarlet Lotus alone. I guess that cunt Julie had taken the hint when I'd told her to get the fuck out last night. At least I thought I'd told her to get out. I remembered fucking her in the ass, because hell yeah, I had to take that trip down memory lane. Too bad Crawford hadn't been there to see it. The look on his face when he'd seen Julie was my date to the ball had been priceless, although not as priceless as it could have been. No doubt because the lucky bastard had had Miss Delaine Talbot on his arm. I should probably say she'd had him on her arm, literally. That cuff bracelet she'd worn had said it all—he'd marked her as his personal property. Which cinched the fact that I had to have her. I just needed to get my game plan together. After our informative conversation the night before, it was obvious she actually had feelings for my ex of a best friend. But even if she hadn't, nabbing a woman like Delaine Talbot was going to take more than empty promises and a fat bank account. Not surprisingly, that was all it had taken with Julie.

I stretched and felt every glorious muscle in my awesomeness of a body groan in protest. One thing was for damn sure: the cushy leather couch that I'd had imported from Italy wasn't doing anything for my back. Too much fucking in my short lifetime had really done a number on it. But hell, as long as I was good at producing the orgasms, I was going to keep doing it. My orgasms, not theirs. Hey, I never gave any guarantees.

I willed my head to stop pounding as I sat up and stretched some more, hoping to get some of the kinks out of my neck and back. Goddamn, I was sore. My head started spinning, but after a moment or two I was able to get the floor to stop moving long enough to stand. Putting one foot in front of the other, I made a zigzag line to my bathroom—admittedly, I was still a little drunk—and grabbed the bottle of painkillers I kept in the cabinet. After popping one in my mouth, and then another for good measure, I ran cold water in my cupped hands and drank out of them.

When I looked in the mirror, I beamed at myself. Any other motherfucker who'd had the same night I had would look like shit, but not me. I always looked good. I reached for the toothbrush that I kept there, because I had a pretty fucking smile that had to be maintained, and made my pearls gleam before jumping in the shower. After toweling off, I headed to my personal closet to grab a fresh set of threads. Yeah, I kept a wardrobe there.

The shower sobered me up quite a bit, which was a good thing because I had a very important appointment that I needed to keep and I needed to be fresh. One glance at my Rolex let me know that I still had plenty of time.

I was shocked, to say the least, when I walked out of my office and saw Crawford stepping off the elevator. He groaned when he saw me as well. I took the groan as a compliment, a definite mark in my favor. Maybe I wasn't the easiest person to get along with when I was on the opposing team, but that fact served its purpose. The more miserable I made him, the more likely he was to eventually give up and turn over his half of the company to yours truly just to get away from me. So if Noah left himself open, you bet your sweet ass I took the shot.

"It's Sunday, Crawford. What are you doing here?"

"I have work to catch up on," he said, pulling out the key to his office. Obviously he was going to blow me off, but I just couldn't let him do that before I'd had my fun.

"You left early last night. No worries, though. I explained to the board members and clients that you had a hot little number that was demanding your attention," I said smugly. He knew the translation; I cut his balls off and handed them over in a paper bag. Score one for the home team. His inattention to them gave me the advantage in the little game we played for control.

He scoffed and shook his head.

"Speaking of . . . she's one hellcat of a woman, that De-laine. Eeeew-eee!" I crowed. "Got a hell of a mouth on her, too. What was it she called me?" I asked, tapping my chin as I recalled her words. "Oh, yeah. A remora. Seems to think your dick is bigger than mine, which might or might not be true, but that didn't stop your other whore from jumping on the David Stone express, now did it? Of course, unlike Julie, Delaine sure was quick to defend her man. Passionate about it, too. I could use someone like her on my list of go-tos."

Bingo! That one had hit home.

Hatred flashed in his eyes. Mistake number one: the more he cared about her, the more I wanted her. He closed the distance between us in half a heartbeat and pinned me against the wall with his forearm to my throat. Mistake number two: assault in the workplace just added another weapon to my arsenal.

"You stay the fuck away from her! Do you hear me?" He seethed, his words forced through clenched teeth as he pointed a finger in my face. "Stay the *fuck* away from her! That is your one and only warning, Stone. I swear to God, I'll kill you with my bare hands."

Mistake number three: terroristic threatening. I might need to get a protection order, you know, because I was terrified for my life and all and shouldn't have to be subjected to a hostile work environment.

I flashed him my winning smile because I had him just where I wanted him. It was exactly that sort of emotional reaction I'd always warned him about when it came to getting attached to women. He wasn't on his A game, wasn't thinking clearly, and he certainly had no idea that he'd given me all the ammunition I needed to ambush him and steal away his pride and joy. Scarlet Lotus was mine for the taking. And take I would.

His cell phone rang. For a moment, he looked like he wasn't going to answer it, but then he swore under his breath and finally backed away, restoring the flow of air through my trachea. I did my best to cover my cough as I rubbed at the spot while he answered his phone. Crawford was no wuss. I knew if we ever went toe-to-toe in a physical altercation, he'd be a formidable foe, but no way was I going to let him know that.

"What?" he barked into the receiver.

I ignored him and started toward the elevator because, quite frankly, I was bored with him. I already had what I needed and still had that appointment, so . . .

"Polly, slow down. Who? . . . Dez? Who the fuck is Dez? . . . Shit, no . . . Oh, God, no. Where is she? . . . No, no, that's fine. University? . . . Okay, just calm down. I'll call Daniel, he's on staff there . . . Yeah, go . . . Just go be with her, Polly."

I had no clue what that one-sided conversation was about, but then again, I didn't really give a fuck. As the elevator dinged and the door opened, he looked back at me briefly and then pulled the phone away from his ear. "I meant what I said, David. Stay away from her," he warned again.

"Oh, yeah. Sure thing. You have my word." I gave him a mock salute as the doors closed. He knew there was nothing doing, but it sounded like he had his hands full with whatever crisis that little gnat had called him about. Which just gave me a wide-open berth to take care of business.

Down in the parking garage, I climbed into my red Viper and cranked the custom stereo before I peeled out of the parking garage with tires squealing. All the more inadequate modes of transportation on the road ahead of me split like the Red Sea to allow me passage. It was plausible that it was just the fact that traffic was normally sparse on an early Sunday morning, but I'd like to think it was because I was a fucking god behind the wheel of that piece of masterful craftsmanship.

"That's right, you sad bastards . . . make room for great-ness."

~$~

I pulled into the parking lot of Foreplay, a popular party spot for the college kids—and a place with big business deals that had been successfully kept on the down low. So down low they were underground. Hos and schmos on the top, real-life whores and business moguls in the pit. It was the perfect framework.

I walked up to the back door and gave two knocks in rapid succession, six in a heartbeat rhythm. Right on cue, Terrence answered the door.

"Mr. Stone! Right on time, as usual," he lied convincingly. I was at least twenty minutes late, but like I said, time stood still for David Stone. "Come in, come in."

I stepped inside the dark entrance and inhaled deeply. "Aw, the sweet, sweet smell of pussy and money in the morning," I crooned. "Is there any better combination?"

"No way, man." He laughed and clapped me on the back. "Mr. Christopher is waiting for you."

Flashing my award-winning smile, I said, "Of course he is. I know the way."

He nodded and went about his business as I walked down the corridor to Scott's office and stepped inside without even bothering to knock. Scott was kicked back in his chair, smok-ing a joint. The day's take was spread out on his desk along with blocks of the latest shipment that he'd yet to distribute to his runners.

"Hey," he lazily greeted me, his eyes barely slivers through squinted lids as he exhaled his ganja smoke.

I shut the door and shrugged out of my jacket before nodding to the fluffy white lines of snow he'd arranged on a little rectangular mirror. "You started the party without me?"

"Just thought I'd get the sample ready in advance." He sat up and butted the joint in the crystal ashtray on the corner of his desk, and then started shuffling the ledgers before him.

Scott Christopher was my business partner, though for my part it was silent. Foreplay belonged to him, but I provided the financial backing and most of the clientele for his trade business. Two trades, to be exact: sex and drugs. Scarlet Lotus was my main source of income, but the auction and cocaine padded my pockets. Nicely, I might add.

Fuck those amateur pimps and dealers on the streets. That was nothing more than chump change. We catered to the elite.

Although I had a solid investment in his dealings, the only reason Scott was able to attract the rich and powerful was through me. Nose candy was the hang-up for a lot of well-to-do types, and I had my finger in the punch bowl on that one. An entrepreneur like Scott would never be able to approach men of the same caliber as the ones with whom I associated. Many of my business luncheons and hobnobbing with clients and prospective investors for Scarlet Lotus provided me with a little side action to boot. My promise of discretion was what brought the big fish in for a nibble. Once they sampled the goods, their business was hook, line, and sinker. They only managed to go deeper inside after that, securing a bit of pussy to satisfy their needs in whatever way their pervy hearts desired. We had a little something for everyone.

The cherry on top was that I knew all of their secrets. I smiled in their faces, shook their hands, and patted them on the back. But at the end of the day, I'd stab them in it if push ever came to shove and mine was against a wall. The need for contracts meant there was a paper trail, proof of their scandalous behavior. However risky those documents were, our clients considered it a worthwhile liability in exchange for the goods. I considered it a surefire bet they'd be team David when I made my move to take Scarlet Lotus for my own.

I loved my fucking life.

"And how are the numbers looking on our other venture?" I hung my jacket on the coat rack and walked over to test the sample of coke for myself.

Bending over the desk, I took the straw and put the tip to my nose and the other end at the base of one of the sculptured lines. Once I closed my other nostril with a finger, I shut my eyes and inhaled the superior white powder. Although it felt like fine sand being shot up my nose, the cut was so pure there was no burn, only an immediate numbing and the high that would make Mighty Mouse feel like the Incredible Hulk.

I slowly opened my eyes as the sensation took the fast track through the rest of my body. "Oh yeah, baby. That's the good shit right there."

On a normal day, I'd feel like I could take on the world. Put a little of the devil's dandruff up my nose, and I knew I could not only take the world, but the universe as well. The rich and powerful craved that feeling, became addicted to it. Given our clientele, it was no surprise our hugely successful and highly profitable cocaine biz was the envy of street dealers the world over.

I took a seat and propped my feet on the corner of Scott's desk. He looked irritated, but he wouldn't say shit about it. "So, the numbers on the auction?"

"Spectacular, thanks to the virgin on the block, but that's nothing compared to my other news." His face lit up with a devious smile. "I've got an interesting bit of information for you."

I arched a brow at him because he was acting like a man who suddenly knew all the answers in life and was about to make me a deal I wouldn't refuse. "Is that right? Do tell."

"How about if I just show you?" He opened the bottom drawer of his desk and pulled out a manila folder that he slid across the desk.

I chuckled when I saw the name Delaine Talbot written in red on the tab.

I could practically see that sexy little smirk on her face from the Scarlet Lotus Ball when she'd torn me down. It gave me some serious wood. I knew word of mouth had been spreading among our customers and their colleagues, so I got pretty fucking curious as to the reason Scott would be holding a folder with my future conquest's name on it. I flipped it open and scanned the singular document inside.

A satisfied smile crept over my face when I scanned what appeared to be a contract promising two years of Delaine's life to one Noah P. Crawford. "Well, fuck me. Noah, Noah, Noah," I tsked.

"Thought you might like that," Scott said with a self-satisfied grin.

"Why didn't you tell me this was going down?"

"I didn't know he'd be here. He's smart. When he called

in, he did it anonymously. Wouldn't give me his name, only a number and a very particular interest. A virgin. I honestly didn't think I'd ever hear from him again because the odds of finding a virgin desperate enough to put her innocence on the menu are nil to none. And then Delaine Talbot," he said with a wave of his hand toward the folder I was holding like it was the holy grail because it fucking was, "signed up on the day before the auction.

"I called him up, and he told me he might make the auction and that I should reserve a room for him just in case. Imagine my surprise when Noah Crawford walked through those doors."

"Yeah, I bet." I laughed as Noah's signature stared back at me, right alongside Delaine's.

I closed the folder and pushed it back across the desk. It took everything in me to do it, but at least I knew where the contract was and had access to it at any time. Scott would never hand it over to me to use in my conquest to blackmail Crawford into giving up his half of Scarlet Lotus. That would be too risky for the rest of his business. All of it: the auction and the coke. Not to mention his suppliers and the power players involved in every aspect would get twitchy if they thought he'd gotten sloppy and their dirty deeds were in danger of being exposed. It was best not to spook them.

I just needed to figure out a way to make my newfound knowledge work in my favor without risking life and limb in the process.

"If you decide to tell Noah you know, you keep my name out of your mouth," Scott said, putting the folder back in his desk. "And if he figures it out, you better make damn sure you give me a heads-up so that I can clean house. I mean it, Stone. These people I deal with do not play well with others."

"You worry too much, Scotty. Crawford isn't about to step into a light that is unfavorable to him. Besides, I'm pretty sure I know how to get what I want without bringing you down in the process."

I wasn't confident my plan would work, but the important thing was that I had finally won. What had happened between Noah and me back at the office earlier that morning was my word against his. And although I would have had a valid case and would have thoroughly enjoyed dragging his name through the mud, there was no way I could prove what had happened. But this? There was just no denying this. I had it all in writing.

Scarlet Lotus was as good as mine.

2

two-for-one special

Lanie

Why were hospital rooms always so cold? It was like death's cruel hand had reached in and stolen all the warmth out of the place. No matter how warm and inviting the hospital attempted to make the room that was likely going to be the last your loved one would ever see, the realization that someone you cared about was in their last days, hours, or even minutes made the décor irrelevant. And then there was the smell: chemicals mixed with bodily fluids, sickness, and death. It made it too real, and I wanted to run away as fast as I could, find Noah, and just not deal with the very real possibility that I was going to lose my mother. But I couldn't. For one, I would never forgive myself if these were in fact her final hours and I wasn't there, and second, Noah had rejected me. Besides, it would be like running away from one problem only to have to face another that might have been every bit as hopeless. I was where I needed to be.

As much a part of my family as I was, Dez was right by my side, as was Polly. Thank goodness she had thought to bring me something warmer than the little red slut attire I'd had on before. My father would have probably keeled over with a heart attack and ended up in a hospital bed next to my mother if he'd seen me in that getup. So there I stood, looking out the window, dressed in a little black sweater dress and black boots. Nothing elaborate, nothing sexy. In fact, it was sort of depressing, but it matched the way I felt on the inside. My heart, vacant and hollow, was still mourning the loss of Noah, but my soul was worried that the bleak blackness covering my body was actually an omen of something even more morbid to come, like the loss of my mother. As devastating as it was to lose the only man I would probably ever love, losing my mother would make it incredibly hard to find the will to live.

The cold spot I felt in the cavern of my chest amplified tenfold with that thought, like the cold of the room had somehow seeped its way into my heart. My mother was my best friend. Always had been. Not the same kind of friend as Dez, or even the same kind of friend Polly had become. My mother was something more. She knew me better than anyone else because I was a living extension of her. That woman could tell what I was thinking or feeling without me having to say a word. And with more experience under her belt, she knew what I needed to hear, when I needed to hear it, and made me listen even if I didn't want to. Most children hated to admit it, but my mom was right nearly a hundred percent of the time. So to never see her warm smile again, never hear her infectious laughter, never feel the warm comfort of her embrace, never smell her white musk scent . . . I couldn't even fathom the thought.

"Lanie? You want some coffee?" my father asked, pulling me away from my thoughts.

I turned and gave him a halfhearted smile. That was Mack's way. His wife was dying and he couldn't do anything to stop the inevitable, so he found something or someone else to take care of instead. I accepted his offering, noting the thinness of his face. His eyes had dark rings under them, and judging from the almost full beard he was sporting, he obviously hadn't shaved in quite some time. I knew lecturing him about taking better care of himself wouldn't do any good, so I let it go.

Looking down at her sleeping form, I clutched the paper cup to my chest in hopes that it might warm the chill in my heart. Realistically, the only thing that would make me feel better would be my mother's full recovery, although the co-coon of Noah's arms around me while his reassuring voice promised everything was going to be okay probably would have helped. I missed him, and I desperately wished he was here with me, but fate had apparently had other plans for us. Funny how things had worked out. Noah had released me from our contract just in time for me to watch my mother die and be able to stay home and take care of my dad for what would surely be a miserable existence without his wife at his side. I wondered if the life of sin I had partaken in with Noah had actually caused karma to swing back around to give me a swift kick in the ass.

"Mr. Talbot?" a familiar voice called from the doorway. I looked up to see a tall brown-haired doctor retrieve a pen from the pocket of his white lab coat and begin to scribble on the clipboard he'd had tucked under his arm. "Hello, I'm Dr. Daniel Crawford, and I'll be conducting the surgery and tak-ing over as the attending physician for your wife. If it's okay with you, that is?"

Daniel Crawford. Noah's hunky uncle. My heart might

have sighed a bit at the sight of him. From relief, not longing. There was only one Crawford man I longed for, and he wasn't present. Another fact that made my heart sigh for a second time.

Daniel looked at my father and then glanced at me with a warm, knowing smile before looking back to Mack again.

Under normal circumstances, my mother would have been the one to make the decision about her health care, but she had been heavily sedated since her arrival. Her regular doctor had assured us that the sedation made her more comfortable and decreased the likelihood that she would get too excited, thereby overexerting her already weakened heart. So that left Mack to make all of her medical decisions. I think the doctors and nurses on staff were relieved that it wasn't me. I might have been a bit in their face when we first arrived, demanding results, demanding they get off their asses and do their job, demanding they save my mother's life. Dez and Polly had done their best to get me to calm down, but ultimately, it was the threat by the rent-a-cop security staff that they would remove me from the premises that finally got me to back off.

"Taking over? What about Dr. Johnson?" my father asked Daniel.

"Dr. Johnson is incompetent," I said. Seeing the disapproving scowl from my father, I added, "What? He is."

I heard a faint chuckle from Daniel as he checked my mother's vitals.

"See? Dr. Crawford agrees."

Mack rubbed the back of his neck and looked down at my mother. "I don't know about changing her doctor at this stage in the game."

"This isn't a game, Dad," I said out loud, which was totally unfair of me. I knew he didn't think of it that way, but I was frustrated, not that it excused my inappropriate comment. My father didn't hold it against me, though, because he was feeling the same way.

"I assure you, I am very qualified," Daniel broke in, slipping his pen back into his breast pocket. "I run the cardiac department here and have performed numerous heart transplants—"

"Wait a minute," I interrupted his list of accomplishments, all of them very great, I was sure. He was a Crawford and greatness probably ran in their bloodline, but there was one teeny-tiny detail—which was actually mega-important—from his earlier introduction that had just hit me. "What surgery?"

My mother had been in intensive care after having coded in the emergency room and then been brought back to fight for her life another day. As far as we knew, that was where she would remain until either a miracle happened and she showed marked improvement and we took her home, or . . . didn't. I had tried to pull every string I could to get her a new heart, now that we had the money for the procedure, but it hadn't mattered because there were too many people on the list ahead of her: proof of Dr. Johnson's incompetence and lack of pull.

Daniel gave us a genuine smile. "We have a donor, Delaine." Apparently he remembered my name from the Scarlet Lotus Ball, where I'd made a complete jackass of myself by not speaking to him—not one word. It had been my way of throwing a very childlike tantrum in response to Noah's order not to speak to any men at the party.

"A d-donor?" my father stuttered, an apprehensive smile drawing up the corner of his mouth. I could tell he was trying hard not to get excited, like he didn't believe what he was hearing. Truthfully, it was hard for me to believe as well, but I had a feeling Noah Crawford might have had something to do with it. I was certain he had everything to do with the fact that his uncle, a world-renowned cardiologist, was standing in the room at that very second. It hadn't dawned on me before that when Noah found out about my mother he would have gone to work behind the scenes trying to ensure that she got the best possible care. He'd already unknowingly contributed two million dollars toward that, and there he was, contributing family members as well. Once again, he was showing his love for me, and I still had no way to prove that I reciprocated his feelings.

"Yes, well, we are a transplant center here, and given Mrs. Talbot's condition, she is a priority case," Daniel explained. "We had a potential donor, and as soon as we got the lab work back, we knew we had a match. Now, there's little more than paperwork to do, and the actual procedure, of course."

"She's getting a new heart. . . ." My father looked dazed.

I thought about Noah again, and again I wished he was here. I needed him here. My mother might have been getting a new heart, but mine was still broken. I highly doubted they were running a two-for-one special.

"Yes, she is." Daniel cleared his throat as a nurse, who looked sort of like Betty Boop with blond hair, walked in. "Mr. Talbot, if you'll just follow Sandra, she'll help you with the paperwork and we can get started. Delaine," he said, nodding his farewell with a warm smile.

"Hell yeah! Mama Talbot's gonna live!" Dez did a fist pump in the air, earning a scowl from my father. "Oh, um, sorry," she said with an embarrassed giggle. She stood and draped her purse over her shoulder. "I don't know about y'all, but all this excitement's made me hungry. I guess I'm going to head down to the cafeteria and grab some hospital slop. If I'm not back in half an hour, check the ER, and I'm not saying that because of the Latino god of an orderly down there, either. Although I just might have to fake a pelvis injury to get him to check me out after I get my belly full. Anyone wanna come with?"

Polly's phone chirped, signaling a message, and I glanced at her, noting the way she frowned before putting her coffee down and saying, "I'll go. I need to check in with Mason anyway." Part of me wondered if that meant she would be checking in with Noah as well, but that might have been wishful thinking on my part.

Mack came over to me and put his arm around my shoulders. "You going to be okay here by yourself while I go do this paperwork?"

"Yeah, go ahead. I'll stay with her." I looked at my mother's sleeping form. The circles under her eyes were even more prominent than the ones under my father's, and she was much thinner than even he. I felt guilty that I'd been living in a mansion fit for a king, and that said king had been coaxing my inner sexual goddess out to play, while the two people who meant the most to me had been suffering. I should've been there for them.

"Hey, she's getting a new heart, a chance to really live again. She's going to be okay, and the second they give the all-clear, I want your ass back at school to get that degree. You hear me? No moping around now."

"Sure, Dad. Whatever you say." I laughed lightly as he

hugged me to his side and then followed the nurse out. He was going to be so disappointed when he found out that I hadn't actually been enrolled at college, and I had no clue how to hide it from him. I probably should've figured that out before I told the lie, but you know what they say about hindsight.

I sat in the chair next to my mother's bed and took her hand in mine. Her skin was cold and had a grayish tint to it but still soft. I noticed that her nail polish was chipped, and I reminisced about the trips to the salon she'd made me take with her before she'd gotten really sick. She'd always said she felt better when she looked good. I pictured her sickly form sitting up in her bed and painting her nails even though she knew she was in no shape to go anywhere where someone besides my father might actually see them. Perhaps she even had my father do it. I laughed inwardly at that picture.

"Hey, Mom," I said quietly to her sleeping form. "You're getting a new heart. Yay!" I mimed shaking pom-poms in the air, a goofy smile on my face. Then seriousness took over. "But before you do, and while you're out like a light and won't really hear anything I'm saying, I have something I want to talk to you about.

"See, I met this guy, and he's wonderful. His name is Noah Crawford." I rolled my eyes, knowing the reaction she would've had to that if she'd been conscious. "Yes, *the* Noah Crawford. Don't let the money and his gorgeous face fool you; he can be a real prick, but that's one of the things that makes him so wonderful. So anyway, we've been seeing each other for a while now, and last night he told me he loves me." My mother would've squealed at that point.

"Yeah, yeah, yeah," I said with another roll of my eyes, even though she couldn't actually see me. "Here's the thing, though . . . this morning, he pretty much told me to get the hell out of his life. I have a feeling he did it because he thinks he knows what's best for me. Men, right? I guess I knew all along that an actual relationship working out between a billionaire and a simple girl from Hillsboro would be nothing short of a fairy tale, and fairy tales simply don't come true. The problem is that Noah makes me feel like maybe they can. I mean, he told me he loves me, so despite my fears, I started to believe things really could work out between us. Only I never got the chance to say how I feel about him." I buried my face in my mother's shoulder and sighed. "I can't stand the fact that he doesn't know, which can really be even more torturous because there's not really anything I can do about it. That's not exactly something you say in a text message or over the phone, right? No, it's gotta be face-to-face. But the problem is, his face isn't here and I don't know if I'll ever get the chance to see it again. You gotta help me, Mom, because I have no clue what to do."

"My face is here now," a familiar voice said from the doorway. My head snapped up, and I turned in his direction. He was there, looking like he'd stepped out of the pages of a magazine. Leaning against the door frame with his hands tucked into the front pockets of his jeans, his words oozed with all his sexy gruff. "Tell me, Delaine. How *do* you feel about me?"

Noah

I'd overheard every word she had said. It wasn't that I was trying to eavesdrop; I just didn't want to interrupt the moment she was having with her mother. I'd even turned to walk away, but when I heard my name, human nature took over and I stuck around because some masochistic part of me needed to hear how much she hated me. What I'd heard hadn't sounded anything like hate, but I wasn't about to make an even bigger ass out of myself by trying to figure it out for myself either.

Delaine looked at me, stunned, but she didn't answer my question. She didn't say anything, in fact. What she did do was leap to her feet and run to where I stood. I righted myself in the nick of time to catch her when she jumped into my arms. Her lips crashed against mine, her pliant body molding to my hard planes as she kissed me like it had been months since we had last seen each other rather than hours.

"Hey, hey, hey," I got out between the onslaught of kisses. I could taste the salt of tears that had dropped onto her lips. She was full-on crying and shaking uncontrollably, so I tucked her head into the crook of my neck and held her tight. "It's okay. I'm here now, kitten. Everything's going to be okay."

"My dad can't see me like this, Noah. He still doesn't know anything about you or what I did, and he can't find out. He just can't," she said frantically.

"Don't worry. I'll take care of it."

Polly stormed into the room like a mama bear on a mission. "Damn it, Noah! What did you do to her? Is she okay?" Normally I'd say her tone was way out of line and I'd give her a stern talking-to, but under the circumstances I understood her abruptness. She and Delaine had grown close, and Polly was only being protective, the same way she was toward me. So I let it go.

"She will be," I answered. "I need to get her out of here."

"No! I can't leave," Delaine protested through her tears, but she still wouldn't look up.

"No, kitten. I'm not going to take you away from the hospital. I just want to take you someplace a little more private so we can talk," I reassured her while stroking her hair.

"Omigod, that's Noah freakin' Crawford!" I looked up to see a leggy chick with a fake rack, a way too skinny waist, and a face concealed by two inches of makeup blocking my escape. She had stars in her eyes at first, and then those stars turned to daggers. If looks could have killed, I would have been murdered, cremated, and had my ashes added to compost. "Get your hands off her before I rip your balls off and shove them down your throat, you bastard!"

"Dez, leave him alone," Delaine mumbled into my neck.

"Ah. Dez. You're the best friend," I said, finally figuring it out. "Listen, you can make me choke on my balls later if you want—I'll even handle my own castration—but right now I've got to take care of Lanie. I need to get her somewhere a little more private before her father sees her. Will you please sit with her mother until I get her calmed down?"

She looked from Lanie back to me, then gave a reluctant nod.

I turned to Polly, still holding my million-dollar baby in my arms. Fuck the million-dollar part—I guess she was just my baby now. "Polly, for some reason I will never understand, you have a way with people. They like you. So can you stay here and run interference with her father?"

"Roger that," she said with a salute and a playful wink. When Polly had a mission to accomplish, she thrived.

I left Dez and Polly to their tasks and carried Lanie down the corridor, ignoring the curious glances of hospital staff and patients alike. When I finally made it to Daniel's office, I knocked on the door, and he called out, "Come in!" At the sight of Lanie in my arms, he stood from his desk, his brow furrowed with concern. "Is she okay?"

"Yes, she's fine. I, uh . . . we just need a little privacy. Do you mind?"

"Not at all. I'm due in the OR to scrub in and start the procedure anyway." He cleared his throat as he passed to leave. "Lock the door and no one will disturb you."

I set Delaine down on the couch after he left, but when I tried to pull away, she grabbed my arms and looked up at me pleadingly. "No, please don't leave me."

"I'm not going anywhere, Lanie. I promise. I'm just going to lock the door, okay?"

She nodded and reluctantly released her hold. I quickly went to the door and turned the bolt before stopping by the mini refrigerator to grab a bottle of water. "Here, drink this," I said, removing the top and handing it to her.

She took a tiny sip and then set it on the table. I'd no sooner sat down beside her than she was crawling into my lap and laying her head on my shoulder. She was still shaking and quite visibly upset, and I had no idea how to calm her down.

"Shh, it's okay, baby. Everything's going to be okay now," I said, rubbing her back and kissing the top of her head. "What's got you so upset? Talk to me."

"Oh, God, Noah, it's not okay. She's dying. Or at least she *was* dying, but now your uncle says they have a donor, and I was such a bitch to him at the ball. But all I knew was that she was dying and Dez came to get me and I had to get here, and I was scared to death that I wouldn't get here fast enough. I didn't want to leave you, but I had to. And I needed you here, but you weren't because you ran away from me this morning and I was so *pissed* at you. I wanted to yell at you. I wanted to smack you upside your beautiful, *stupid* head and you weren't there, but you weren't here, either. And I still kind of want to yell at you and punch you, but I can't because you're here now and I just want to be in your arms. You left me. . . ."

She was hyperventilating and ranting incoherently at the same time, and the tears were back in full force, but I understood every word she'd said. She was upset and scared, and I hadn't been there when she needed me the most. She was right: I was stupid. And she had way too fucking much on her plate to have to deal with my shit on top of it.

"I know, kitten. I'm sorry," I said, and I fucking meant it. "I'm here now, and I'm not going anywhere until you tell me you don't want me here anymore."

"Good. Because I swear to God, Noah Patrick Crawford, if you leave me again, I'm going to be the one holding you down while Dez cuts your balls off," she said, and then there were more tears.

I sat there with her, rocking her back and forth while she got it all out. Her tears, her rants, her frustrations, her sadness, all of it. After a while she grew quiet, and at first I thought she'd fallen asleep, but then she looked up at me through swollen eyes and smiled. I kissed the tip of her little nose, tinged pink from her crying, before returning her smile.

"I've ruined your shirt," she said with a hoarse voice.

"It's only a shirt, Lanie. It'll be fine," I said, rubbing her arm. "I'm more worried about you."

"I'm sorry I broke down on you like that, taking you hostage on board the train to Crazy Town. Not many people know this about me, but I take regular trips there, just so you know," she said with an embarrassed shrug. She reached forward and grabbed a tissue out of the box on the table.

I chuckled lightly in response. "It's not a secret. But I happen to find that trait very endearing about you."

She laughed halfheartedly and dabbed at her tearstained cheeks. "How long have you been here?"

"Not long enough." I took the tissue and finished the job for her. "Congratulations on having gotten a donor, by the way."

"You did that, didn't you?"

Looking at myself through her eyes should've made me feel twenty feet tall, but I knew the truth, and so should she. "I hardly have that kind of power, Lanie."

"Bullcrap. You can do anything, Noah Crawford. You got Daniel to come, didn't you?"

"I may have asked him to oversee your mother's care, yes."

"Then you're her savior by default, because if he hadn't stepped in, Mom wouldn't have gotten that donor heart."

I sighed and took her chin in my hand and looked into her eyes. "I'm no superhero, Lanie. But I'd take a speeding bullet for you, maybe face down a powerful locomotive with nothing but a raised hand in defense, or even leap tall buildings in a single bound to get to you. Anything it takes to make you happy . . . because I love you, and that's all the reason I need."

"I love you, too," she whispered.

The blood in my veins surged and my heart swelled to the point I thought it might burst right out of my chest. She loved me. My million-dollar baby loved me.

"I may not have all kinds of pretty words to express it like you do, but—"

"Hey," I said, stopping her rambling before she got going again. "That's all I need—to know you love me."

Lanie closed her eyes and exhaled slowly. When she opened them again, she looked into mine and said, "Noah Crawford, I love you so much sometimes it's like I can't breathe because my heart is smothering my lungs."

That did it for me.

Slowly leaning forward, I nipped at her bottom lip before taking it between my own for a sensual kiss. She fisted my shirt as I pulled away slightly and then kissed her again and again, each time deepening it a little more. It wasn't enough for her, and truthfully, it wasn't enough for me, either. Thankful the door was still locked, I maneuvered out from under her so she could lie back on the couch before settling on one bended knee between her legs. Just as anxious as I, Lanie tugged on my shirt, pulling me down to her until our chests were flush.

We were making out like a couple of teenagers on the couch in my uncle's office, and I felt so alive. My hand traveled up her thigh and under the hem of her dress, and I stopped abruptly when I got to her hip. Something was very much out of place.

I hooked my fingers under the elastic band there and snapped it. "What the hell is this, Miss Talbot?" I asked against her lips.

"Panties," she answered breathlessly and then started a trail of suckling kisses down my neck.

"I know that. What are they doing on your body?" Panties had been expressly forbidden after Lanie had decided to throw a bitch tantrum and destroyed the very expensive collection of undergarments I had purchased for her. True, she had done it because the shop owner was my ex-lover and Lanie had been jealous of her, but the no-panties rule had remained in effect.

"Polly brought them to me along with the dress." She cupped my ass and pulled my hips into hers.

"But you didn't have to put them on," I said, cupping her ass as well—her bare ass. Well, at least it was a thong.

She cursed and arched her back when I nipped at her neck and sucked languidly. "No, but you left me, and even though I didn't really think you'd get a chance to see them, in my head, I'd gotten a little bit even. Besides, you ripped up the contract." Her breathing was ragged, just like mine.

"Contract be damned, you still belong to me," I said, grinding against her center and eliciting a moan from her to prove my point. "And you've been a naughty little girl, De-laine."

She wrapped her legs around my hips. "Mmm, I love it when you get all possessive and threatening."

This was what I loved about our relationship. We'd just confessed our undying love for each other, and there we were, about to get all kinds of kinky in my uncle's office.

"Kitten, I would love nothing more than to dole out your punishment, but we have to stop before we get carried away," I said, pulling back.

Lanie sighed and let her head fall onto the armrest, unwrapping her legs from around my waist. "You're right." With closed eyes, she took a deep breath to calm herself. Without warning, she huffed, shoved on my chest, and then scrambled into a sitting position to right her clothes. "See? This is the kind of stuff you do to me, Noah Crawford. You come in here and get me all riled up, knowing that we can't do anything about it, and my mother's right down the hall, about to go into surgery. I have half a mind to tell my father all about how you've taken advantage of his sweet, innocent little girl and turned her into a walking poster for teenage hormones."

She stopped abruptly. "Crap! Mack!"

I laughed. "What about him?"

"How am I going to explain you to him?"

"How about 'Dad, this is my very rich, very hot boyfriend. He's got a colossal cock and a wicked tongue'?" I licked my bottom lip to tease her, but she grabbed my tongue to stop me and narrowed her eyes at me.

"I'm serious, Noah."

Pulling back, I made to nip at her fingers until she finally released me. "So am I, and I think I've already proven the validity of that statement, but I can always refresh your memory," I said with an evil grin and a waggle of my brows. I slid my hand up the inside of her thigh, prepared to do that very thing.

"Noah!" She slapped my hand away and stood to pace the room. "My father thinks I've been away at college, not Noah Crawford's House for Daughter Deflowering. How am I going to say we met?"

With a shrug, I offered up the most logical solution. "I'll leave. That way he doesn't have to know anything about me."

She stopped dead in her tracks and turned on me with a finger aimed in my direction. "You're not going anywhere! I swear, Noah. I can't even think about—"

"Okay, calm down," I said, cutting her rant off and throwing my hands up in surrender.

Appeased, Lanie dropped her hands to her hips and started chewing on her bottom lip. If she didn't stop doing that, we weren't going to make it out of there without fucking like bunnies. I stood and crossed the room, forcing her to release the meaty morsel from between her teeth and then cupping her face. "I'll think of something. Just go back to your mother's room and find some way to tell Polly and Dez to meet me here without your father knowing."

"What are you going to do?"

"I don't know yet, but I'm sure if the three of us put our heads together, we'll come up with something believable."

"Okay."

I gave her a chaste yet soft kiss and walked her to the door.

"Hey," I said, stopping her before she left. She turned to look at me. "I love you."

The smile she gave me was so electric it could've powered the entire city of Chicago. "I love you, too."

3

hors d'oeuvres

Noah

We had a plan. It took us four hours to come up with it, but we finally had one. Of course, some of that time was spent waiting on my cousin Lexi, because Polly had decided we needed reinforcements.

"You're a disgusting pig, you know that?" Lexi said to me after having sat through the explanation of why we needed her there.

Normally, I wouldn't let anyone get away with talking to me like that, but this situation was different. Even if it hadn't been, one chose their battles with my cousin carefully. To the public eye, Alexis Mavis was a business savvy lady who garnered much respect from men and women alike among society's upper crust. But to those of us who knew her best, she was still that tomboy climbing trees and wading through dirty creek water in her white Sunday best to catch a toad. She said what was on her mind when it was on her mind, and she didn't give a rat's ass who liked it or not.

"Yes, I do," I agreed, because it was true, but it was also irrelevant at that moment. "Regardless, it's not like that now.

I love her and she loves me, and she's sitting in there with her father, unwilling to let me leave because she doesn't want to have to go through all this shit by herself. Nor do I want her to. Now, are you going to help us or not?"

"Yes," she finally agreed, and then gave me her signature bitch look. "But I'm only doing this for her because you obviously took advantage of the situation. She doesn't deserve to go down in flames for something that you're equally as guilty of, you enabler."

I was fine with that, because she was right.

Lexi was actually the one who came up with the ingenious plan. I had no contribution to make because I couldn't get the thought of Delaine wearing panties out of my head. It was a blatant disregard for my rule, a cheap shot, and she had to be punished—soon. I was looking forward to it.

"All right, team, let's get out there and bring home the win," Dez said. But when I made as if to leave the room, she blocked my way. She had the whole intimidating stare-down thing going on. "You and I still need to have a little chitchat, don't you think?"

I might have been a tad afraid, because Dez looked like she'd eaten the head off a prison guard or two in her day after having fucked them stupid, praying-mantis style. Plus Lexi was poised for the tag-in.

"Can it wait? I don't want to spend another moment away from Lanie."

"Aww, how sweet are you?" she asked, her tone saccharine. I didn't fall for the trick because I was a smart guy. Dez narrowed her eyes. "No, it can't wait. You hurt her. I don't care who you are or how much money you have—you shouldn't be allowed to get away with that. Lanie loves you, though, so my hands are tied." She stepped into my personal space, coming nose to nose with me. "But make her cry again and I will set fire to your testicles."

I heard the flick of a lighter and immediately looked down to find she'd somehow managed to pickpocket and use my own damn lighter to drive her point home. I jumped back and grabbed my boys to make sure they were okay. Dez laughed, closing the lid on my lighter and slapping it to my chest.

"You should've seen your face!" Dez turned around and high-fived Lexi, aka my traitor of a cousin. Obviously blood was not thicker than water. Despite that, I was happy Lanie had someone else who would fight tooth and nail to protect her.

We finally made it out of Daniel's office and were on our way toward Faye's room when Dez sidled up to Lexi and linked arms with her. "So . . . sports agent, huh? You must have a lot of connections. Any chance you can get me into the Gators' locker room? It's sort of my lifelong dream. Okay, so maybe not my lifelong dream, but hello? Locker room, big manly men, nakedness . . . *so* my thing."

Lexi chuckled. "Is that even a real question? Those college kids all think they're the next big thing, so they're usually champing at the bit to get me to visit their locker room. And FYI, they have no shame, but they do have teeny, tiny towels. So yeah, I can get you in. We should make a weekend of it."

Dez covered her mouth with her hands and gasped. "You shut your dirty whorish mouth."

"I will not," Lexi laughed. "Brad isn't keen on me making those trips without him. Not because he's insecure, but because he knows they're ogling what belongs to him and he's a stingy little boy who doesn't like to share his toys. Doesn't matter, though, because he doesn't get to tell me what to do. Tell you what. Since I really like you and all, I'll set it up and give you a call. The whole trip will be my treat."

"Alexis Mavis, from the bottom of my fatherfucking heart, I want to have your babies," Dez said, completely serious. "No way am I going to get my hoohah all distorted to do so, but I'm pretty sure we could pay a doctor enough to make it so that I can push one out of my asshole for you. We could name him, her, it, whatever . . . Asstasia, or Buttford, or Derrierick," she said, flaring her hands out with each name as if they were spelled out in lights on Broadway.

"Or you could just have a C-section," Polly offered. All three of them burst out into a fit of giggles, drawing attention from the nurses and orderlies at the nurses' station.

"Shh," I hushed them, because we were nearing Faye's room. "Okay, Lexi, go do your thing," I said, putting my hand on the small of her back and giving her a push toward the door.

"Wait a minute, asshat!" At least she whispered it. Lexi turned on me and thumped me on the forehead. Lucky for her, she was family. "Delicate shit like this takes finesse and preparation. You can't just go rushing in without looking the part. Polly? Dez?"

I sighed in defeat and watched as Polly scurried off toward the water fountain with a paper cup. Lexi turned toward Dez, who started bunching Lexi's clothes up in her hands while Lexi pinched and smacked at her own cheeks. When Polly returned, she drew her arm back as if to hurl the contents of the paper cup at Lexi, but Lexi stopped her. "Jesus Christ, Polly

Pocket! I'm supposed to look like I've been rushing, not like the winner of a wet T-shirt contest!"

"Oh, right. My bad," Polly said with a sheepish grin.

"Okay. Now . . ." Lexi mussed her hair, threw her shoulders back, and then lifted her chin. "Drizzle me, baby. Make me sweat."

There were about a million rude and crude things I could've said in response to that comment, but the short-lived satisfaction from the zing wouldn't have been worth it in the end. Lexi was the reigning queen of a very long game of guerrilla wordfare, a game in which verbal assault was our weapon of choice. We'd been playing it since we were kids, so I knew she would most definitely get her revenge and we didn't have time for that. Plus, I was pretty sure Lanie would've tied me to a car bumper, stomped on the gas pedal, and dragged my ass down the middle of the street until my balls had a thorough case of road rash for insulting her friend. The thought of picking tiny pebbles out of my sack with tweezers for the next year of my life was not the least bit appealing, so I let it go.

Polly dipped the tips of her fingers into the cup and flicked them toward Lexi's face, neck, and chest until she looked, very convincingly, like she'd been rushing around in a panic. Afterward, Lexi breathed in and out rapidly until she was practically panting. Then she turned toward the door and yanked it open with a purpose that perfectly mimicked the plan we had set in motion.

Lanie

The wait was excruciating; sort of like waiting to see if the little white stick you just peed all over was going to show one line or two after a drunken one-night stand where the person you ended up going home with was a scrub with no job, no money, and no control over their bodily functions. Okay, so I didn't really know anything about that, but I had an imagination and I watched a lot of cable television. My mother was in surgery, my father was sitting patiently beside me as he read the local newspaper, and Noah was somewhere in the building concocting God only knew what sort of plan to explain his presence in my little corner of the western hemisphere. My fingernails couldn't withstand the torture my gnawing teeth were putting on them for much longer, and I was pretty sure that if you put a lump of coal between my ass cheeks you were going to get a diamond the size of a baseball.

Sandra, aka Nurse Barbie, had come into the room moments earlier to let us know that everything was well with my mother and that she was in recovery. Daniel would be in soon to give us the rest of the details. It was fantastic news, but I still had the other drama to worry about. My dad might have been a bit off his game, but he was so skilled at detecting bullshit that I knew we weren't going to get away with anything as far as he was concerned. I just hoped Noah's plan would be as flawless as his face and that Daddy wasn't carrying his firearm.

Suddenly the door flew open and I jumped so high out of my chair that I listed sideways and hit my head on the wall. That smarted, too.

"Oh my God, Lanie! We came as soon as we could," Lexi said as she rushed into the room and wrapped her arms around me. "Are you okay? Is your mom okay? What's going on?"

"Lexi? What are you doing here?" I asked, confused.

"Saving your ass," she whispered into my ear.

It was then that I looked over her shoulder and saw Noah

stroll in with all the swagger and grace of a runway model. No, scratch that. He looked more like a rock star turned sex god on a rocket ship to planet Orgasm. His right hand was wedged into the front pocket of his jeans and the fingers of his other were casually stroking the edge of his impossibly chiseled jaw. The pad of his thumb caressed his bottom lip and a hint of his talented tongue peeked out to wave a how-do-you-do.

The Cooch started bouncing up and down while clapping. And when Noah casually adjusted himself in his jeans, she put the back of her hand to her forehead and swooned. Yeah, that was the effect the man had on my body. And my mom was okay, so my reaction to him wasn't the least bit indecent, thank you very much.

"Omigod, is this your dad?" Lexi abruptly turned me loose and sashayed over to him. Yes, she sashayed, which made me wonder if the ingenious plan the four of them had come up with had anything to do with infidelity, because she was laying it on pretty thick, batting her lashes and jiggling her cleavage. I was pretty sure the curtains were going to part to reveal a stripper's pole, a stage, and a DJ. I didn't know if I should tackle her to the ground and pound her face with my fist or dig into my wallet for all the dollar bills I could find.

"It's so nice to meet you, Mr. Talbot," she said, offering my dad her hand. "I'm Alexis Mavis, Lanie's roommate." My roommate? Yeah, that threw me for a loop, but I decided I should probably keep my mouth shut and see how it all played out. One look at Polly and Dez holding their breath let me know I was right.

Mack was awestruck by Lexi, and I sort of wanted to punch him for salivating over her like that when his wife, my mother, was lying in a recovery room down the hall. Not that I really thought Mack would cheat on her. And to be fair, it wasn't like it was his fault. I ventured a guess that Lexi had that power over any man not related to her, so his reaction was pretty normal. Plus, he recovered from his boob-induced trance quickly enough, so I had to at least give him credit for that.

"Alexis Mavis the sports agent? Your husband is NFL player Brad Mavis, right?" my dad asked with an awed expression. Aha, so that would explain the salivating. The only other thing that could make a man react that way would be sports, and my dad was a fanatic.

"One and the same," Lexi said with a red-carpet smile in place.

Oh, she was good.

Mack looked as confused as I was. I think I covered mine fairly well, mostly because I was distracted by the way Noah was breathing. Well, it wasn't so much the way he was breathing as the fact he just was. Add to that the fact he was there and that he loved me, and I was pretty much done for in the coherency department.

"Didn't Lanie tell you?" Lexi asked, looking to me and then back at my dad. She sighed and rolled her eyes in exasperation when I shrugged dumbly. "When Lanie got to campus, it turned out there was some mix-up on the dorm assignments—as in one less bed than they had originally thought. And well, since she was so late to report on her scholarship, she was pretty much left to fend for herself.

"I'm an NYU alum, and my husband and I were there to have lunch with the dean, but as we were leaving, we overheard all the fuss and wanted to help. Lucky for Lanie, we just happened to have an extra room in our penthouse off campus," Lexi explained—quite convincingly, I might add.

"And you didn't call us because . . . ?" Mack asked, tilting his head to the side while giving me the same look he'd given me when I was younger and had gotten into something I had no business getting into.

"I, um . . ." I looked to Lexi for help.

"She was actually going to pack up and go back home, but I'm a strong believer in the importance of a good education, and I couldn't let her give up because of a technicality." I'd say she was laying it on a little too thick, but if it worked, I'd give her a standing ovation and nominate her for an Emmy. "Besides, Brad's away for games a lot and I could use the company. She's my date to a lot of social functions that Brad can't make because of his schedule, which is where she met my dear, sweet cousin Noah."

"Noah?" Mack asked, turning toward me. "Who's Noah?"

"That would be me, sir." Noah stepped forward with his hand outstretched. "Noah Crawford. It's nice to finally meet you. Lanie's told me so much about you and your wife."

"She has, has she?" Mack asked, giving me another sideways glance. "Well, I wish I could say the same about you."

I could practically hear his bullshit meter screaming high-pitched alarms.

"Yeah, um, sorry about that, Dad." I stood and walked toward Noah to make a proper introduction and do some damage control. Noah put his arm around my waist and pulled me into his side, a sign that we were forming a united front, but really it was just incredibly distracting because I could both feel and smell him.

"Dad, I'd like for you to meet my . . . um, boyfriend, Noah Crawford," I said, not really sure what to call him, which is probably why the whole thing came out sounding more like a question rather than a statement.

Mack looked at me and then Noah and then Noah's arm, which was placed around my waist in a way that spoke volumes about our familiarity, and then down to Noah's outstretched hand before he finally shook it. "*The* Noah Crawford, huh?"

"Of Scarlet Lotus," Noah acknowledged before pulling his hand back and tucking it away in his pocket. "I'm really sorry to hear of your wife's illness. Can I ask how she is?"

"She's doing exceptionally well," a voice said from behind us.

Everyone turned to see Daniel walk into the room with what I assumed was my mother's chart in hand. He pulled up short when he saw Lexi standing beside my father. "I see you've met my daughter and my nephew," he said with a grin. "Small world, eh?"

"Yeah, it would appear so," my father replied, his tone signaling to me that he knew he was being bullshitted. "So about my wife?"

"The transplant was textbook smooth," Daniel replied, his demeanor utterly professional. "From here, it's a waiting game to make sure her body doesn't reject her new heart."

"Can we see her?" I asked.

"Right now, rest is imperative to her recovery. Any sort of excitement," he said, looking pointedly at the various people in the room before settling on me and Noah, "won't be good. So how about if we limit it to just you for now, Mr. Talbot? Sandra will take you to her in a few minutes."

"But Lanie is her daughter," Mack started to protest.

"I want to see her," I said adamantly.

"And you will," Daniel answered. "Just please, be patient. One at a time for now."

"You go first, Lanie," Mack offered, even though it was etched in every fine line of his face how badly he wanted to be at her side.

I gave him a reassuring smile. "It's okay, Dad. I'll get to see her later."

"Why don't I take you to get something to eat?" Noah kissed me on the temple and rubbed my back soothingly. "I was worried you would be so upset that you'd forget to, and I was right."

He gave me that irresistibly sexy smirk, and I bit down on my bottom lip, trying not to attack him on the spot. My dad wouldn't have appreciated that little porno moment.

"We'll go with you," Polly offered, linking her arm through Dez's. It really warmed my heart to see my two worlds coming together so seamlessly.

It seemed silly to me now that I'd ever thought Noah's life and mine were too different for us to ever have a life together. After all, when you took away the money and the fancy houses, cars, and clothes, weren't we all still just human underneath? Money truly cannot buy you love, and even though it could change some people, that didn't mean everyone who had a little of it were snobs. Truth be known, I was the snob for thinking Noah and his loved ones weren't good enough to live in my world. Not only were they good enough, but they had already become a permanent fixture of it. I couldn't remember my life before Noah, and I didn't want to imagine the future of my life without him in it.

"Yeah, I think I like that idea. We'll all go together," I said as I pulled away from Noah and took his hand instead before I turned back to my father. "Tell Mom I love her and I'll be in to see her as soon as I'm allowed, okay?"

"Sure thing, sweetie," he answered.

Daniel gave Noah and me a knowing grin and then took his leave. Lexi, Dez, and Polly followed close behind, but as Noah and I turned toward the door, my father stopped us.

"Lanie, a word please?" he asked, and then looked at Noah. "In private?"

I gave Noah an apologetic yet nervous smile. As much as I hated to watch him walk away, I couldn't deny my father the audience he requested. Besides, Noah was here to stay for as long as I wanted him, per his own words. I hoped he realized how long a lifetime really did last.

As if reading my mind, Noah cupped my cheek and kissed me gently on the forehead. "I'll be waiting for you at the elevator," he said before following our friends out.

I took a deep breath to still my nerves and then turned to face my dad, a smile plastered on my face. "What's up?"

"What took you so long to come see your mother?"

"What do you mean? I came as soon as Dez told me."

Mack picked up the newspaper he'd been reading earlier and held it out to me. There, on the front page of the entertainment section of that day's *Chicago Times,* was a picture of me and Noah on the red carpet at the Scarlet Lotus Ball. The caption read: "Chicago's most eligible bachelor, off the market?"

"Dad, I can explain—" I started.

Mack threw his hands up and stopped me. "No need to, Lanie. All I know is that you were in town, and even if I hadn't seen that article, I was already questioning how the hell you managed to make it here so quickly from New York. I've been so preoccupied with worrying about your mother that I didn't even notice how suspicious it was that you just happened to get a full scholarship at the last moment and whisked yourself away to New York at the drop of a hat. Then a couple million dollars shows up in our bank account with no clue as to where it came from, and your mother's doctor is taken off the case in favor of a prestigious cardiologist, who just so happens to be the father of your quote-unquote roommate, who just so happens to be the cousin of"—he motioned toward the newspaper again with a flick of his hand—"Chicago's most eligible bachelor. The man's got more money than he knows what to do with, and my daughter, a kid who was so shy she didn't even go to her own prom, is dating him and has her picture plastered all over the newspaper?"

Mack sighed and shook his head. "It doesn't make any sense, but right now I don't care. We've been given a miracle, and I suspect all these *coincidences*," he said, using air quotes around the word, "have everything to do with it, but I won't question that miracle because it means I get to hold on to my wife a while longer. Just don't make me regret it."

A smile so huge it hurt my cheeks spread across my face. "I won't, Daddy." I hadn't called my father that since I was seven. I went over and gave him a big, fat hug because he deserved it and because we both needed it. "Thank you."

"Yeah, yeah, yeah. Get out of here and go get something to eat. You're too skinny," he said, waving me off. "And when all of this is over with and your mother's back home, I want the two of you to come over for dinner and a proper introduction."

Translation: he wanted to introduce Noah to his Smith and Wesson.

Despite the fact he was letting me off the hook, I gave him my best please-don't-pull-out-the-shotgun-and-embarrass-me look. Noah was important to me, and the last thing I needed was for Mack to pull the protective-father routine. I was twenty-four years old and more than capable of taking care of myself. Mack might argue that point if he knew the lengths to which I'd gone to help my family, but I saw what I'd done as a show of strength, not weakness. Regardless, I knew once they got to know Noah, he'd sweep them off their feet the same way he did me.

"It's a date," I told Mack. "I'll be back in a bit to check on Mom."

Once I'd left the room, I blew out a huge puff of air and sighed in relief before I made my way toward the elevators. I hadn't gone far when a pair of hands shot out from an opened doorway and grabbed me, dragging me inside. There was no squeak of protest, no fighting off my would-be attacker, because I smelled him even before I saw him.

"Noah, what are you doing?" I laughed as he put my back against the wall and pinned me in place with his body.

He started devouring my neck with kisses. "I told you I was hungry."

"No, you didn't. I said I was hungry," I corrected him with a giggle.

He shrugged, securing my hands above my head with just one of his. "Po-tay-to, po-tah-to."

My body relaxed under his touch. "You're insatiable, Mr. Crawford."

"Ah, so finally you're catching on, Miss Talbot," he said as his free hand cupped my right breast and began to massage it.

"So what are we doing here then?"

"I think you're in need of some . . . what did you call it? Stress management?" His hand moved down my side until he slipped it underneath my skirt and down the front of my panties. I moaned the second his fingers came into contact with the soft flesh there and began to manipulate my clit. The Cooch shivered in delight.

"Mmm, yeah. You needed this, didn't you?" His tongue wrapped around my earlobe and he sucked it into his mouth.

The Cooch bobbed her head emphatically and wept from his touch.

I tried to pull my hands down so I could immerse them in his thick hair, but he held me firmly in place. "Uh-uh, Lanie. No touching. Only feeling."

He accentuated the last word by dipping a long, broad finger inside me, languidly pushing it in before pulling it back out again just as slowly. The heel of his palm pressed against my clit, massaging it with his movements until I felt like my knees would buckle and I'd fall to the floor. But there was no danger of that because Noah was very capable of holding me up.

I felt a second finger push inside and then he stroked the walls of my pussy until I rolled my pelvis against his hand. Back and forth he flicked his fingers, maddeningly slow and then fast before slowing down again. It was enough yet too much, all at the same time, and I felt my body coiling with sensation, ready to spring with just the right stroke.

"Not yet," he whispered against my lips, then claimed my mouth in a searing kiss. Noah removed his fingers, leaving me wanting. When I groaned in protest, he broke the kiss and looked down on me with that evil little smirk that always made my girly bits break into a chorus of hallelujahs.

"Patience, kitten. You know I always take care of you."

True story.

Noah pulled his body away from mine, and moved my arms down until my hands were planted flat against the wall at my sides. He hummed in contemplation as he looked me over and then bit down on his bottom lip. "I'm going to let go of your hands now, Delaine, but I want you to keep them in place. If you move them, you will not get your release. Do you understand me?"

"I really hate you for this," I said, but knew I would do anything he asked. So did he.

He smirked again. "No, you don't. You already told me you love me, and you can't take it back." He kissed the tip of my nose and then slowly pulled his hands away.

Noah

Sinking to my knees, I slipped my hands beneath the hem of Lanie's dress and pushed the skirt up and over her hips. I couldn't help the overwhelming urge to nuzzle her center, so I flicked my tongue out to sample the sweet taste of her arousal that had seeped through the black silk material. "Mmm, hors d'oeuvres. I think I'll keep these for later." I ripped her panties from her body. Those fuckers had been outlawed and had no business creating a barrier between me and what I wanted.

Lanie gasped in surprise and I smirked up at her. "Never know when I might get hungry again," I said with a shrug.

"Not that I've forgotten your blatant disregard for the no-panties rule, Miss Talbot. You will pay for that. Later."

I tucked her panties in the front pocket of my jeans. Once they were securely in place, I put my hands on the inside of her knees and pushed, spreading her creamy thighs wide for invasion. I didn't take my time, didn't make it slow or sensual; I buried my face between her thighs and attacked. Lanie's back arched and her knees buckled, but I held her in place with my hands firmly grasping her hips. There was no escaping me or my mouth until I was ready to release her.

I pulled back minutely, mixing the coaxing with the demanding, and saw her fingers twitch out of the corner of my eye. "Please don't move those hands, kitten. I'd hate to have to stop before I give you what you want, but I'm a man of my word, and I will, so don't test me," I warned with my lips grazing her sensitive spot.

"Please, Noah. Please, I need to . . ." I fucking loved to hear her beg for what only I could give to her. It made my cock impossibly hard, and I was overcome with the urge to get it wet.

Really, there was no reason we couldn't both be appeased at the same time—kill two birds with one stone, or cock, as it were. Getting dental was a necessity first, though, so I nipped at her clit, letting her guttural groan linger and then grow into something altogether animalistic as I sucked on the taut knot with a vigorous hunger. Giving her delectable little pussy one last, long lick, I stood before her and planted my hands against the wall on either side of her head. When I pressed my body against Lanie's, I made damn sure she could feel my hardness.

"This is what you fucking do to me. It's really quite painful, but I assure you, the pleasure is also there," I told her, relishing her moans of appreciation as I continued to work myself against her very naked, very wet cunt. The purpose was to drive her crazy, which it did, but I was also insane and unwilling to wait any longer.

Quickly stepping back, I made fast work of my belt and jeans before pulling them down far enough to let my dick spring free. Then I slipped my hands between her thighs and onto the wall, forcing them to spread as I lifted her until she was at the perfect height with her legs draped over my forearms.

"I'm going to take my time with you once I get you back home, but for now, this will have to be quick. Hold on to me, kitten," I said, finally giving her permission to touch me.

Lanie hooked her arms under mine and grabbed the top of my shoulders with her hands and I entered her . . . deep. When we both moaned out in pleasure, I was forced to muffle our sounds with my mouth or risk drawing unwanted attention or causing some nosy nurse—or, God forbid, her father—to come investigate. I most definitely did not want to kick off my official relationship with the woman I loved by having her father threaten to send me to the morgue. Although apparently rigor mortis had already set in, at least in my cock—I was that fucking hard for her.

Not to worry, I was buried balls deep inside my Lanie, and that was more than enough to take care of the issue at large. Over and over again, I thrust into her, going deeper and deeper with each urgent stab. She sank her nails into my shoulder, and I could feel the bite from them digging through my shirt, but it didn't deter me because that shit felt good when I knew it was derived from the pleasure I was giving to her. My girl's kisses became needy, my thrusts frenzied until finally I felt her walls clench around my cock with a throbbing pulse and she moaned into my mouth. Her body stiffened and her thighs attempted to clamp shut of their own accord as she shuddered in my arms with her orgasm. It was all the permission I needed to finally let go myself and spill my seed into her with a final strangled grunt, my hips jerky with incomplete strokes until I was spent.

Hands down, best quickie ever. I'll admit to feeling like a douche for taking her that way the first time after our confessions of love, but I would most definitely be making it up to her later. Over and over again, until she was thoroughly satisfied. And then start at the beginning again, because like my girl pointed out, I was insatiable.

I pulled out of Lanie and eased her down the wall until her feet touched the floor. She swayed a little lethargically in my arms, so I gathered her back up to me. "Easy, kitten. You okay?"

She sighed contentedly. "Oh yeah, I'm really okay."

I chuckled at her response. She had the same effect on me—not that I was all that surprised, because it had been that way from the very first week we'd spent together, and it always would be.

Always? Was I thinking long-term about our relationship?

Damn straight I was. She was mine.

4

envy me, bitches

Lanie

"He did not!" my mother squealed.

Dez laughed at her reaction. "Oh yes he did. You should've seen him, Momma Faye. He was all"—Dez tucked her chin to her chest and spread her shoulders to mimic my father—" 'That's my wife, boy, and I'll be goddamned if I'm gonna sit by and let some pimply-faced orderly who's just barely reached puberty and still jacked up on teenage hormones give her a sponge bath! I'm the only man who touches those goodies! Leave the sponge and the tub, and walk away slowly, son, before someone gets hurt.' "

My mother was full-on laughing by the time Dez was finished with her less than accurate impersonation, and the peal was music to my ears. I hadn't heard her laugh like that in so long I'd nearly forgotten what it sounded like. Of course, had my father heard Dez's mockery, he wouldn't have found it quite so humorous. Good thing he was at the house getting things ready for my mother's return.

It had been ten days since her transplant, and so far so good. All her color was back, and she was sitting up, laughing, eating, smiling . . . living. The scar on her chest was an angry red in color, but it, too, had healed significantly, and she claimed that it only hurt a little if she coughed. That may or may not have been true, but the sparkle was back in her eye and she was soaking up every single bit of information she could about how to maintain her health so her body wouldn't reject her new heart.

The only source of worry I could find was Faye's concern for the family of the young lady who had given her another chance to live. She wanted to offer her condolences and thank them properly, as we all did, but Daniel said it was the family's choice not to have their information disclosed. Upon his suggestion, I sat down with my mother and we wrote them a letter that he agreed to deliver, hoping they would one day find peace with their loss. I'd also hoped my mother would find peace with her gain, but she was a sentimental person and I knew the idea that someone else had had to die in order for her to live would haunt her for the rest of her life.

"Well, it wasn't exactly like that," Polly chimed in.

"It *was* exactly like that," Dez argued.

I knew better. "Mack does not say 'goodies.' "

My mother interrupted with a devilish grin. "Um, yes, he does."

"Oh, gross! Mom!" I did not need those mental images. I contemplated checking the janitor's closet to see if there was some bleach—or whatever it was hospitals used to keep everything so sterile—I could use to scrub my brain. It was definitely going to take something industrial-strength and then I'd probably still be scarred for life.

She scoffed. "Oh, please, Lanie. How do you think you got

here? I assure you, it wasn't by immaculate conception." She got this dreamy look in her eye like she was reminiscing. "We sure did have a lot of fun making you. The things your father can do with his—"

I plugged my ears with my fingers and started singing to drown her out. It didn't work. I could still hear her over my own hideous screeching.

" . . . your dad has this fascination with the Statue of Liberty, so I have this outfit—"

"Stop! Stop! Stop! Pleeeeease stop," I begged.

Faye finally fell silent at my outburst and gave me a look. "Don't act like you're so innocent," she said, smoothing the sheets over her midsection. "I've seen that piece of man meat you've been wearing. You two haven't been able to keep your hands off each other. I bet he's good in the sack, too, isn't he? I mean, he's Noah Crawford, Chicago's most eligible bachelor."

"Seriously? I'm going to puke," Lexi said in a bored tone as she examined her nails. Then she sighed and straightened in her chair. "I love my cousin and all, but I really don't want to hear this."

My mom did that thing where she tried to be less like a mom and more like one of the girls. "You shush it, girlie. I want to know everything," she told Lexi, then turned back to me. "So just how big is the big spender?"

"I'm soooo not going to answer that question," I said, appalled and embarrassed. I wanted to curl up into a fetal position and suck my thumb until it all just went away. "What are you, some kind of cougar? Need I remind you that I'm your daughter, and this is beyond inappropriate?"

Dez came to my mother's defense. "Stop being such a prude, Sandra Dee, and let your inner Cha Cha DiGregorio shine through. You've shimmied your way into your painted-on leather, strapped on your peep-toe heels, colored your lips red, and snagged Danny Zuko." Her obsession with *Grease* bordered on insanity.

"Let us live vicariously through you. I mean, you've scored the jackpot, honey, so the least you could do is gloat about it for the less fortunate." Dez crossed her legs, propped her elbow on her knee, and rested her chin in her palm. "What's he working with? And don't try to lie, either. I've seen the size of his feet *and* his hands."

"Oh my God! I can't believe this is happening," I mumbled, running my hands over my face. "I'm being punked, aren't I? Where are the cameras?"

Dez made a fist with one hand and started rotating the other as if she were holding a movie camera aimed straight at me. "Lanie Marie Talbot, this is your life," she said with a game show host's intonation. "So tell us . . . Vienna sausage or Peterbilt truck?"

"Just tell us," Polly chimed in. I was shocked. She sounded like I was about to reveal the secret to eternal life or something. Noah was her boss, and her husband was probably the closest friend Noah had, yet she was all up in my business, wanting to know how long his schlong was.

Lexi sighed and rolled her eyes. "Tell them, for God's sake, so that we can move on from this horrendous topic."

"Fine!" I yelled, throwing my hands up in defeat. "He's colossal, okay? Huge! And the sex is epic! He knocks it out of the park each and every time he's at bat. He's got me speaking in tongues and my head spinning around on my shoulders like I'm possessed or something. If the absolute greatest sex in the universe were to manifest into a physical being, it would clone itself after Noah Crawford. He is the poster child for massive orgasms, the alpha and omega of cocks everywhere. His junk should be stuffed and mounted like a trophy over a fireplace, put on display behind bulletproof glass with heat-sensitive alarms and motion detectors at the Smithsonian of Cockdom! It is the holy grail of penises everywhere, and only he has the ability to harness its full power. In short, Noah Crawford is the epitome of sex. He makes my toes curl and my body convulse. There. Are you happy?"

The room was so quiet you could hear a pin drop. My mother's jaw was slack and Polly's eyes were bulging out of her head. And then there was Dez . . .

"So if you had to put a specific measurement on it, what would it be?"

I heard a throat clear at the doorway and my head snapped in that direction to find Noah leaning against the door frame with his hands in his pockets. Judging by the egotistical smirk on his face, I'd say he'd heard just enough of my speech to make him impossible to live with.

"Sorry to interrupt, ladies," he said as he straightened and walked into the room. "Mrs. Talbot, you're looking very well."

"I, uh . . . Well, um, thank you," my mother stuttered, apparently picturing my boyfriend naked, which was oh so Jerry Springer of her.

When I'd first seen my mother in the recovery room ten days earlier, Noah had been right by my side, and I remembered the way her jaw had nearly dropped to the floor and how she repeatedly rubbed her eyes as if she couldn't possibly have been seeing what she was seeing. She beamed like the mother of a beauty pageant contestant who'd mopped the floor with all those other wanna-bes. Not that my mother had ever treated me that way, but she knew who Noah Crawford was, and she was stoked that her baby girl was dating him.

"I missed you." Noah squatted behind me and leaned in to give my neck a very sweet, chaste kiss. Then he wrapped his arms around my shoulders from behind and addressed my mother. "I spoke with Mr. Talbot on the way over and he said all the medical equipment arrived today and has been set up. Looks like you're good to go when Daniel gives you the green light."

"Actually, Dr. Crawford said that, barring any unforeseen complications, I can go home tomorrow." Faye beamed excitedly. "I want to thank you for making all of this possible. I know you'll probably never claim responsibility, but I also know that if it hadn't been for you, I wouldn't be here right now, and my daughter wouldn't be nearly as happy as she finally seems to be. You've touched the life of each member of our family, Noah, and we can never repay you for that."

He hugged me tighter. "I'd do anything for Lanie. Besides, I only did what any decent human being would do if given the resources, Mrs. Talbot. I'm no saint."

"Well, in my eyes you are, and I won't soon forget what you've done," my mother said with misty eyes. She took a deep breath and collected herself before starting again. "Now, Lanie, what are your plans? Are you going back to school?"

Yeah, she and Mack still thought I was legitimately enrolled at NYU. How was I going to get out of that mess?

Lexi came to the rescue. "Actually, I pulled some strings with the dean's office and got him to agree to let Lanie drop her classes for this semester and reenroll for the next, without it affecting her *scholarship*," she said, giving me a look that said I should go with what she was saying. "So she's free to stick around here for a while."

My mom clasped her hands together. "That's great! You'll be coming home, then?"

"Um . . ." That caught me off guard. I hadn't really thought about what I would do, or where I would go once she was free to leave. I turned to look at Noah, hoping he'd saddle up on his white horse and come to my rescue yet again, but his defeated expression offered me no solace or hope of being able to go back home with him. I could tell by the way he nodded and offered a smile that our separation wasn't what he wanted, either. But at the same time, he had to have known this would happen, which meant he was sacrificing, yet again, for me and my family. I wished he'd been selfish and demanded I stay with him, but I knew he wouldn't.

I turned back to my mother so that I wouldn't have to see his pretty face, in hopes that I'd have the strength to say what he and I both knew I had to say. "Yeah, Mom, I'm coming home." I gave her a halfhearted smile that I hoped looked convincing enough.

What kind of daughter had I become? I should've wanted to be there to help her on her road to recovery because she still had quite a way to go. But I couldn't fathom the idea of sleeping in my cold bed—the very same bed in which I'd spent night after night wondering if I was doomed to never know what it felt like to have a warm body cuddled up next to me, to never know the fire that boiled in my veins from a lover's touch, to never know what it felt like to be adored by someone of worth.

I could feel Noah's warm breath on the shell of my ear as his husky voice spoke from just over my shoulder. "If it's okay with you, Mrs. Talbot, I'd like to steal her away from you for the evening. Unless you need her here, of course."

Always the fucking considerate gentleman. *Throw me over your shoulder like a Neanderthal, damn it! Whisk me away to your cave with grunted warnings for anyone who might dare try to take me away from you!* God knew the man didn't seem to have a problem behaving that way when he'd decided he knew what was best for me time and time again before. It may have been seriously fucked up of me, but part of me wanted that Noah back again. At least in that moment.

"No, no, no. Lanie's been with her sick old mother every single day and night since I got here," Faye said. "She needs to get out. You two kids go and, um . . . have fun." She tried to contain her giggles, but then Dez, Polly, and Lexi started snickering, and all bets were off.

How very junior high of them, I thought. But it became very evident that I was never going to live down the whole Noah-is-a-sex-god rant. I imagined the episode of *The Jerry Springer Show* we could all appear on: "My Mother Wants to Sleep with My Boyfriend, but He's Too Busy Boinking His Cousin, His Married Assistant Dreams of His Penis Size, and My Best Friend Might Be Pregnant with His Baby."

Intent on capitalizing on my newfound realization and making them all suffer for embarrassing me, I shook those disturbing thoughts out of my head and stood. After kissing my mother on the cheek, I grabbed Noah's hand and dragged him behind me as I turned for the door.

"Where are you going?" Polly asked.

I stopped short, looked back over my shoulder at my friends, and with a knowing smirk said, "The Smithsonian. Envy me, bitches."

~$~

"The alpha and omega of cocks everywhere, huh?" Noah asked as we stepped into the empty elevator and the doors closed behind us.

I inhaled deeply, letting the scent of him that had permeated the air in the small space envelop my senses. I think I purred. "Something like that."

Noah suddenly had me pinned against the wall, his body pressed firmly to mine, and his mouth engaging my own in a searing kiss. His hands were everywhere: fondling my breast, cupping my ass, stroking the sweet spot just under the crotch seam of my jeans. His attack was so fast and furious that I hadn't even had a chance to take a breath. Oxygen was over-rated, right? I was pretty sure I could live without it because as long as Noah continued to do things that made my pulse race, it meant my heart was still beating. Sure, I would probably be a little brain-damaged from the lack of oxygen to the old cranium when he was done, but it would be worth it.

The bell dinged, signaling our stop at another floor. Before the doors opened, Noah pulled away and stood by my side. A nurse stepped on, carrying a food tray. Judging by the way her eyes widened when she took in my appearance, I'd say she knew exactly what we'd been up to. My chest was heaving, I was sure my hair looked every bit as disheveled as my clothes, and I could feel the flush on my skin. When Nurse Observant finally stopped staring at me, she swept her eyes over Noah . . . and gasped. I turned to find the cause of her reaction, but he seemed perfectly normal to me. I was about to chalk it up to it being merely the effect his gorgeousness had on women when I suddenly noticed the enormous bulge in the front of his pants. I quickly stepped in front of him to block Nurse Observant's view of the colossal cock. Just then another nurse stepped onto the elevator, and the two soon were engaging in conversation, which meant I wasn't going to have to spoon the bitch's eyes out for ogling my man.

Noah put his arm around my waist and pulled me back against him so that my ass was firmly planted against his erection. He nuzzled my ear with his nose and grinded against me, whispering, "Jealous, Lanie?"

I shook my head.

He chuckled quietly and gave my exposed neck a soft kiss. "Yes, you are." His warm breath caressed my ear. "I want to fuck you. Right now. Right here. In this elevator. With them watching."

My heart literally skipped a beat. I'd never thought of myself as kinky, but I wasn't really surprised that exhibitionism turned out to be a turn-on for me. Noah had already shown me so many different sides of the person I truly was on the inside—someone that I hadn't known existed before. Damned if I didn't want him to do it just as badly as he wanted to. And I knew it wasn't only so those hussies would know he belonged to me, either.

The elevator finally stopped on the ground floor, and Noah led me out the front doors to where Samuel was waiting with the limousine. Once we were inside, Noah pulled me to him and kissed me deeply.

"I missed you," he said, breaking the kiss.

Noah had been by my side throughout the entire ordeal with my mother and we hadn't gone one day without seeing each other, but I knew what he meant. With the exception of the one time, we hadn't been able to hide away to, um, take care of business. We were both wound up pretty tightly, and it seemed yet another separation was on the horizon, what with me going home to stay with my parents and all. I hoped we'd have a lot more alone time despite that, though, because I was not one bit averse to sneaking out into the woods with him and doing it like a couple of adolescent teens.

"Me too," I whispered, stroking his cheek.

A mischievous smile crept up on his face. "And don't think I've forgotten about your punishment, either."

I sighed and rolled my eyes. "Not with the stupid panties again."

"Oh, yes," he said, grabbing my hair roughly and forcing me to look at him, which really turned me on. Holy crapola, did it ever. "It was a cheap shot, and you know it, so you must be punished."

"And what might my punishment be, Mr. Crawford?" I asked, eagerly playing along.

"I might have an idea. Hungry?" he asked, and I nodded. "Good, because I've got something for you right here."

I heard the clinking of his belt buckle and then the metal against metal as his zipper was released.

"I missed your lips," he said, kissing me chastely. Then he sighed heavily. "And I really missed your mouth."

He wasn't talking about my sarcastic wit, either, and it kind of made me all giddy inside because I knew I could take care of that for him, gladly.

With his hand still fisted in my hair, he pushed my head down toward his crotch, where his cock was already free and giving me a *Hey! How are ya? I'm the piece of meat that's about to get crammed down the back of your throat when my man, Noah, there forces you headfirst into his lap so that he can fuck your mouth. Tsk, tsk, tsk. Shouldn't have worn the panties, woman.*

I stifled a giggle because it wasn't like I was the least bit intimidated by the threat. How could something I wanted be considered punishment? I was getting off easy. Or, rather, he was going to be the one to get off. And maybe that was his angle.

"I love you," I whimpered, hoping to change his mind if in fact he had no intention of letting me get mine.

"Mmm-hmm. I love you, too, kitten. Now suck my cock," he said, pushing my head into his lap.

I loved that he hadn't lost that domineering edge just because admissions of love had been spoken. It wouldn't have been the same. *He* wouldn't have been the same, and I didn't want him to change who he really was.

The angle I was approaching from wasn't exactly prime, so I slid onto the floor between his legs and took him in my hand. His skin felt silky smooth and hot, yet he was as solid as marble, and I couldn't help but admire his cock. He was all I had bragged that he was, and I'd missed him so.

I took him into my mouth and hummed at finally having him back there. He was right; I did enjoy having his cock in my mouth a little too much.

"Fuck, yeah. You love this, don't you? Bad girls like to suck cock, don't they? Let me see." He groaned as he gathered my hair up into his hand so that he could have a better view to watch what I was doing.

I hummed again in answer and bobbed my head more earnestly, wanting to make him happy. Saliva was dripping down his shaft, making it easier for me to exaggerate my motions and take him deeper.

Noah hissed. "Goddamn, that feels so fucking perfect. I love to hear those wet sounds when you're sucking my cock real good and proper like that."

I started to move faster, spurred on by his dirty talk and a growl from somewhere deep within his chest erupted. Noah pulled hard on my hair and immobilized me. Then he started thrusting his hips, his dick quickly moving back and forth inside my mouth. I could feel him hit the back of my throat with each stroke, and he pulled nearly all the way out before pushing back in again. It was all I could do to control my gag reflex, but I loved it when he fucked my mouth.

"I wish everyone else could see how fucking good you look sucking my cock," he grunted.

I have no idea what came over me; perhaps it was the realization from the elevator moments before, or the fact that I wanted everyone to see how good I made this man feel, but whatever the reason, I reached my hand up and pressed the button that controlled the window. The tinted glass slid down, giving greater Chicago front-row seats to our little show. I felt like a porn star who'd just won the Golden Cock, even though the only thing anyone could see was my head bobbing up and down and Noah's face with its expression of orgasmic pleasure. But make no mistake, anyone who pulled up next to us would definitely know what was up in the back seat of that limousine.

"Oh, God, I really fucking love you, woman." Noah moaned, the city lights spilling in through the opened window and casting moving shadows across his chiseled face.

I took as much of him as I could, swallowing the head of his dick down the back of my throat before releasing him again.

"That's right, baby. You keep sucking my cock like that, and when I get you home, I'm going to give you what you've been wanting." He growled, shoving my head down and then rolling his hips upward before releasing to let me do my thing again. "I'm going to make love to that tight little pussy of yours, and then I'm going to fuck that pretty ass."

Game, set, match. Hole in one. Touchdown. Swish—nothing but net. Goal. Home run . . . Whatever. All I knew was that my eye was on the prize and I wanted the win.

I gave him and that colossal cock all I had, going to town on that bad boy like I hadn't eaten for days and had stumbled upon an all-you-can-eat buffet. All my hard work—yeah, right; 'twas my pleasure—paid off big-time. Noah thrust his hips up while shoving my head down so that his cock was lodged in the back of my throat, and then he came, spewing his hot semen into my mouth like a volcanic eruption. I swallowed as quickly as I could, not really wanting to taste the salty goo, but loving the feral moans of ecstasy that spilled from his succulent lips nonetheless.

"Christ, woman." He was still panting when his body finally relaxed and I released his dick. "I would've fucked you one way or the other, but that? Fucking hell, there just are no words."

I giggled. "So does that mean I'm forgiven for the panty thing?"

He smiled while tucking his dick away. "Yeah, you're forgiven. But don't ever let that shit happen again, because I will be only too happy to do a reenactment of your punishment."

"Promises, promises," I cooed, wiping the corners of my mouth.

The car rolled to a stop and I looked out the opened window and realized we were home. I suddenly felt a little sick to my stomach, not knowing how long I was going to have to be without him, or whether or not our separation would have an effect on the way he felt about me. I mean, he had his work and home in Chicago, and I would be in bum-fucked Hillsboro. Not exactly in another state, but with his schedule, how often could I really expect to see him?

"Hey, what's wrong?" Noah asked, lifting my chin to look into my eyes.

"I don't know if I can do it."

"Do what?"

"Be away from you."

"I'm not going anywhere, Lanie."

"Yeah, but I am," I said, pulling my chin from his grasp and straightening myself. "And you're horny all the time, which is exactly the reason you bought me in the first place—"

I stopped abruptly when I saw his face contort like I'd just slapped him.

"I'm sorry, I didn't mean that. I just . . . God, it's killing me, you know?"

Noah sighed. "Yeah, I do," he said quietly. "But there's always the weekends, and I'll make a trip to Hillsboro every chance I get."

I crossed my arms over my chest in a pout. "Sure, it'll be that way for a little while, and then you'll get tired of it and the trips will become more infrequent until you're just doing it every now and then out of habit. You'll start to resent me, and before I know it, you won't be there at all because you'll have moved on." I wrapped my arms tighter, hugging myself and already beginning to feel the hole developing in my heart.

"Don't," he said, all business.

"Don't what?"

"Don't start dooming us already." He ran his hands through his hair in exasperation. "I love you, Lanie. It took me a long time to be able to open myself up like this again, and I'm not about to let you go that easily. I'm yours and you're mine, and we're going to make the best of the time we have together. Now get out of the fucking car."

Noah opened the door and stepped out, holding his hand out for me. My thoughts drifted back to my first night there, when I would never have been able to imagine what we'd since become to each other. I took his outstretched hand, a symbol that we were in this thing together and that together we would find a way to make it work.

I'd no sooner stepped onto the ground than Noah snatched me up, threw me over his shoulder, and carried me up the steps to the door. I giggled, no longer feeling the pangs of separation, content to live in the moment. If little stolen moments were all we had for the time being, I was going to live them to the fullest and hope for the best.

Once we were inside, Noah carried me to his office, opened

a drawer, and pulled something out that I couldn't see since I was hanging upside down, face-to-face with the Ridonkabutt. All the blood was rushing to my head, but the view was fabulous, so I wasn't complaining.

"What are you doing?" I laughed.

"You'll see," he said, then turned to leave the office.

Up the stairs and down the hall he carried me. I knew the route well; he was taking me to the bedroom for some happy-happy, joy-joy playtime. When he finally set me down on my feet, the blood drained from my head and flowed back into the rest of my body, making me suddenly dizzy.

"First things first," Noah said, steadying me. In his hand was a ruler. "If you're going to be bragging about me, I think you should have the facts."

"A ruler?" I questioned.

He smirked. "Right. Perhaps a yardstick would be more appropriate?"

He wanted me to measure his penis? *And so the egomania begins* . . .

I shrugged. If you can't beat 'em, might as well join 'em. Plus, I was more than a little curious to know the exact number myself.

I took the ruler and reached for his pants.

"Whoa, whoa, whoa!" Noah stopped me, taking a step back. "You can't measure it limp, Delaine. You have to wait until I'm hard."

"Hmm, I see," I said, and then closed the gap between us. "Well, let's see if we can't take care of that. In the interest of presenting the facts, that is."

I backed him up against the wall and began kissing along the length of his neck. At the same time, I cupped him through

his jeans and massaged his cock. Even limp, he was still an impressive size, but it didn't take long before the bulge in his
pants grew thick and hard under my manipulations. I couldn't
help the self-satisfied grin that spread across my face.

Noah moaned. "You're . . . very talented."

"I have a great teacher." I took a step back and made fast
work of his pants. "I think you're up to snuff now, big boy."

The Wonder Peen sprang free, and I wrapped my hand
around it, steadying it so that I could take a proper measurement. I was impressed. Like, really impressed. Noah measured
in at a little over nine inches and all that, had been inside me,
and was about to be inside my ass. Admittedly, I was a bit intimidated.

"And there you have it," he said with a cocky grin and a
twinkle in his eye. "Proof that your boyfriend's cock truly is
the holy grail of penises everywhere."

I rolled my eyes and tossed the ruler to the side. "Just how
much of that speech did you hear?"

"All of it." He stepped toward me and took the bottom of
my shirt, pulling it over my head.

"And now you've got a big head over it, huh?" I asked,
unbuttoning his shirt. I kissed the newly exposed skin, inhaling
his scent and memorizing each indentation of the muscles in
his chest.

"Well, I think we just proved that, now didn't we?" He
kicked his shoes off and reached forward, flicking the clasp at
the front of my bra and releasing it so that the straps could fall
down my arms. "And it's all yours, baby," he said before cupping my breasts and suckling at one of the nipples. "Jesus
Christ, I want you so fucking bad."

It didn't take either of us much longer to have the other completely undressed, and before I knew it, I was sprawled out on top of the bed with Noah's head between my thighs.

"Mmm, you taste so sweet, kitten," he mumbled against my soaked flesh.

His tongue flicked at my clit rapidly before he covered it with his mouth and sucked gently, all while still manipulating it with his very talented tongue. I brought my knees up and closed my thighs around his head, moaning at the sensation of his scruffy beard against my sensitive skin as he worked me over. Two fingers pushed and pulled inside me, while two more worked my back entrance. He was priming me for the invasion, so I relaxed as much as I could, enjoying the other sensations he gave me as a distraction. Before long, I found myself actually pushing forward to meet the thrust of his fingers, wanting even more.

"Yeah, you want it, too, don't you?" I could only whimper in response. "Don't worry, kitten. I'm going to give it to you. I just need to make sure you're ready first."

I came hard, rocking my hips back and forth and then stiffening as the orgasm took over my body and rendered me unable to move. Noah carefully removed his fingers and crawled up the bed to lie on his side next to me. Tender kisses were placed along my shoulder and neck until my breathing finally evened out and I could see straight again. Noah gathered me up into his arms and turned me so that my back was to him. And then he entered me from behind, in the traditional sense.

He made love to me slowly—holding me tight as he whispered words of admiration and love into my ear.

"I love you so much," I told him, kissing the palm of his

hand, because it was one of the very few parts of him to which I had access.

"I know you do, baby." He nuzzled the sensitive skin on the back of my neck. "I love you, too. Jesus, you feel so unbelievably good."

But I could give him more. "Noah, I'm ready," I told him, sensing he was waiting for my permission before going any further.

"Are you sure?" He kissed along the length of my neck to my ear. "I want to . . . really fucking bad, but I don't want to hurt you."

"You and I both know that you could never hurt me," I reassured him. "Please?"

Noah reached over me and grabbed the bottle of lubricant he'd brought up from his office. He didn't pull away from me as he squirted a little on his fingertips and then spread it around my rear opening. All the while, he was still moving inside me.

"This will be a first for me, too," he whispered, kissing my shoulder. He pulled out of me and began to coat himself with the lubricant.

"You've never done this before?" I asked, stunned.

"No. So if it hurts too much, I need you to tell me. Okay?" I could feel the head of his dick at my entrance, applying a little pressure.

I nodded, holding my breath because I was nervous, but I really wanted this first for both of us. Finally, something he and I would have that no one else could ever take away.

I felt him push forward slowly, more pressure. And then with one very quick, very short thrust, he was inside me. I gasped at the burning sensation and stiffened, holding my breath once again and willing the fire of the stretching pain to subside. Tears sprang to my eyes unbeckoned, like a little girl who'd just fallen and scraped her knee, only this was so much bigger than that. My body's natural instinct was to push him out, but I held still and squeezed my eyes shut instead, unwilling to move or breathe for fear it would only make it worse.

"Breathe, kitten. You have to breathe." Noah's strained voice was almost a whisper as his shaky hands stroked my arms lovingly and peppered my shoulders with tender kisses. "Just breathe and try to relax. It'll get better."

I exhaled a long breath and tried my damnedest to loosen the muscles in my body. He was right—once I started to relax, the pain subsided a bit.

"Keep going," I told him.

Noah's voice was raspy, his body trembling. "Are you sure? I'm not even all the way in yet. That was only the head."

What!?

I nodded my head quickly, my jaw feeling the pressure of my clenched teeth. I inhaled deeply and then exhaled again, readying myself for yet more pain. I could do this. I could do it for him. "Just . . . go slow," I said, unable to keep the strain out of my voice.

"I'm hurting you. We're not doing this," he said, and I felt him back away as if he were about to pull out, which I absolutely could not let happen.

"No! I want this. Please, Noah, let me give this to you. Give this to me," I begged, and then pushed back into him slightly to prove how much I wanted it.

I heard him groan. A groan of pleasure, not frustration. I did that to him. Then I felt his warm, soft, wet lips along my shoulders again as he began to move inside me, oh so slowly, once more. It wasn't nearly as painful, just uncomfortable. But the more he moved, the deeper he went, the more I loosened up and started to enjoy the sensations. An involuntary moan escaped my lips, and I felt his arms tighten around me and his breathing became heavier. I wanted to know that it felt good to him, too; I wanted to hear him *say* it.

"What does it feel like?" I asked. "Do you like it?"

"Oh, God, kitten. You have no idea," he moaned in that husky voice, his hot breath spilling over the skin on the back of my neck. "You feel so fucking good."

"More. Give me more," I urged him on, knowing he was holding back for fear of hurting me. But I wanted him to get the full effect, and in truth, I sort of liked it. I knew I wouldn't get off this first time, but that was okay, too.

Noah held me firmly in place as he rolled his hips, moving deeper still, faster.

"That's it, baby," I spurred him on. "Do what feels good to you. I want you to come so fucking hard."

"Shit! I love it when you say naughty things to me," he managed between heavy breaths.

That was all he needed to say. If he loved it, I was going to give him more of it.

"Noah, your massive cock is in my ass," I moaned, wanting him to get the mental effect as well as the physical. "Oh, God, baby. You're fucking me in my ass, owning me completely."

That must have done it.

"Fuck, fuck, fuck!" he growled through clenched teeth. "I can't . . . stop. Oh, God. I'm gonna . . . Fuck, I'm gonna come, kitten."

Noah thrust into me, his hips slapping against my ass and his hand clutching my hip so hard I knew there would be a bruise there by morning. He bit into the flesh on the back of my neck and growled out his release, furiously animalistic. All I could do was hold on, all the while grinning like the cat that ate the canary. *I* did that for him. *I* gave him what no one else ever had—or ever would again, if I had anything to say about it. And I'd do it a thousand more times. Because I could.

It hurt like a motherfucker. But the discomfort I experienced was worth it in the end, because it was a connection only he and I shared. I could feel how much pleasure it gave him, and I reveled in the fact that a man who seemingly was always in control wasn't when it came to me. It was a freedom he deserved, and I always wanted him to feel like that.

I'd come to Noah a virgin in every sense of the word, physically and emotionally, and he had introduced me to a world of unspeakable pleasure. He might have paid two million dollars for me, but I owed him so much more than that for what he had given to me in return. I owed him my heart, my soul, my body—and they were all his.

"I love you so much, Noah Crawford." My voice was barely a whisper. I reached around and caressed his bare ass with the palm of my hand. "Thank you."

"I love you, too, Delaine Talbot," he whispered back. I could feel his heart pounding against my back as his chest rose and fell with his labored breaths. "I can't imagine ever sharing something so intimate with anyone but you. Thank you for trusting me."

5

the red flower blooms

Noah

Making love to Lanie was the easiest thing in the world to do, because I loved her with everything that I was, or ever would be. But bringing her pain for the sake of my pleasure was torture.

I had wanted it so badly. It was forbidden, and that made it all the more alluring. But when I'd entered her there for the first time and heard her suck in a sharp breath and felt her body stiffen . . . well, I'd expected it to hurt her at first, but I obviously hadn't been fully prepared for just how much it would, and I couldn't do that to her. I had every intention of calling the whole thing off, but then she practically begged me to keep going. It was her plea for me to let her have that moment, that first with me, my first, even though she was receiving nothing but pain in return, that cinched the deal and made me continue on despite my reservations.

I would've given her anything she asked for. I would've snatched the moon out of the night sky and laid it at her delicate feet, gathered the universe up into a neat little ball and placed it in her tiny hands—anything she wanted. Because she deserved so much more than that, and I would sacrifice my entire life to make sure she fucking had it all.

But I'd never be able to make up for treating her like a whore, for treating her like she was nothing more than a piece of ass that was solely there to satisfy my cravings for pussy, for treating her like she was no more than another toy I'd acquired, a piece of property. For stealing her innocence. How were we ever going to make it when our relationship was born out of the fucking bowels of impure intentions to begin with?

I had to have faith we would, because if what we had was wrong, then I didn't want to be right. Yeah, it was a corny line, but the words rang undeniably true. See? I was turning into a total bitch for her, pussy-whipped to the extreme.

Let me prove my point . . .

During the actual deed, I was a nervous wreck. My body shook both from my fear of hurting Lanie and from having to hold back and not plow into her. It felt that good. Not that her pussy didn't; it was experiencing the forbidden dance with her that was such a turn-on. You only share something like that with someone you trust, someone you plan to spend the rest of your life with, someone with whom you have a sacred motherfucking bond.

What I had walked in on between Julie and David hadn't been anything like the intimacy of the moment Lanie and I had just experienced together. That was nothing more than two whoremongers fucking for the sake of fucking, for the sake of gutting me and leaving me to bleed out onto the floor. They could search the rest of their pathetic lives and never come close to finding what I had with my Lanie. My Lanie.

We needed it, that level of intimacy, before our separation.

And although I knew I needed to remain strong for her, it was killing me on the inside to know she wouldn't be there when I returned home in the evenings, that she wouldn't be lying next to me naked in my bed every night, that I wouldn't see that look in her eyes on a daily basis. That look that said more than a thousand words ever could. That look that said I was her world, just like she was mine. Lips were capable of saying anything, but the eyes never lied. And what I saw there reflected what I felt in every fiber of my being. She loved me. She really loved me. Not my money, not my status. Me. And come hell or high water, I was going to make it fucking work. Somehow.

Delaine moved her ass against me, reminding me that my dick was still inside her, flaccid but becoming more aroused the longer it remained in place, and if she kept moving like that, it was going to be harder and harder to make myself pull out of her. Although I would definitely love to have another round, I knew she was already going to be sore, and I didn't want to take advantage of her need to give me even more of herself. Her presence in my life was enough, and it was time for me to give her something in return. So before my dick became too engorged and hurt her even more, I pulled out . . . hoping that the quick movement would make it more bearable.

I felt a stabbing sense of guilt pierce my chest when she winced, and my mind immediately went into caregiver mode. I would worship that woman, show her my appreciation and take care of her for a change, just like she took care of everyone else around her, including me.

"I'm sorry, kitten," I said, rolling her over and gathering her to me. "I'm so fucking sorry I hurt you."

My girl could've sobbed into my chest, could've beaten the

shit out of me with my permission—she could've done anything she wanted or needed in retaliation for the pain I'd inflicted on her. But she didn't do any of that. Instead, Lanie wedged her thigh between mine, wrapped her arm around my waist to palm my ass, and then attacked my neck.

"Shut up, Noah," she mumbled between kisses. "You're overthinking this and killing my buzz. And just so you know, I definitely want to do that again."

I'd said it before, and I'd say it again: I fucking loved my girl so much it hurt.

She tilted her head back to look up at me, a spark of wicked intent in her eyes. I had definitely created a monster. But I wasn't an insensitive ass. My girl was hurting, and she was trying to mask her pain so I wouldn't feel bad about it, which was insane because of course I felt like a douche. How could I not?

I leaned forward and took her succulent lips with mine, deepening the kiss with all the love and adoration I could manifest. It was when I felt myself hardening again that I broke the connection. She would take that as a sign that I wanted her again, which I did. However, her needs were so much more important than mine, and right then, she needed me to take care of her, whether she wanted to admit it or not.

It took a lot for me to do it, but I finally managed to pull away from her and slip out of the bed.

Lanie groaned in protest and reached out to grab my hand. "Noooo. Where are you going?"

I knew exactly how she felt; I couldn't stand to be away from her for even a second, either. The thought alone made me feel empty inside, and I missed her already. How was I going to tear myself away? My selfish side reared its ugly head temporarily, and I almost asked her not to go. I knew that she'd stay with me if I asked, but I just couldn't bring myself to do it. I'd already taken too much from her.

"Not far. Never far." With one last tender kiss, I pulled away, severing our physical connection, but the invisible tether that stretched from the bed where she lay to my heart kept us bound across the distance. I'd never felt anything like it before—so connected, so absorbed in just one person—it was an enigma of which I didn't want to find the solution.

It gave me hope.

I quickly ran a bath for her, taking care to be sure the water was neither too hot nor too cold. I was thankful to see that Polly had stocked the bathroom with some girly soaps, and I chose one whose label promised a tranquil, soothing calm. It damn well better or I was going to sue the bastards for false advertisement. Only the best for my girl.

I managed to walk back in to her, only because running might make me look like an even bigger bitch than I already was. My cock was at half staff and flopped back and forth on my thighs as I made my way to the bed where she lay. She was ogling the piece of meat as if it were a sausage link hanging in the front window of a butcher's shop and she were a stray pup looking for its next meal.

"I'm really trying to show some restraint here. You know, be a caring, gentle boyfriend? A real Prince Charming. But if you keep licking your chops like that, the prince might turn into an ogre. And I really don't think that would be a good idea right now," I said, pulling the sheets from her naked body and sweeping her up into my arms.

As I walked with her, Lanie put her arms around my shoulders and nuzzled the crook of my neck. "I can take it," she said, lifting her chin slightly so that her sultry voice ghosted over the shell of my ear. A shiver shot down my spine and straight to my cock, which was not helping matters in the least.

I took a deep breath in and let it out slowly, composing myself. "Somehow I don't doubt that," I said, stepping into the bathtub with her weightless body in my arms.

I slowly lowered myself into a sitting position with her resting in my lap. When she started squirming while kissing along the length of my neck and moaning, I knew it was only a matter of time before I'd slip my dick inside her, and that was the last thing she needed at the moment. So I quickly maneuvered her tiny frame so that she sat between my outstretched legs, effectively improving the odds of being able to make it through her bath without fucking her again.

Delaine was turning into a nymphomaniac. I blamed myself for her corruption, but I wanted her to know that what was between us wasn't just about fucking anymore. I thought back to how upset she'd looked in the car earlier, how unsure she seemed to be that we were going to be okay, given the separation and all. I needed her to know that even though we had to be apart for a little while, the way I felt about her wasn't going to change. She needed to have faith in me, in us.

"I love you," I whispered into her ear while wrapping my arms around her waist and hugging her to me. "So fucking much. Do you know that?" Now that those three little words had found their way out of my mouth, I just couldn't stop saying them.

"I love you, too," she whispered. Her fingertips caressed my arms beneath the water.

"That's not what I asked," I corrected her. "Do you *know* that I love you? Because if we're going to have to be apart for any length of time, I need there to be no doubt about how very important you are to me. And if what they say is true about absence making the heart grow fonder and all that other fluffy shit, then the way I feel about you is only going to intensify even more. I won't let anyone come between us."

"Are you trying to tell me you're a closet stalker, Noah?" she joked as she rolled her head to the side, exposing the creamy skin of her neck to me.

"I assure you, I am quite serious," I said, and then began a trail of kisses along the length of her graceful neck. I stopped when I reached her ear and whispered, "Every moment we're apart, I will be thinking of you. Every night you aren't lying in my bed next to me, I will be dreaming of you. Every time I smell fucking bacon," I went on, referring to the time I'd had my way with her while she cooked my breakfast, "I'll have a hard-on for you, and I'll touch myself while calling out your name. I'll call you with no purpose at all other than to hear your voice. I'll drop by unannounced just so that I can see your eyes light up when you catch sight of me. And I'll steal you away just so that I can have a taste. Because I'll be hungry for you, Lanie. So very hungry."

She sucked in a breath and then her lips parted slightly, a soft moan spilling forth. Her eyes closed and her legs opened to me as if my words had commanded them to.

"So if you call that stalking, then yeah, I guess I'll be stalking you." I moved my hand over her abdomen to the mound that resided below it, and she rolled her hips into my touch, another soft moan escaping her lips.

"I'm a strong believer in the three P's: proclaim, protect, and provide. I will give you everything you need. *Every*thing," I said, slipping my fingers inside her while my thumb applied pressure to her sweet spot. "You are mine to take care of. So if I find another guy sniffing around what belongs to me, I'm going to go after him, and I will inflict pain. Are you sure you're ready for that level of commitment, Delaine?"

"Oh, God. Yes, Noah." She moaned as I curled my fingers back and forth inside her.

"I am a god, ruler of my world, and *you* are my world," I told her, moving my other hand to her breast and manipulating one taut peak. "I can and will give you everything you need to feel good. But I'm a jealous, vengeful god, Lanie."

She moved a hand between her legs to cover mine as I finger-fucked her, and the other palmed the back of my neck. "I'm . . . shit . . . I'm yours, Noah. Just . . . oh, God . . . yours."

"Good. I'm glad we agree," I said, pushing my fingers in further and with more purpose. "Do you want to come?"

She nodded.

"Hmm, I'm not so sure you do," I said, toying with her. "Beg for it."

"Please," she said breathlessly.

"Oh, come on. Surely you can do better than that," I said, rolling her nipple between my fingertips. "Convince me."

She arched her back while digging her nails into my neck and pushing down on the hand I had between her legs.

My fingers worked steadfastly, but when her walls began to tighten, I pulled back, halting my efforts. "I don't think so, kitten. Not until you convince me."

She whimpered. "Please, Noah. Give it to me. Let me come on your fingers."

Goddamn, I wanted her. But I needed her release to fill me, sustain me until I could have her again.

"Oh, you will come, Lanie, but not on my fingers." I released her, only to pick her up and turn her so that her ass was perched on the edge of the stone-tiled wall surrounding the bathtub. A nice, fluffy towel was already there, so she wouldn't be too uncomfortable, given what I'd just done to her a little while ago.

I was so anxious to give her what she wanted, to taste her, that I wasn't quite as careful spreading her knees apart to allow me access to her pretty little kitty. But there were no cries of protest, only a cry of pleasure as I buried my face between her thighs and began to lap at her silken folds with the flattened part of my tongue. She fisted her hands in my hair—damn if I didn't fucking love it when she did that—and then she hooked her legs over my shoulders with her knees falling to the side, giving me full access.

I looked up at her and she was watching me, so I made a big show of letting her see my long, thick tongue work her juicy little clit.

"Fuck," she whispered, and then bit down on her bottom lip. She lovingly pushed her fingers through the locks of hair on the side of my head. "That feels so unbelievably fantastic. Do you like the way I taste, Noah?"

I closed my eyes and let out an "Mmm . . ." before giving her slit tender kisses.

I heard her suck in a breath of air, and I looked back up at her, making sure she was still watching me. She was. Reaching my arm around her thigh, I used my fingers to pull back the hood of skin at her apex to reveal the fleshy meat hidden beneath. She needed to have the full view to really appreciate what I was doing, and I gave it to her.

I leaned forward again and sucked her engorged bud into

my mouth, pulling back my head and letting it go before doing it again and again.

"Jesus," she said in a hiss. "Come up here and fuck me, Noah. I need you inside me."

I ignored her, completely enthralled by the effect I was having on her not just physically but mentally and emotionally. My eyes were trained on her face, watching every little detailed expression of pleasure, because knowing I was making her feel good . . . it just fucking did things to me.

She was enthralled by what I was doing to her as well, her eyes following with rapt fascination every move I made. I bared my teeth, scraping her clit with them before the pointed end of my tongue slowly flicked back and forth over the delicious little nub. She sucked in a stuttered breath, her grip tightening in my hair as I encompassed the pert bud with my lips and gave her a wink.

I meant to drive her insane, and apparently I was on the right track.

"Oh, God. You have to stop, baby. You're going to make me come, and I want your cock inside me."

No way—no fucking way was I going to deprive myself of the sweet nectar I knew awaited me as my reward. I didn't stop. Instead, I drove her to the edge, flicking my tongue back and forth over her little pleasure bud with lightning speed, sucking it into my mouth and stroking it with my lips, coaxing her orgasm out.

"No. Don't," she said, cursing under her breath while pulling on my hair in a vain attempt to make me stop. I ate that pussy like I'd never have a chance to again, although I knew damn well that I would. I'd make sure of it.

"You're going to make me . . ." She pushed and pulled on my head, trying to get me to release her, but I didn't give an inch. Her body was going to give me the result I was looking for, and I wasn't going to stop until I got it.

"Damn it! No . . . ," she half moaned, half growled, then she pushed on the back of my head so that my face was completely buried in her treasure trove. Her thighs slammed shut, putting my head in a viselike grip as her body stiffened and her juices gushed onto my awaiting tongue. I licked, I sucked, I swallowed. All of it. Mine, all mine.

As the orgasm I gave her subsided, the grip she had on my hair loosened and her thighs became lax. She cupped each side of my face in her hands and forced me to look up at her. "You are so infuriating," she said between labored breaths.

"I'm pretty sure we've gone over this before, Delaine. I'm insatiable. Don't ever try to deny me what I want, because I'll always get it in the end," I said with a smirk as her chest heaved and I pulled her back into the bath.

Lanie surprised me by pushing on my chest until I was flush with the opposite wall of the tub. "And don't you ever try to deny me what I want, Noah Crawford. Because in the end, I'll take it," she said, and then she climbed into my lap, grabbed my dick and . . .

"Lanie, don't. You're—"

Too late. She sank down on top of my cock, which was hardened to titanium strength, and took all of me in.

"Goddamn," I growled, my head falling back as I felt her tight walls envelop me.

Lanie giggled at my reaction, a cocky sort of sound, and I snapped my head up only to be met with a cocky grin to match. *My* cocky grin. It was almost like looking into a mirror, and I wasn't sure how the fuck I felt about that, but I supposed I was to blame. Yeah, I had definitely created a monster. Tit for motherfucking tat, just like I had suspected from that very first time we had been together in that respect, the night I took her virginity. I knew then that I'd have my hands full, and she was proving me right. She was impossibly stubborn, always having to prove me wrong. I couldn't fault her for that, because I was the same damn way, and she had been learning from watching me. So I let it go, let her do her thing, let her make me feel good, because in the end she would have her way anyway.

And that was just fine with me.

~$~

The smell of hyacinths surrounded me, a cool breeze twirling the fragrance around my body. I could hear the sounds of a string quartet and the buzzing laughter of friends and families as they gathered. The sun was warm on my face and hands. It would have been stifling had it not been for the light breeze.

I was happy. This was a momentous occasion, even if I couldn't quite put my finger on what exactly was happening.

"Oh, Noah, she's spectacular. Just the type of girl I'd always hoped you'd meet," a soft voice cooed from behind me. I knew that voice. I turned quickly, and there she stood: my mother, amid the tall grass, sprigs of purple, white, and yellow flowers blooming up around her red gown. Her arm was linked through my father's, who was standing by her side with a proud grin on his face, his hair still black on top, white along the temples. My mother was right; it did make him look very distinguished indeed.

"Mom? Dad? What are you doing here?" I asked, confused.

While part of me felt it only natural for them to be, another part registered that they shouldn't have been.

"She's a sassy one, too. Kind of reminds me of your mother." My father looked at his wife adoringly.

My mother laughed, then kissed him on the cheek. "That's a good thing. You Crawford men need a strong woman to keep you in line."

Suddenly they were right in front of me. I hadn't even registered the movement. My mother turned to me and smiled gently as she cupped my face with one hand. "She's one in a million, Noah. Don't ever let her go. Remember: From mud and murk, the red flower blooms, overcoming all to stretch toward the moon."

I remembered her saying that all the time when I was younger, but back then I'd had no clue what it meant, and I still didn't.

"The scarlet lotus," I whispered.

She nodded once and grinned widely, obviously happy that I remembered. "We love you, Noah. You've made us so proud."

My father cleared his throat beside her, and I turned to him.

"We have to go now, son. We can't stay."

Go? Go where?

"We just wanted to give you our congratulations." He reached one arm around my shoulder and hugged me. "Oh, and thanks for the drink," he whispered into my ear.

My mother kissed my cheek and I closed my eyes, inhaling the familiar scent of her floral perfume. When I opened them again, they were gone. I turned back and forth, all around in a circle, looking for them, but they were nowhere to be found. I stopped dead in my tracks when off in the distance I saw a woman dressed in white, her back turned toward me. Her hair was swept up and a veil fell over her face as she turned her head to the side and fidgeted with her dress. A bouquet of red flowers was in one hand. The breeze picked up again, carrying her scent toward me, confirming what I already knew to be true. I could tell who she was by the way my heart swelled in my chest as if it were about to burst. A huge smile spread across my face in anticipation. It was her.

"Delaine?" I called out, but she didn't answer. She looked up at me, and although I couldn't see her smile, I felt it warm my heart. But then she turned back around and ran away, her ghostly giggle tickling my ear.

"Lanie!" I called out, and then started to run after her, confused. "Why are you running away from me?"

I ran and ran, my legs heavy, my feet weighed down with what felt like cement bricks. When I thought I'd caught up to her, my hand reached out, but the fragile fabric of her dress slipped through my fingers and she was gone again.

She let out another ghostly giggle, playing with me, challenging me. "Come on, Noah. Catch me."

With all the strength I could muster, I leaped forward, catching Lanie around the waist and pulling her into my arms. Even through the filmy veil, I could see her eyes, alight with childlike joy when she looked up at me. Her head fell back and a joyous laughter bubbled up into the warm air around us. Her body was soft and supple as it melted against mine. "Just where do you think you're going, kitten?" I asked, holding her to me.

I could feel the warmth of her hand on my biceps and the

delicate tickle of her fingers as she ran them through my hair. "Kiss me, Noah. Make me yours forever," she whispered.

I reached for her veil, lifting it to gaze upon her unadulterated beauty and seek out my prize. When my lips brushed against hers, she disappeared.

"Noah, wake up. Wake up, Noah, you're dreaming."

I was jostled awake, still feeling the remnants of sleep in my partially paralyzed body. My eyes snapped open and she was there, her body pressed against mine, one hand on my arm while her fingertips gently massaged my scalp at the side of my head.

It was just a dream.

She looked down at me with a warm smile lighting up her flawless face. "Are you okay?"

"Yeah," I croaked in a sleepy voice. I rubbed at my eyes. "I'm good. Did I wake you?"

"You could say that," she said with a playful grin. "You were holding me so tight I was finding it a wee bit hard to breathe. Lack of oxygen kind of has a tendency to wake you up. I think it's called survival instinct." She laughed.

I swept a stray lock of hair away from her face and tucked it behind her ear, then kissed the tip of her button nose. "I'm sorry."

"Hey, I'm not complaining. I kind of like your possessive side," she said, petting the scruff of my jaw. "Want to tell me about your dream?"

It wasn't that there was anything terrible about the dream; it hadn't been a nightmare. But it felt real, and that freaked me out a little bit. I needed time to process it for myself before I shared it with her, if I ever shared it with her. No use in freaking her out, too. So however noncommunicative it might have been, I shook my head, choosing to hold on to the dream for myself a little while longer.

Just then the alarm clock on the bedside table went off, its deafening screech piercing through the silence of the room and effectively ending the moment. Lanie pressed her forehead to my chest and we both groaned in protest, knowing it was symbolic of our separation. I had to go to work, and she had to go be with her family. Neither of us was happy about it, but it was what we had to do until we could be together on a more permanent basis.

I smacked at the alarm clock, shutting it the fuck up as it fell to the floor with a thud. We didn't need the reminder, but it was there, looming like a guillotine in front of a prisoner on death row. Because that was what it felt like. To be without her would be just like having my head severed from my body. Or maybe having my heart ripped out would be a more apt description, because she was definitely taking it with her.

"I love you," she mumbled into my chest as I rubbed the satin skin of her naked back.

"I know," I answered, kissing the crown of her head. "I love you, too."

She looked up at me, her eyes set on mine with a look of conviction. "I know," she said, and the weight of the world melted away as we sealed our declaration with a kiss.

It wasn't a kiss to say goodbye, and it wasn't a kiss meant to arouse each other, although I was most certainly sporting a hard-on of epic proportions. That kiss was a promise. It said we knew we'd be together, that we meant all the words we'd uttered, that we were in love, and that we would overcome any and every obstacle that stood in our way, no matter what life threw at us. Because however fucked up things between us might have started out, from mud and murk the red flower would bloom.

I finally got it.

6
busted!

Lanie

I did my best to hold the tears at bay as I finished packing up the last of my things. I knew I'd be back, but it was still hard. I had made yet another trip into the closet to get the last of my jeans when the white shirt I'd worn the night Noah decided to have me for dessert caught my eye. I let my fingers dance along the sleeve, remembering the look on his face when I'd walked in wearing nothing but that. I'd hated him at the time, but even I couldn't deny the sexual attraction that hung thick in the air between us. The Cooch fully agreed and encouraged me to swipe the shirt off the hanger and pack it, too. I did. Noah would never miss it. He had a ton of clothes, and to him, that one shirt was like a single snowflake among an avalanche of others. To me, it was priceless.

Noah came out of the bathroom wearing a V-necked T-shirt, a pair of jeans, and sneakers. His hair was still wet from our morning shower, sticking up in every different direction. He'd obviously decided to forgo the shave, but I wasn't complaining. I loved his scruffiness.

"A little underdressed for the office, don't you think?" I

smiled at him as I stuffed his shirt and the last of my clothes inside my bag and zipped it.

He wrapped his arms around my waist from behind and hugged me close. I could smell the light scent of cologne and body wash, and I inhaled deeply, committing every little nuance to memory. Like I'd ever forget.

"Yes, but it's the perfect attire for taking my girl back to her folks' house."

I covered his arms with mine and turned my head to look at him. "You're playing hooky?"

"Mmm-hmm." He kissed the tip of my nose. "I want to spend every last second I can with you. They can do without me for another day." Noah rested his chin on my shoulder and looked down at my bag. "How in the world did you manage to fit all of your clothes in there?"

"I didn't pack everything," I said with a shrug. "Fancy clothes aren't exactly a necessity in Hillsboro. It's just a little town. We don't even have a mall. Can you see me walking around the grocery store in spike heels and a short skirt?"

Noah hummed dreamily and pushed his hips into my backside. I took that as a yes, as did the little hoochie between my legs. The Cooch purred and tried like hell to get me to rub up against his cock like a kitten searching for attention. He would've given it, too, which would have been counterproductive to ever leaving the bedroom again. Not that I had any qualms about having yet another round with the Wonder Peen, but my mother needed someone at home to help out, and my dad deserved the break.

"We're never going to make it out of here if you keep doing stuff like that," I warned.

The Cooch was all, *Yeah that's sort of the point, dumbass. Scrogg his ever-loving brains out for Christ's sake!*

Realizing that I really hadn't packed much, and wanting to mess with Noah a bit, I exaggerated a sigh. "I will eventually have to go shopping, since you discarded all the things I brought with me originally."

Noah buried his face in my neck and groaned, which made me giggle. He clearly felt like a jerk for doing it, which I happened to find incredibly cute. I turned in his arms and cupped his face in my hands.

"I love you," I reminded him.

Noah looked at me adoringly. "And I'll never get tired of hearing you say those words. Here," he said, reaching into his back pocket and pulling out his wallet. He plucked a little black metal card out and handed it to me. "I want you to have this for clothes or anything else you might need or want."

"A credit card, Noah? Don't you think you've given me enough already?"

"Hey," he said, taking my chin in his fingers. "I thought we already went over this. You're my woman to take care of, and I intend to do so quite thoroughly. I don't want to hear any complaints about it."

He gave me a chaste kiss and then grabbed the strap of my bag and hooked it over his shoulder. Holding his hand out for mine, he said, "Ready?"

I took his offered hand because I always would. I had no idea what was ahead for us, but I knew that as long as he was holding my hand, I'd follow him through the darkest of nights, because somewhere at the end of our journey, there would be light.

Noah stopped dead in his tracks at the door and turned around. "What?" I asked when he gave no indication of what he was up to.

He walked to the bedside table, opened the drawer and then reached inside. With a disapproving scowl he held up the vibrator he'd given me, which we'd nicknamed the "Crawford bullet." "Forgot something, didn't you?"

"Well, I didn't think I'd need it," I answered, confused.

He smirked and stuffed it into my bag. "Oh, you'll need it all right."

He was happy, and I was reminded that I did that for him. The Cooch reminded me she had a little something to do with that also, which was probably true, but I mentally reminded her that it wasn't just about sex between Noah and me any-more. Not that I was demanding she hang up her hooker heels or donate the Super Cooch outfit to Goodwill or anything. They'd come in handy someday soon. Of that I was positive.

Once my bag was loaded in the trunk of the car and Noah and I were settled in the backseat, we were off. I watched the house disappear from sight. Sensing my sadness, Noah wrapped his arms around me and pulled me into his side so that I could rest my head on his shoulder.

He kissed the top of my head. "It'll be nothing but a vast waste of space until you return, and then it'll feel like home again."

I felt the same way. Home was wherever Noah was, whether it was in an enormous mansion surrounded by Edward Scis-sorhands sculptures or a cardboard box in an alley. It didn't matter. All that mattered was whether or not he was with me.

I fell asleep sometime during the long drive to Hillsboro.

All I remembered was Noah petting my hair lovingly and then encouraging me to put my head in his lap. At first I thought it was his way of hinting for a blow job, and so did the Cooch, but it turned out he just wanted to get cuddly. Don't get me wrong, it was nice, but I felt like he was holding back a part of him, the domineering, forceful side that made the Cooch go all fangirl for the bad boy. Maybe it was because he thought it was what he was supposed to do since we'd gotten all sticky sweet with our declarations and all. I would've protested against his insistence that I get some rest—or been a little more assertive with my offering of the blow job—but truth be known, he'd worn my ass out the night before and I really could have used a little more sleep. I guess my tired brain won the battle after the Cooch threw down the gauntlet, because before I knew it, I was out like a light.

Noah woke me up quite a while later. He complained that having my face in his lap had given him a major hard-on, and his balls just couldn't take it anymore. Served him right. He adjusted himself in his jeans while I looked around to see where we were. We were on the outskirts of Hillsboro—I recognized the surroundings because I'd traveled that road with my folks so many times. When I was a kid, I used to stare out the window and make up all these different stories about the landscape. My favorite was pretending I was a poor maiden who had been locked up in a little cottage, forced to pass the days alone while waiting for my Prince Charming to ride up on his white stallion and sweep me off my feet.

I snorted at myself internally. What little girl didn't have that fantasy?

That memory was so vivid in my mind that I still remembered most of the details. In fact, just around the bend there would be a . . .

"Stop the car!" I yelled, and then started pounding on the glass divider that separated us from Samuel.

"Why? What's wrong?" Noah asked in a panic.

"We have to stop! Please, Noah, we have to!" I said, a little louder than was necessary since he was sitting right beside me. Even though he winced at my shrieking, he got the urgency.

Noah pushed a button and the window rolled down. "Samuel, pull over." He was all business, and normally that would kind of turn me on while simultaneously pissing me off, but now was not the time.

Once the car rolled to a stop on the shoulder of the road, I fumbled with the door handle until I finally pushed it open and jumped out.

"Lanie!" Noah called out from behind as he followed me out. "Why are you running away from me?"

I couldn't stop to answer him. It was there, the little country cottage that I'd always pretended was mine. It had a stone chimney, flower boxes filled with hyacinths under the arched windows, and a door of knotty wood, and it was sitting in the middle of a meadow to boot. The grass was tall and green, littered with little purple, white, and yellow flowers, and the air smelled crisp and clean. It was perfect—and, as I'd just noticed, it was for sale.

I ran as fast as my legs could carry me. I had to touch it, to know that it was real and not merely a part of my imagination. The wind blew through my hair, and I suddenly felt like that little girl again, alight with childlike joy. Seriously, my cheeks hurt from smiling so hard.

I felt Noah's fingertips when he reached out and barely skimmed the skin on my arm, but I kept running, giggling like a fool. I turned to look over my shoulder at him and with another giggle called out, "Come on, Noah. Catch me!"

Just as I reached the porch of the cottage, his arms hooked around my waist and he pulled me to him. I laughed—oh God, I laughed. Everything was perfect. I was standing in front of the little cottage, and I was wrapped in the arms of my very own knight in shining armor.

My knight smiled down at me. "Just where do you think you're going, kitten?"

His head, with its fantastic sex hair, blocked out the sun in the sky behind him, creating a halo effect and casting a soft shadow across his face. He was beautiful. I reached up and softly ran my fingers through his hair, my heart swelling with everything that was good and right in the world. "Kiss me, Noah."

His eyes widened and his body stiffened. "Whoa . . . déjà vu." His voice was barely a whisper, and the expression on his face was weird.

"What?"

Noah shook his head slightly. "Nothing." He leaned down and brushed his lips across mine.

Usually our kisses were full of fire and passion, hungry. But this one? This one was sweet and delicate, controlled. And it made me horny as hell.

"Mmm," I sighed in perfect contentment, and then opened my eyes to see him staring down at me with this look I'd never seen before. I'd always heard the eyes were the doorway to the soul, and right then I believed it.

"What are you thinking?" I asked him.

Noah smiled and shook his head. "About mud and blooming flowers. Let's just leave it at that."

Well, that certainly was an odd thing to say, but Noah was quirky in his own little way, and I was bouncing like a little girl on the inside, so I didn't question him any further.

"Come on," I said, taking his hand and pulling him behind me to peer into the windows.

"What are we doing here? What is this place?"

"When I was a little girl, I used to pretend I lived here," I told him as I looked through the window and found the room on the other side empty. I tugged on his hand to drag him around to the side of the house so I could do the same thing there. "It's magical, don't you think?"

"Magical?" he asked.

"Yeah, like straight out of a fairy tale." I cupped my hands around my face to block the reflection of the sun on the window and gasped when I finally achieved a clear view. "Oh, the fireplace is breathtaking!"

Nothing on the inside looked modern. It had more of a quaint, rustic appeal, like it belonged in the pages of *Country Living* rather than *Modern Home:* arched doorways, wooden floors, wavy glass windows. I could just imagine Noah and me snuggled up on the couch, or making love on a soft rug in the glow of the fireplace. Of course I was getting way ahead of myself, lost in my own world of make-believe once again. *Such a dreamer you are, Lanie Talbot.*

Noah surveyed the place with his brow furrowed. "It's a little run-down, don't you think?"

"Noah Crawford!" I smacked his arm. "How dare you talk

like that about my dream home? Besides, it's nothing a little love and elbow grease couldn't fix."

He was right, but it wasn't that bad. Some of the shingles on the roof were missing, everything was caked in dust and grime, and judging by the way the wind whistled through the panes of the windows, they'd probably need to be replaced as well. But all in all, it was still picture perfect.

"Oh! I've always wanted to see the backyard," I squealed and tugged him along yet again.

When we made it around to the back of the house, I stopped dead in my tracks. The view was breathtaking. There was a little pond about fifty yards or so from the house with a family of ducks paddling through the water. A small gazebo sat beside the pond with a white wooden swing swaying to and fro in its center. A circular flower garden surrounded it, and a stone walkway led to the house. And since it was facing the west, that meant it was the perfect place to view the setting sun.

Without warning, Noah pushed my back to the stone wall of the house. One hand landed on the stones to my right, while the other cupped my ass and pulled me to him. Our bodies pressed together, our foreheads touching, Noah looked into my eyes and said, "That look on your face . . . I want you so fucking bad right now."

He kissed my neck while kneading my ass and grinding his hips into me. He wasn't kidding. I could feel his hardened length against my abdomen, and I wondered how in the hell he was able to keep it from busting through the tight denim of his jeans.

His hand was suddenly at my waist, and he popped the button of my pants before slipping his hand inside. When his fingers found the Cooch, we both moaned and my head fell back against the house.

"Noah, we can't," I said unconvincingly as I pulled at his arm in vain. "Samuel . . ."

"He's at the car. He won't come back here," he mumbled against my neck as he continued to assault it with hot kisses.

"Neighbors," I tried again, seeing the house through the trees on the east side of the house.

"Let them watch. I want you. Now."

I heard the unmistakable sound of metal against metal as he lowered his zipper. "It'll be quick. I promise," he whispered against my ear. "Turn around, kitten."

I took another look at the house across the way and, seeing no one out and about, I did as he asked. Admittedly, I was excited about the precarious position we'd found ourselves in, our need for instant gratification taking precedence over the possibility we could get caught.

The chilly air nipped at my bare skin when Noah lowered my pants down my thighs. His body covered mine and his hand drifted over the swell of my ass and between my legs.

"Goddamnit, Delaine. Always so wet for me," he said, and then he sank to his knees.

My hands were pressed against the side of the house, my legs ensnared by my jeans, and there was nothing I could do to stop him. He pulled my hips out and away from the wall as his tongue sought out my pussy.

"Oh, God, Noah." I moaned, closing my eyes and biting down on my bottom lip.

Just a taste was all he wanted. His tongue snaked its way through my soaked folds, finding that little pleasure bud and teasing it only for a moment before he directed his attention elsewhere. He gave my pussy one long lick from front to back, but then he kept going until . . .

"Holy shit!" I felt his tongue swirl around my rear opening, lapping at it with an unbelievable pressure. Moaning like a shameless hussy, I arched my body and pushed back against his mouth, begging for more. Noah gave my new favorite body part a sensual open-mouth kiss before he stood back up.

His husky voice was at my ear. "Liked that, did you?" I felt him rub the head of his dick back and forth between my legs in search of my opening.

Was I supposed to like that? Oh, God, I really liked that. "Uh-huh," was all I managed.

Noah entered me, his cock slowly sliding inside my core until he was fully sheathed. He rolled his hips, pulling back a bit before pushing forward again. He was merely getting the feel of the angle, but it drove me absolutely insane.

"Ready, kitten?"

"Uh-huh." Obviously my vocabulary had decided to take a hike, and my voice sounded like the wind had been knocked out of me.

Noah chuckled at my reaction and kissed the spot just below my ear. Then he held my hips and started a steady rhythm of in and out thrusts. "Fucking A," he moaned. "It's like dipping my dick in the honey pot. So soft, so warm, so sweet. What did I ever do to deserve you?"

Of course I knew I should've been the one to ask that question, and he should've already known the answer to his own, but even if I said it a million times, I'd never make him believe it.

"You saved my mother's life . . . and mine," I answered him. Feeling a little wicked, I tacked on, "Plus I love how you lick my pussy."

I heard that growl I loved so much rumble from his chest. A hand latched onto my shoulder to keep me steady and his thrusts increased in pace and roughness. "In that case, I guess I do deserve you."

I turned toward the thicket of woods to the east in time to see a man step out of the sliding glass doors of the house next door. He carried a tray of something toward what looked like a barbecue and lifted the lid.

"Noah," I whispered. "A guy just walked out of the neighbor's house."

"Then I guess you better be quiet, huh?" His grunts were quieter than normal, but he continued to fuck me without so much as a pause in his stroke. "You make a sound, you'll draw his attention. Unless you *want* him to hear you."

Noah found my clit and began to work the little oh-my-God-that-feels-so-fucking-good spot with an expert rhythm. He sucked the lobe of my ear into his mouth and bit down on it. I couldn't stop the resulting moan and my head fell onto his shoulder.

"Shh, he'll see you." It helped matters not a bit that Noah's voice was all sexified. "And once he sees how good you look being fucked from behind, he's going to want you for himself. Remember what I said about not making me hurt someone, Lanie?"

Turning my head to the side, I bit into the flesh of Noah's hand at my shoulder to stifle my sounds. He'd do it; I really believed that. Noah was possessive and ruthless, and judging from what he'd gone through in his past, there was no doubt in my mind he'd do whatever he felt necessary to make sure he never had to endure that type of heartache again. And I wasn't a bit spooked by it. In fact, I coveted his possessive nature because I wanted to be possessed. Screw anybody that said it wasn't a healthy relationship. If it worked for us, what business was it of theirs anyway?

"Just a little bit more, kitten. Just a little . . . bit . . . more," Noah whispered into my ear as his hips met my backside.

I could feel my walls tightening, squeezing his cock while that unbelievable pressure in the pit of my stomach continued to build and build, ready to snap. I knew I needed to get off quick because Noah would hold out on getting his until I came first, increasing the odds that we would get caught. He was such a selfless lover. And he didn't mind if we got busted, but I did.

I held my body away from the unforgiving stone exterior of the house with one hand, and maneuvered my other down to join Noah's. We worked together to bring me to my boiling point, and then the lid rattled on the pot.

I bit down harder on Noah's hand with a moan that was nowhere near quiet, but it was the best I could do under the circumstances. The neighbor apparently heard something, as he looked around, but never in our direction. I supposed the fact the house was empty played to our advantage, as he obviously hadn't expected the noise to come from the cottage.

"Fuck, I love it when you get dental. Harder, kitten," he urged me, and I complied with his request. I could hear his grunted breaths at my ear, the urgency of his thrusts matching the intensity of my bite. He was ready, his control slipping.

"Come on, kitten," he growled into my ear. "Give it to me. Come on my cock."

That was all it took. My walls clamped down around him and constricted rhythmically with my orgasm, and I couldn't say for certain that I wasn't drawing blood with the force of my bite. Noah came, hard but silent. His hips jerked to and fro and I could feel his cock pulse inside me with each wave of orgasmic release. And then the weight of his body fell against my back.

"Hey! What are you two doing over there?" I heard a male voice call out. Both Noah and I snapped our heads in the direction of the neighbor's house to see the man starting in our direction with his hand poised over his eyes to shield them from the sun.

"Oh my God!" I shrieked.

"Guess it's time to go." Noah laughed as he quickly pulled his dick out of me and we both scrambled to pull our pants up.

Once I had my jeans over my butt, I took off toward the safety of the limousine, adjusting my clothes as I ran along and hoping I didn't fall flat on my face. Noah was laughing his head off as he followed behind. If I hadn't been terrified the neighbor would catch up to us and see who we were, I would've turned around and tackled him for almost getting us caught.

It was a good thing the other house was so far away. Hillsboro was a very small town, a town where everyone knew everyone else. That meant the neighbor guy very likely knew my father. I didn't really think Mack would appreciate the fact that Noah was scrogging his daughter in broad daylight. And in public to boot. My mother would probably be all teen-girl squealy, but my dad? He had lots of guns in the house—guns that went boom and made your heart stop beating.

So there I was, running for my ever-loving life without the ability to clean up after our quickie, which probably meant my jeans would be stuck to me like glue and I'd have to peel them off later. Samuel was standing at the opened door to the limousine with an I-know-what-you-two-little-slut-puppies-were-just-doing look on his face. Noah was laughing behind me, and a man who was perfectly capable of ratting me out to my father and ending Noah's life as we both knew it—or at the very least, causing the beheading of the Wonder Peen, which I was definitely not cool with (the Cooch seconded that)—was potentially chasing after us. My heart was beating a gazillion miles an hour, and I was pretty positive that wasn't normal. As soon as I reached the car, I avoided Samuel's knowing eyes and dove into the backseat. My hand flew to my chest in a vain attempt to calm my wildly beating heart.

I needed to exercise more, and a little bit of Jesus in my life probably wouldn't have hurt either.

Noah plopped down in the seat next to me, unable to catch his breath because he was laughing like a stupid hyena. I smacked his shoulder, and he crossed his arms to shield his face like he knew that was target numero dos, all while still laughing.

"Stop it! It's not funny, Noah!"

"I'm . . . sorry," he managed to get out between deep breaths. "You were so scared . . . and running . . . and it was just so damn cute."

I crossed my arms over my chest and turned away from him. Yes, I pouted, a fact I was not very proud of, but I did it nonetheless.

"Aww, come here, kitten," Noah cooed as he wrapped his

arms around my unforgiving body and pulled me into him. "I love you."

"My dad would cut your balls off and eat them for breakfast, and I'm a little partial to them," I whined.

Yep, that's right, whined. But it was Noah Crawford and his colossal cock. Do the math and tell me you wouldn't have whined at the prospect of it going bye-bye.

"Yeah, I'm sort of attached to them, too." He chuckled again, but cut it off abruptly when I gave him the evil eye.

"Hardy-har-har," I deadpanned. "Maybe I should tell Mack what you just made his precious baby girl do. I bet you wouldn't find it so funny then."

"Hmm, I don't recall forcing you to do anything you didn't want to do," Noah countered. "You wanted it, Lanie. You wanted my *cock*." He emphasized the last word, which made my still-racing heart skip a beat. "Admit it."

"No."

"Admiiiiit it," he drawled out playfully as his fingers found my rib cage and gave it a tickle.

I laughed involuntarily and tried to squirm away, but Noah pulled me into his lap and locked his arms around me so I couldn't move.

"We're two consenting adults, Lanie. And one day soon your daddy is going to have to let his baby girl go," he said with a serious look on his face. His long finger caressed my cheek delicately and he sighed. "Because you're *my* baby now."

I couldn't help but smile. Who wouldn't be happy to have Noah Crawford murmur those heart-stopping words to them?

Pleased with my reaction, Noah tilted his head up and kissed me sweetly.

There was never a dull moment between the two of us, and I prayed there never would be. But even if we grew old and gray together, sitting on a little white wooden swing in a gazebo, feeding a family of ducks as the sun set before us, I'd still be happy.

7

say what?

Noah

It had been nearly two weeks since I'd seen her. Two very long, very unbearable weeks since I'd taken Lanie back to Hillsboro. I was irritable at best. The absence of the girl he loves will do that to a man.

I'd talked to her every day, though. Some normalcy had returned to their household. Her mother was up and about and seemed to be faring well, her father was back at the factory, and that was a good thing. Even I had to admit Mack deserved the break. And, according to Lanie, he wasn't nearly as grumpy, but he still hated to leave his wife. Although it was for different reasons entirely, I understood how the man felt; I hated not being by Lanie's side.

As if the first week without her hadn't been bad enough, I had been called out of town on business and had to miss our weekend together. I would've just said fuck the whole son of a cock-blocking whore of a trip and gone to her anyway, but there was a board meeting coming up and I'd already missed so much work. And that didn't look good for me at all, especially considering the intensity with which David Stone was breathing down my neck.

He had been acting even more arrogant than he normally did, if that was even possible, and I was beginning to get suspicious. It was like he knew something I didn't. Something big. I chalked it up to his threat of tattling on me to the board about our little run-in the morning after the Scarlet Lotus Ball. I wasn't concerned. The board members had a lot of respect for my parents, which trickled down to me by default. More than likely they'd say he deserved it.

I had half a mind to go ahead and sell my half of the company to the bastard so I could move closer to Lanie, but I couldn't do that to my parents. Scarlet Lotus had been their dream, and although I knew my happiness would have meant more to them, I couldn't be that selfish.

Yeah, I know; all of a sudden, I was a real saint. But since admitting my feelings to Lanie, I wanted to be the kind of man she deserved—a man who was just as self-sacrificing as she was.

Lanie was very understanding, insisting that I go on my trip and get my work done, but I knew it was all a façade, one that she put up because she knew it was something I had to do. Still, the way she covered the heartbreaking crack in her voice with a perkiness that sounded more like Polly was a dead giveaway, proof that the hardship of our separation was affecting her the same way it was affecting me. It was torture. Pure, unadulterated torture. But the anticipation of how great it was going to be when we finally did get to be together again was enough to keep us both going.

I'd tried to busy myself with work to take my mind off the fact that she wasn't there, but that hadn't been successful, either. Admittedly, I was a bit snippy with my employees, Mason, Polly, and Samuel included. Polly snapped right back at me, which really wasn't a very good idea, but I respected her for it.

She wasn't one to put up with my bullshit when she knew it was uncalled for. I granted her a reprieve because I knew she missed Lanie almost as much as I did. Her friend was gone, and she didn't have many. Being an annoying pissant sort of limited the number of people who were willing to put up with her ass. Plus I'd sort of forced Mason to go along with me on my business trip. She really hated me for that, but she'd gotten over it. I think.

Two more days.

Two more excruciating, miserable days until the weekend, when I would get to see her again. Hold her in my arms, taste her luscious lips, feel her soft skin. It would be enough to get me through at least a few hours.

Yeah, I was an optimistic motherfucker.

I finished looking over the reports Mason had prepared regarding the new clients I'd managed to sign on despite my preoccupied mind, and packed up my things for the day.

Mason came into my office with the agenda for the meeting. "You out of here, boss?"

"Yeah, I'm calling it a day. Good work on the reports, by the way. They look great."

Mason drew his head back, eyes wide with disbelief at my kind words. The poor man had really taken a beating from me over the previous days, and it wasn't right. He didn't deserve it. So channeling my newfound theory about being self-sacrificing, I offered up an apology.

"Hey, I'm sorry if I've been hard on you lately, it's just that with Lanie gone and all—"

"No worries, man. Polly has been the same way," he interrupted, letting me off the hook.

"So you're getting it from both ends, huh?"

Mason nodded. "I guess I never realized the effect that little gal has had on so many lives."

I hadn't, either, but he was right. Even Lexi had been calling me a lot more lately, which wasn't at all like her, and it was always to see how Lanie was doing. I'd told her to call her herself, that Lanie would love to hear from her, but Lexi didn't want to be intrusive. Yeah right, like that held an ounce of truth.

"Well, you don't deserve all the shit you've been getting." I shrugged my coat on and clapped him on the shoulder on my way out the door. "Have a good night, man."

The weather had turned chilly over the last couple of days, which was right on time with the season, but part of me wondered if it hadn't been more obvious to me because Lanie wasn't there to keep me warm. Seriously, it was like all the warmth had been sucked out of the space around me. My own personal sunshine was miles away, and I was left feeling desolate and cold.

"Hey, Crawford!" David called out as I made my way toward the elevator. Speaking of cold and desolate . . .

I didn't stop to shoot the shit with him because I really didn't have anything to say. Besides, I had a telephone date with my girl, and I had no intention whatsoever of missing it.

"What do you want, Stone?" I snapped.

"I just wanted to make sure you're planning on being at the next board meeting, that's all." David's words were ones of casual curiosity, but it wasn't hard to see the cutting look his dark eyes reflected, or the scornful sneer that played along his lips. My right hand started to close into a fist. I wanted to knock the fucker out cold and wipe that butt-ugly mug along the floor to remove his cocky perma-grin.

"Why wouldn't I be there?" I sighed in annoyance and punched the down button for my personal elevator, imagining it was his face.

"Well, since you've been MIA so much lately, I wasn't sure. You don't want to miss this meeting, Crawford. It's going to be entertaining as hell." He flashed his toothy grin and then winked at me before he finally got out of my face.

Entertaining. The asshat really thought I'd get ousted over threatening to kill him? People said stuff like that every day. And while it might not be appropriate for the workplace, it certainly wasn't enough to make me lose my own company to the likes of him. Besides, it was his word against mine, and I highly doubted he was wired at the time.

I rushed home like a madman. Well, as much rushing as a madman could do in bumper-to-bumper traffic. Sitting in the back of the limo for so long drove me crazy. I swore I could still smell Lanie's delicious scent from the trysts we'd had there.

Once inside the sprawling mansion I'd called home for all my life, the emptiness and longing set in yet again. Lanie had a way of filling the room with a presence that was larger than life, yet so intimate it felt like she and I were the only two people left on the planet. And I was really into the prospect of the two of us doing all we could to repopulate the damn place. You know, for the sake of mankind and all. And that was when it dawned on me: I wanted kids with her. Lots and lots of kids.

When Lanie and I last spoke, she had claimed she was going to give me a real workout the next time we saw each other. I had to chuckle to myself at the thought. She had become the insatiable one. Once a kitten that trembled under my stare, she had morphed into a lioness, a sleek predator whose need to satiate her hunger made her desperate and bold. The tables had turned—where she had become the predator, I had become the prey.

Well, not really, but I wasn't averse to letting her think so if it meant she was going to be more adventurous. I admired her for knowing what she wanted and not being ashamed to take it, even if I was a willing participant.

I grabbed a quick bite to eat and a shower while I waited for her call. I had just stepped out of the bathroom when my phone rang. I dropped my towel to lunge at it from the other side of the room, completely naked as I crashed onto the bed in an awkward position. Damn, but that hurt.

"Oh, shit! Goddamnit!" Yes, those were the first words that came out of my mouth when I answered the phone. "Hey, kitten."

"What's wrong?" Lanie asked, worry lacing her tone.

"I think I broke my dick," I told her as I rolled onto my back.

Lanie attempted to stifle her giggle from the other end of the line. "Were you doing your cockarobics?"

"Yeah," I chuckled, playing along. "Only my dick refuses to bend that way."

"Aw, poor baby," she cooed. "Want me to kiss it and make it better?"

Had my cock not been on a perma-leash, I was sure it would've attempted to lunge through the phone to get at her.

"You're an evil little minx. You know damn well I would

love nothing more than to fuck your mouth. Now I'm hard from the thought, and there's not a goddamn thing I can do about it."

"Oh, I don't know about that." Her voice was all deep and sultry and shit. Not helping matters at all. "What are you wearing?"

"I'm lying in bed. What do you think I'm wearing?" I asked in a husky voice, knowing damn well she knew I slept in the nude.

"Mmm, show me."

"What?" I asked, confused.

"Look at your cell."

My phone vibrated on my nightstand and I reached over my head and grabbed it. Sure enough, there was a text from my girl. When I opened it, I nearly fell off the bed. There she was, naked as the day she was born, leaving absolutely nothing to the imagination. She was propped up against her headboard, her luxurious hair cascading over her shoulders, her breasts full, and nipples taut. Her knees were lifted and spread to the sides, giving me a glorious vision of the tender pink flesh between her thighs. And her eyes. Dear Lord, her eyes were all hooded and she was biting down on that plump, bottom lip like she was craving my touch.

"I showed you mine. Now, show me yours," she practically purred into the phone.

"Oh, so you want to play, do you?" I asked with a smirk I knew she could hear even though she couldn't see it.

"Does this sound like I want to play?" I heard the click of a button and then the unmistakable vibration of the Crawford bullet I had gifted her. "I need you. I can't wait any longer. Make me come, Noah."

"Jesus Christ . . ." I was more than happy to make her come, even if it was going to have to be by a piece of goddamn metal instead of any real part of my body. "Is that my bullet, kitten?" I asked, already sure of the answer.

"No, but this is." Another, higher-pitched vibration joined the low hum of the previous one, and I raised an eyebrow.

"So, what's that other thing you got there, Lanie?"

She giggled. "Dez made me go to this little shop with her today. An adult shop. I never even knew it existed. Probably because it was tucked away in a back alley."

"You bought a vibrator?" I hoped like fucking hell she used my credit card to buy the best they had to offer, even though the motherfucking thing was going in the trash as soon as I got her back in my bed where she belonged. No cock, real or fake, was going anywhere near my pussy when I was perfectly capable of taking care of her needs myself. The Crawford bullet was an exception only because it was an enhancer, not a cock replacement.

"Mmm-hmm. Of course, it's nowhere near as big as the real thing, but since I can't have you, it'll have to do."

Yeah, my head grew about ten times its normal size. Both of them.

"Tell me what to do with it, Noah. Tell me how to make myself feel good. What would you do to me if I was there with you right now?"

I ogled her picture on my cell phone and I knew exactly what I would've done. "I'd throw your ass on this bed and bury my face between those beautiful thighs to feast on you. That's what the fuck I'd do if you were here."

She moaned into the phone and my dick twitched on my stomach. Goddamn, but that woman could turn me inside out.

"But since you're not sprawled naked on my bed, we'll have to make do. That vibrator will play the part of me for the evening. We'll call it mini-me. I want you to put it to the side and get the bullet, kitten. Move it down your body and let it rest just over your clit. Not on it. Above it."

She moaned again, obviously approving of the light vibrations that were teasing her nerve endings.

"Leave it there. No matter how badly you want to move it down further, don't," I directed her. "Now, palm those beautiful breasts and massage them. God, they feel so good, don't they? Lick your fingers for me, Lanie. Push your breasts together, and then use those wet fingers to pull and tug on those pert little nipples. That's my mouth, hot and wet, sucking and teasing. I alternate between each one, my tongue flicking and circling, then both of them at the same time. Scrape your nipples with your fingernails. That's my teeth. Damn, I want to bite them so bad. Do you feel me, kitten?"

"Oh, God, yes."

"Fuck, when you say it like that . . ." I closed my eyes and could almost see her hands manipulating her own body. I made a mental note to make that a reality in the very near future. Maybe I'd even watch her pleasure herself with her little toy as well. I should reconsider letting her keep it after all.

"Touch yourself for me. Slip your fingers between your pussy lips and feel how soft and warm you are," I continued to toy with her. "Are you wet for me, Lanie?"

She moaned. "So fucking wet."

My voice was deep and throaty to my own ears, blood pumping through my veins and going straight to my engorged cock. "That's good, kitten. Take the mini-me and put it in your mouth. I want you to suck my cock. Get me wet and ready to slide inside that tight pussy."

The hum that came from the other end of the line was muffled, and I could tell she'd done exactly what I'd asked of her. Wet, slurping sounds mixed with greedy moans of satisfaction, and I wanted to feel what the fuck she was doing for real, not just imagine it.

"That's enough, Lanie. You don't want to make me jealous, do you?"

"Will it make you fuck me hard?" Her voice was teasing, hoping my answer would be yes.

"You like it when I fuck you hard?"

Lanie mewled on the other end of the line, and my breathing accelerated from the sound alone. My cock was about as hard as it could get and I feared I might seriously burst a blood vessel if I didn't release some of the tension soon. My hand had a mind of its own at that point and I began to stroke myself.

"I love it when my pussy feels so good to you that you just can't help yourself."

When my girl said *pussy*, it just motherfucking did things to me. A growl erupted from my chest and escaped through my clenched teeth. "Say it again."

"Say what?"

She knew what the fuck I wanted to hear. She was playing with me, and I was slightly annoyed by it. Mostly because she was there and I wasn't, and I was hornier than a nymphomaniac on the set of a porno. "You know what. Say it again."

"Puuuuusssyyyy."

"Goddamnit, woman. If you were here right now, I'd have

no mercy on you. I'd fuck you so hard you'd be seeing stars."
And I meant every word of it, too.

"Now who's the tease? Tell me what to do next, Noah."

Oh, right. She was holding a dildo in her hands. So many places my mind could've gone with that thought. It was about to hit on at least one of those.

"Turn it on, kitten. Feel me vibrating in your hands. I want you to run the head of my dick up and down those wet folds. Soak me in your wetness."

"Mmm, that feels so good."

I shouldered my phone and reached behind me to fumble around with my hand until I found the lubricant in the drawer of the nightstand. Then I squirted a generous amount into my palm before throwing the bottle to the side so I could watch my hand go to work on my cock.

"Feel me there, teasing your opening with my cock. I'm ready for you. I want to fuck you hard and fast. I want to make you scream my name."

"God, yes, Noah," she moaned, her breathing labored to match my own.

"Sit up on your knees, kitten. Can you do that for me? I want you to turn the speakerphone on, sit up on your knees and hold on to the headboard with your free hand."

I heard a shuffling noise from the other end of the line, and then her voice again, a little more distant than before. "Okay, what now?"

"You're going to ride my cock, Lanie. Put a pillow between your legs and prop that thing on it. Now spread your knees until you're low enough that you can feel it at your opening."

"I want you so bad," she whined.

"Then take me. Lower yourself onto my cock and ride me hard, just the way you like it." Wanting to feel the sensation with her, I squeezed the head of my dick between my thumb and forefinger before bucking my hips to push the rest of my cock through the grip of my hand.

My eyes shut as the mental picture of entering her mixed with the memory of how I knew it felt. "Oh, fuck, Lanie. You feel so good. Do you like that?"

"You're so *thick*," she enunciated the last word.

"Kitten, you gotta stop saying stuff like that before I get in the fucking car and drive my ass to Hillsboro to kidnap you." And I was a ball's hair away from doing it, too.

"Will you bring your thick cock?"

Her words sent me into a frenzied state. My hands tightened on my dick as I stroked it faster, the lubricant warming with the friction from my palm. I closed my eyes and imagined it was her pussy wrapped around me, constricting and releasing as she rocked her hips above me.

I wanted to see her looking down at me, her mouth slightly agape while her fingernails dug into the muscles on my chest. Her hair creating a curtain around us. Her hips undulating against mine as she stroked that little nub against my groin.

She moaned and groaned on the other end of the line, quietly so as not to disturb the rest of the household, but she was reeling and I could tell she needed more.

"Ride me, Lanie. Harder." I imagined her ass slapping against my thighs as her tits bounced with her movements. My hand quickened and I bit into my lip so hard I thought for sure I had split it.

"Feels so good," she moaned quietly. I could hear her breaths and the soft tap of her headboard as she rode the dildo beneath her.

"Hold on, kitten. Just hold on," I urged her, almost there myself.

"Noah, I need you. Please?" she begged, seeking her release. "Give me more."

"I promised to give you everything you need. Remember? Didn't I promise you that? Let go of the headboard, Lanie. Use your fingers. Find the spot, the one that needs that little something more. Work it with your fingers and when I tell you to, I want you to pinch it."

Her breathing was heavy, a keening sound building on the other end of the line until it went throaty.

"Now, kitten. Pinch it now."

"Oh, fuck!" she called out, her voice a husky whisper as she tried to be quiet. I could practically see her head fall back and her body go rigid under the power of her orgasm.

And that vision took me exactly where I needed to go as well. "Right there. Right . . . fucking . . . there." I growled out my release, my hips bucking into my fisted hand. Squeezing my cock tight and pressing the pad of my thumb to the tip, semen shot out like thick, molten lava from a spewing eruption and landed on my stomach. I milked my cock, my hips pumping in uneven intervals until the job was done.

"Noah, are you still there?" Lanie said, picking up the phone and turning off the speaker. She was still panting, but her voice was rich and smooth.

I threw my arm over my face and fought to regain my composure. "Yeah, kitten. I'm here."

"I miss you."

Yeah, I fucking missed her, too.

~$~

It took about four hours to get to Hillsboro, eight hours round trip. Which meant I had enough time to get there and be back in time for work. I'd gone over the calculation at least a dozen times in my head as I lay there watching the minutes on the clock count down to midnight. Despite the release I'd had two hours prior, I found it impossible to sleep . . . yet again. There was a thin line between love and obsession, and I was afraid I was dangerously close to stepping over it (although it could've been a pesky little thing called sleep deprivation that made me think like that). I needed a cure, soon, and I knew I had two more days to wait for it. The problem was that I had absolutely no intention of wasting any of the couple of days I had with her on sleep, so the cycle was just going to keep repeating itself until we figured out some way to be together. Or I went crazy, whichever came first.

I climbed out of bed and slipped on a pair of jeans before I went downstairs to grab a glass of milk or a shot of Patrón—whatever the hell was going to work best to get me to fall asleep. Only I was distracted when I reached the bottom floor, because everywhere my eyes fell, I saw a vision of her. Lanie on her knees in front of the door; Lanie storming through said door after torching the lingerie she clearly didn't want; Lanie descending the stairs looking like Cinderella on her way to the ball; Lanie on the stairs, tears streaming down her face after I'd just fucked her there angrily. I closed my eyes to that image and was rewarded with one of Lanie in my shower immediately afterward, her beautiful body soaked and trembling as she held me under the spray.

I walked through the house until I reached the piano room, and she was there, too, splayed across my baby grand, cradled in my lap on the bench as we made love. In my office, there was Lanie wearing nothing but my silk tie as she stood in the doorway.

I missed her so much. My heart ached as my mind sifted through countless images of her, some innocent, some not so much: her beautiful smiles, the sexy little sneers from a time when she hated me, the erotic expression on her face as she came for me over and over again, the look of contentment when she told me she loved me—everything. Maybe I could survive without her by my side, but I sure as hell didn't want to.

Distance be damned—I needed to see her.

With bare feet and no shirt, I rushed out to the foyer, grabbed my keys and wallet from the dish on the side table, and ran to my Lamborghini. A few sprinkles of rain dotted my windshield as I pulled out of the garage and made my way toward Hillsboro, toward her.

I sped like a maniac. Wet roads were not exactly prime driving conditions for a sleek sports car, but I didn't care. I had to make it to her with time to spare to hold her in my arms before I had to turn back around and leave her again, and the Lamborghini was my fastest means of transportation at the time. I made a mental note to invest in a helicopter the very next day.

The rain started to fall harder along the drive, and with each slosh of water under my tires, with each swipe of the blade across the windshield, I lost myself further and further into thoughts of Lanie.

I was haunted by the dream of her, and by the reality that had unfolded the day I took her back to her parents' house two weeks earlier. That cottage, the meadow, her laughter, the smile on her face—it was like the dream had come to life before my very eyes.

I could still hear the sound of her voice, sad and lonely as she said she missed me. It echoed through my mind and caused a tightening in my chest. I was sad and lonely for her, too. And I didn't give a good goddamn if that meant I was pussy-whipped. I couldn't think of any other pussy I'd rather be whipped by.

I stepped on the gas pedal, forcing the Lamborghini to speed even faster down the road toward my destination.

Night surrounded me as I sped along the empty roads, my headlights reflecting off the wet pavement before me. I was nearly there—just a few short miles and I'd have her in my arms.

By the time I pulled onto her street, the rain outside had already become a torrential downpour. I killed my headlights, not wanting to alert Lanie or her parents to my presence, and parked a bit down from her house. There was a dim, flickering light from Lanie's bedroom window, casting shadows like dancing images across her wall—obviously a candle. The rest of the house was dark, and not a soul was stirring on the street.

I got out of the car and closed the door as quietly as I could, but apparently even that was too loud. First one dog and then another began to bark until it sounded like a whole pack of the fuckers surrounded me.

Cold rain pelted my bare skin, the merciless wind whipping it into sheets. Within seconds I was drenched from head to toe and freezing my balls off, but I gave not a flying fuck. My body began to shiver under the elements, but I only had one thing on my mind: my girl. Of course, if I'd used one ounce of that energy to think out my plan a little more thoroughly, I would've known what my next step was going to be. I couldn't very well ring the doorbell because I'd be greeted by the barrel of Mack's shotgun aimed at my boys.

I examined the tree that sprouted from the ground below Lanie's window and calculated my odds of being able to scale it to make it to her room. There were a couple of low-lying branches, so I figured my chances were pretty good. That is, until I actually tried to climb it.

Thanks to bare feet and moss-covered bark, I couldn't get a foothold on the damn thing. I grabbed the branch overhead and pulled myself up and was nearly close enough to straddle it when it broke under my weight, sending me thudding back to the ground. The wind was knocked out of me briefly, but I hadn't driven four hours to give up that easily. Just as I stood to make another attempt, I saw the curtains shift behind Lanie's window, and the sash rose to reveal her standing there.

"Noah?" Lanie's confused voice called down, having apparently been roused by the sound of the cracking limb. "Are you crazy? What are you doing here?"

My face turned toward the darkened sky. Raindrops fell into my eyes and I blinked against them to keep her in my sights. I stared in awe, unable to take my eyes off the woman of my dreams. Her hair was in a messy ponytail, a few tendrils having fallen loose to cradle her face, and her eyes were slightly puffy with sleep. She looked perfectly imperfect, and I wanted to make her mine for all time. And then two little words tumbled from my lips, unplanned and unabated.

It wasn't a question. It wasn't an order. Hell, it was a plea.

"Marry me."

8
the bubble is popped

Lanie

I stood there at my window looking down at Noah. He was half naked. No shirt, no shoes, just a pair of soaked jeans that were molded to his scrumptious form. His hair was plastered to his forehead, his long lashes batting raindrops away, his tongue darting out to capture one of the perfect beads that hung from his bottom lip precariously. And he was looking up at me like I was the second coming, even though I knew I looked like death warmed over.

"Marry me."

His words drifted up to me, cutting through the unforgiving wind that threatened to pummel him until he was left beaten and battered.

My heart felt like someone had used defibrillation paddles on me. My knees went weak and the floor beneath my feet seemed to fall away, so I tightened my grip on the windowsill to try to keep my balance.

Tried and failed.

I teetered forward, nearly falling from the open window, but I caught myself on the branch before me just in time.

"Lanie!" Noah called up to me, fear evident in his hoarse voice.

I had to get to him, jump into his arms, and wrap myself around him. Taking the stairs would've taken too long, and hell, it was just too damned traditional for us. Screw it, I figured—since I was already halfway hanging on to the branch before me, I crawled out onto the limb, icy raindrops pricking my bare skin and soaking through the white shirt I wore—Noah's, the one I had taken with me.

"Get back in that fucking window, Lanie, before you break your goddamn neck!" Noah ordered. But since when had I ever listened to him?

I'd made it off one branch and down to another with only one more to go before I could jump down to him. And that's when the klutz in me decided to wake up. Yeah, there I was trying to make some sort of grand gesture, and that psycho bitch decided to rear her ugly, deformed head.

"Oh, shit!" I lost my footing.

Imagine my surprise when my body met not the cold, hard ground but a wall of flesh instead. Noah had broken my fall with his body, but the impact sent us both tumbling.

I propped myself up and looked down at him, still amazed that he was there in the first place. A rumble of thunder sounded in the distance, but no words passed between us. We lay there in the mud looking at each other. His gaze was intent on mine, and I searched his eyes to see if I could find an ounce of regret about his unexpected proposal.

I saw none.

What I did see was a longing that matched mine, a certainty that dispelled any doubt, truth that mirrored my own. I loved that man, and he loved me, and it was right.

The muscles in his jaw tensed. He reached up and cupped my face in his hands. Then he exhaled a breath slowly and swept a wet lock of hair from my forehead. "I don't ever want to be away from you again. I *can't* do it." His voice was broken, shaken.

I felt the same way, but the words were lodged in my throat, engulfed by a myriad of fathomless emotions. So since my verbal communication skill was clearly broken, I did my best to convey my feelings through other means. I kissed him like I'd never kissed him before. I was lost in Noah Crawford. Everything else in the world ceased to exist: the unrelenting storm, the fact that it was four o'clock in the morning, the barking neighborhood dogs.

Noah rolled us over until I was writhing beneath him, doing everything I could to get closer. Sensing my desperation, he hitched my bare leg over his hip. The soaked denim of his jeans pressed against my center and I moaned into his mouth. He always knew what I needed, and he would always take care of me like he'd promised.

My hands roamed over his naked chest, his muscular shoulders, his thick biceps, every inch of him wet and slick under my touch. I wrapped my other leg around him, holding him captive, unwilling to ever let him go again.

Noah cupped my ass in one hand and rolled his hips, his kiss hot and demanding. When his lips finally left mine, his talented mouth trailed along the underside of my jaw until he reached the sensitive spot below my ear.

And then he stopped, pulling back abruptly as he looked down at me. His brows were furrowed, his lips parted, and he just stared at me with a confused expression. Rain hung like teardrops from the tips of his hair, and one fell onto my cheek only to slide down the side of my face. Funny how a gazillion other raindrops were pummeling us, but that was the one that caused me to shiver and my skin to pebble.

"What's wrong?" I asked, unsure why he had stopped.

"You didn't answer my question."

I giggled and rolled my eyes. "Noah, I climbed out a window and fell out of a tree, nearly breaking my neck, just to get to you. Do you really need me to say it?"

"Well, yeah, I kind of do." The expression on his face was so sincere. "I'm asking you to be my wife, to bear my children, to grow old with me by your side. I'm asking you to marry me, Delaine Marie Talbot, for better or worse, in sickness and health, for richer or poorer, until death do we part. Does that sound like something you might want to do for the rest of your life?"

I bit down on my lip to stop the goofy grin that spread across my face and shrugged nonchalantly. "Maybe."

He smiled down at me, his teeth all perfect and white. I wanted to lick them. "Just maybe?"

"I'm crazy about you, Noah Crawford. And I'm pretty sure that's because I'm in love with you, and not because you actually do drive me crazy. So yeah, I think that sounds like something I might want to do for the rest of my life."

"Is that a yes?"

I laughed at his persistence. "Yes, Noah."

He looked relieved, and his smile became celestial. "Okay, good."

I pushed my fingers through his wet hair. "Very good." My eyes drifted over the features of his face. His hazel eyes held so much love and adoration. He was happy, and I did that for him.

I traced his prominent jaw, feeling it tense beneath my touch until I moved on to feel the softness of his lips. Noah closed his eyes and kissed my fingertips, his neck arching as I continued down his chin, and further still, to lightly caress his Adam's apple. His neck was thick and muscular, the artery that resided beneath the skin throbbing with the life essence that flowed through his perfect body. It almost wasn't fair how beautiful the man was. But I wasn't complaining, because he was going to be mine forever.

"Make love to me?"

Noah opened his eyes, and with unquestionable certainty, said, "Always, but we need to get you out of the rain." He stood and pulled me up with him. "Mack's probably going to have my nuts for this."

Despite my protests, he wrapped his arms around my shoulders so that I was huddled into his side, and he led me to the front door. And then it dawned on me as he tried the handle: I'd climbed out of the window and the front door was locked.

"Um, it's locked," I told him, stating the obvious.

"Well, you're not climbing back up the damn tree, that's for sure." He looked around again to find another avenue. "Back door?"

"Locked."

Noah looked back toward his car. "You'll have to call them to let you in then. I'll go get my phone . . ." His voice drifted off and he swore, running his hands through his wet hair. "Shit! I'm such an idiot. I left my phone at home."

"You drove all the way here without your phone?"

"Without my phone, my shoes, my shirt," he said with a devilish glint in his eye. "If I hadn't already had my pants on, I would've left those, too. See how crazy you make me?"

I stood up on my tiptoes and kissed the tip of his nose. "Okay, so let's survey the situation. We're both half naked, it's dark, it's raining, we have no way to get inside, and I want you . . . *now*. Come with me."

I took his hand and pulled him down the porch steps and toward the small grove of trees next to my house.

"Where are we going?"

"You'll see," I said, giving him an impish grin.

Once we stepped through the threshold of the thick trees, I led him to a clearing in the center. I stopped and looked up, drawing his attention to the lush canopy of trees overhead that formed a barrier against the elements.

"What now?" he asked as I stepped close to him.

"Now," I said, tugging at the button of his jeans, "we get you out of these wet pants before you catch your death of cold."

Noah sighed and reached for the top button on my shirt. "Well, we can't have that, now can we?"

I shook my head and then leaned up to suck on the skin over the throbbing vein in his neck as we both worked to rid each other of the remainder of our clothes. Once all barriers had been discarded, Noah picked me up so that I could wrap my legs around his waist while our lips found each other again. He slowly lowered us down to the ground until his back rested against the trunk of a tree and I sat comfortably in his lap.

As my tongue sought out his, my hand traveled down his chest and abdomen to find his cock wedged between our bodies. He hissed and threw his head back when I finally touched him, giving me ample access to his neck and shoulders. I didn't waste a second of time, bathing his delicious skin with my tongue, my lips, my teeth. His cock was titanium smoothness in my palm, and I pressed him against myself, coating him in my wetness.

Then his hands cupped my ass, and he lifted me as I guided him to my opening. Noah filled me completely, just like he'd always done, just like he always would. We both moaned at the sensation of our bodies coming together like puzzle pieces perfectly matched to each other. For the first time in a couple of weeks I could ride the real him and not just some synthetic version that could never really compare.

Noah released my hair from the band holding it in place, and then he dipped his head to capture one of my nipples with his mouth. His teeth scraped the hardened peak as his lips sucked and his tongue flicked back and forth at a maddening pace. I arched my back and took him in fully, riding him. Slowly, tenderly, we made love as we each whispered words of forever.

It didn't take long for either of us to reach our climax. Having spent so much time away from each other had both of us wound pretty tightly. Plus, the turn our relationship had taken—the promise of many years spent in the company of the one we loved, our soul mate—had driven us both to such a point that we only wanted to be consumed by the other.

Consummation had its perks.

Before long, I was cuddled in his arms, the heat of our bodies providing all the warmth we needed. We were completely spent, undeniably satiated.

"I have to go." Noah's voice was a reluctant whisper. "I don't want to, but Stone is up to something, and I can't risk missing another day of work before the board meeting on Monday."

I straightened and gave him a soft kiss. "It's okay. I understand."

His hands brushed my damp hair from my shoulders, and then he cupped my face to kiss me more deeply. I actually whimpered when he pulled away.

"How are we going to get you back inside?"

I shrugged. "You leave, and I'll bang the door down."

"And what, pray tell, are you going to tell Mack when he asks how you got locked out in nothing but my shirt? Which looks so very fucking good on you, by the way."

"Don't worry about my dad. I can handle him," I said, having no clue whatsoever how I was going to explain it to him, but I'd come up with something. "Hey, I'm the future Mrs. Delaine Crawford. Some of your ingenuity has to have rubbed off on me, right?"

Noah bit down on his lip, his eyes fixated on my mouth. "Jesus, that sounds good." He hugged me close and then stole my breath away with a hungry kiss.

Moments later, after much prodding to make Noah get his Ridonkabutt in gear so that he wouldn't be late for work, I found myself standing on the front porch of my parents' house, my fist banging on the door. As I expected, Mack sleepily wrenched the door open. His eyes widened when he saw me standing there.

"Lanie? What the hell are you doing outside in the rain in the middle of the night?"

I pushed past him and he closed the door, turning toward me for an answer.

My mother appeared from the hallway, obviously having been roused from her sleep as well. "What's going on out here?" she asked, wiping the sleep from her eyes. Standing there against the door jamb, she looked the picture of perfect health.

"I was just about to find out the answer to that myself," Mack told her, his stare never leaving me. "Lanie?"

So I told them the truth.

"Noah showed up, and asked me to marry him."

"He what?" Faye's eyes went wide with excitement, and a huge smile spread across her face.

"He what?" my dad also asked, his voice not sounding near as pleased as my mother's.

I turned toward him and set my chin in determination. "He asked me to marry him, and I said yes."

"That's wonderful!" my mother squealed as she came to hug me.

Mack raked his hands over his face in exasperation. "And how the hell did you end up locked outside in the rain?"

"I climbed down the tree to get to him," I said matter-of-factly.

"Oh, that is so romantic." My mother had a dreamy tone in her voice.

"That is so stupid!" Mack countered. "You could've broken your neck, young lady. Where is he?"

"Oh, stow it, Mack," my mom said, coming to my rescue. "This is great news, and I'm not going to let you ruin it for us."

I knew that my mother had never really had what you'd call a romantic proposal. The way she told the story, Mack had picked her up for a date, turned to look at her, and said, "So you wanna get hitched?" She told him sure, and he said, "Well, all right then," before turning back to start the car. She hadn't been complaining; it was just the way they were. Exactly like how Noah's proposal, and my acceptance, was the way *we* were.

"Let's grab some coffee," my mother said, dragging me toward the kitchen. "You have to tell me everything."

My father sighed in resignation and rolled his eyes. "I'm going back to bed."

Faye and I were still sitting in the kitchen when the storm finally subsided and the sun peeked over the horizon. I told her the whole story, even the part where we made love under the canopy of trees next door. She hung on my every word like she was a kid and I was telling her the story of Santa Claus.

"Let me see the ring," she said, lifting my hand up to see none there.

I shrugged. "It was sort of spur-of-the-moment. Besides, I don't really need a ring."

"Lanie, he's Noah Crawford. He's going to make sure you have one."

"Either way, it doesn't matter. Just to know he loves me is enough." And it was. I'd never been the flashy type, but my mother was right: Noah was going to make certain I had a ring. I only hoped it wasn't going to be something huge that cost way too much. Heck, he could give me a secret decoder ring out of a Cracker Jack box and it would suit me just fine.

Polly and Lexi would probably go batshit over it, but I wouldn't care.

"Baby," my mother said with sincerity as she took my hand in hers, "you have to go to him. You can't stay here."

"Mom, he's cool with it," I said, cutting her off. "When you're better, that's when I'll go."

"Now you listen to me, Delaine Talbot," she said, her voice taking on that motherly tone. "I'm doing just fine. In fact, I've never felt better. It's time you stop living your life around me and your father and go live your own. That man is crazy about you, and you're just as crazy about him. Go. I insist."

"You're kicking me out?" I asked in mock outrage.

"Yes, I am," she said, playing along. "Get your shit and get the hell out of my house."

We had a good laugh and hugged. I was all kinds of giddy inside, knowing that Noah and I would finally be together without anything keeping us apart. The Cooch was mighty excited about that prospect as well. She and the Wonder Peen were going to be reunited, and the only thing that stood in the way of their happiness was the Cooch's obsession with the Ridonkabutt. However, I didn't doubt they'd somehow work things out so that she could enjoy the best of both worlds.

Noah had called to let me know he'd made it back okay and was on his way into work. I decided not to tell him I was coming home to him, or that I had told my folks about our upcoming nuptials. I wanted to see the look of surprise on his face when I showed up and made the announcement.

I called Dez at her parents' house and woke her lazy ass up to tell her the good news. After about three straight minutes of listening to her bitching about me waking her up, I finally cut her off and just blurted the words out.

The first thing she said to me was, "And I suppose you want me to be your maid of honor?"

I laughed at her nonchalance. "If you're not too terribly busy, I'd love that."

Dez sighed. "I guess I can do that, but you better know now that there will definitely be strippers at the bridal shower."

"You mean the bachelorette party?"

"Yeah, that too."

I laughed. "Hey, do you get a discount since you've slept with all of them?"

"Fuck you very much, and I damn well better." She laughed with me, and then she got serious. "I'm really happy for you, Lanie. But I'm still going to set his balls on fire if he fucks up."

"Aw, you're so sweet. Now get your butt over here. I need you to drive me to Chicago."

"You're lucky I don't have to work until tonight," she huffed. "I'll be there in two shakes of a donkey's dick, trick."

I had just finished packing my things and stacking them by the front door when I wandered into the kitchen and saw my father sitting there having his lunch. He glanced up at me, his eyes full of sadness, and then returned his attention to his sandwich.

I knew he was upset but holding his tongue for my mother's sake.

"Dad?" I said, walking into the kitchen and taking the seat next to him.

He cleared his throat and sat back in his chair, attempting to look nonchalant. "What's on your mind, baby girl?"

"You know I'm going to be okay, right?"

"Let me tell you what I know," he said, crossing his arms defensively over his chest. "Nothing, that's what I know. You go off to college, money shows up out of nowhere in our account, your mother gets the best heart surgeon in the state—hell, in the country, for that matter—you show up with this bohunk who has more money than he knows what to do with, and all of a sudden my baby girl is running off to marry him. Hell, he didn't even ask me for your hand in marriage. Now you tell me, Lanie, what's there for me to be worried about?"

"You have to trust me. I'm not a little girl anymore. I know what I'm doing."

He turned his head to look out the window and then sighed again. "Do you love him?"

I laid my hand on his shoulder, and he turned to look back at me. "More than I ever thought possible. And he loves me, too, *so* much."

Silence stretched between us before he finally said, "You know, when I first held your tiny body in my arms, I swore to protect and keep you safe from everything this cruel world has to offer. But I also promised myself that I wouldn't be so overprotective that I keep you from being happy."

"Noah makes me happy, Daddy," I told him, trying to convey my sincerity through my eyes. "I'm miserable without him. I want to spend the rest of my life loving him and letting him love me. But I can't be truly happy without your blessing. I want you to walk me down the aisle and give me away to Noah, knowing I'll be safe with him. So do we have your blessing?"

Mack looked down at the table as he picked up a potato chip and shrugged. "I guess. But if he steps even a millimeter out of line, I'm going to be up his ass like a pogo stick," he said, and then popped the chip into his mouth.

I threw my arms around his neck and hugged him tightly. "Thank you, Dad! I'll always love you best."

~$~

"Holy torpedo in a Speedo!" Dez gasped as we walked through the front doors of Scarlet Lotus.

"Wow, this is . . . impressive," I said, looking around at the ornate fixtures of the lobby. "The man I'm about to marry is doing very well, indeed."

"I really hate you right now," Dez said, her eyes narrowed at me in jealousy. "Just remember that what's yours is mine."

"This won't be mine, Dez." I spotted Polly and she waved us over. "I don't want anything from Noah other than his love. And maybe—no, definitely—his body."

"Congratulations!" Polly squealed when we reached her, and then she threw her arms around me for one heck of a bear hug. She sure was strong for such a tiny little thing. I guess it was true what they said about ants being able to carry fifty times their own weight.

I thought Dez was going to pull a knife on Polly when she did the same to her, but luckily Polly was too quick. When she pulled back, she got that excited look in her eyes. "Come on. Let's get you upstairs to your fiancé."

She led us to an elevator and we stepped inside while she punched the button for the floor with Noah's office. The entire ride up, she kept asking about the wedding; who was going to plan it, who was going to cater, the date, and the list went on and on. I could see the aggravation on her face when my answer to every question was, "I don't know."

"Polly, he just asked me to marry him a few hours ago. When did I have time to plan a wedding?"

"Pfft," she said with a dismissive wave of her hand. "Honey, I had my wedding planned since I was, like, three."

Somehow I didn't doubt that.

The elevator dinged, signaling our arrival to our destination, and the doors pulled back so we could step off. We followed Polly down a hallway, and I noticed that everyone stopped and stared after us like we were on display. I recognized some of the faces from the ball, but it still made me feel slightly uncomfortable.

"Hey, wifey! What are you doing here?" Mason asked in surprise when we walked into his office. And then his eyes nearly bugged out when I stepped out from behind Polly. "Holy shit! What are *you* doing here?"

"Shh," Polly said, cupping her hand over his mouth. "Is he in?"

Mason only nodded because that was all he could do. "Well? What are you waiting for? Go get him," Polly directed me with a nod toward Noah's office.

I walked over and cracked the door open. He was sitting at his desk, his back turned toward the door as he looked out his window like he was a million miles away. His hair was disheveled and his jaw was slightly scruffier than normal. Apparently his little impromptu trip to Hillsboro had left him with no time to shave.

I closed the door behind me. "Having second thoughts?"

Noah swung around in his chair, his brow raised and eyes wide.

"Surprise," I said, walking toward him.

"Lanie? What are you doing here?"

"I figured two can play the whole surprise-visit game," I told him as I took a seat in his lap. "Only I'm not leaving. I'm here to stay. My mother swears she's fine, and my father . . . well, we have his blessing."

I felt his whole body relax around me, as if every ounce of tension that our separation had caused him had suddenly melted away with my words. His hold tightened when I leaned in and nuzzled his ear. "Looks like you're stuck with me," I whispered.

Noah cupped my face in his hands, his lips brushing against mine when he said, "Welcome home, kitten." And then he gave me a searing kiss.

I melted against him, into him, as his words permeated my skin and became a part of me. I was back where I belonged, in the arms of the man who'd captured my heart for an eternity. My mother was healing, my father was back to work, and all was right with the world. Nothing could penetrate the happy little bubble I'd found myself in.

"Yo, Crawford!" The door to Noah's office swung open, disrupting our happily-ever-after moment as a voice I wished I could have forgotten tainted our pure air with obnoxygen.

Noah growled, ire thick in his voice, "What do you want, Stone? And what the fuck are you doing barging into my office unannounced?"

"Oh, wow. Were you two about to get it on in here? Because I'm pretty sure that's against company policy. We can always ask the board at the meeting on Monday to be sure."

I turned the full force of my glare on him, and he actually took a step back. "Come in search of your dinner, crumb snatcher?" I asked.

"Delaine!" he said, smiling widely in greeting. "Slumming

it again? When are you gonna drop Crawford and give Big Daddy Dick a go?"

Noah attempted to lunge from his chair, but I managed to hold him in place, barely. As much as I'd have loved to see Noah beat the crap out of the man, David Stone simply wasn't worth losing Scarlet Lotus over. "Let it go, baby. He's not worth it. He's just suffering from penis envy."

"Ouch, my feelings," David whined with his hand over his heart and his bottom lip out in a pout.

I ignored him and stood, turning to face Noah. "I'm going to the house to unpack. I'll see you when you get home." Intent on making sure David knew who was buttering my bread, I gave Noah a kiss that was so hot it made my own toes curl. "I love you," I told Noah, and then walked toward the door.

"Move," I told David.

He was smart enough to step to one side, but not without giving me a sarcastic grin. "I love you, too, sweetums."

Dez, Polly, and Mason had just walked back into Mason's office, all three carrying fresh coffee.

Mason sighed when he saw David's back before he closed the door. "Oh, shit."

"Hold the phone. Who is that piece of tall, dark, and ooh-la-la?" Dez asked, checking him out.

"He is what we like to refer to as pathetic scum," Polly answered.

"No, seriously. Who is he?" Dez asked again. "I think I know him."

"Let's hope not," I said. "He's David Stone. He owns the other half of Scarlet Lotus."

"Are you sure? Because he looks awfully familiar."

Mason sat on the corner of his desk and pulled Polly to

stand between his legs. "No offense, Dez, but I hardly think he'd be running in the same circles as you."

"Well, never mind. It doesn't matter anyway," she said, shrugging it off. Then she turned toward me. "You ready to go? I don't have much time before I have to be at work."

"Yeah, I'm ready," I told her, and then bid farewell to Polly and Mason. Of course Polly promised she'd be over first thing the next morning to start wedding preparations. I shuddered at the thought.

Dez and I made it back to the mansion and, with Samuel's help, got all my things unloaded and stacked in Noah's bedroom. Shortly afterward, I saw Dez off for her shift at Foreplay, the meat market where Noah and I first met. I had just gone to the kitchen to pour myself a glass of ice water when the doorbell rang. As I walked back toward the foyer, I spotted Dez's scarf where she had discarded it earlier.

Snatching it up because I knew it was the reason Dez had come back, I opened the door to hand it to her. "Forgot your sc—" My voice caught in my throat when I realized it wasn't Dez on the other side of the door.

"Honey, I'm home." David Stone stood there with a slimy smile on his mug.

"Noah's not in from the office yet." I attempted to slam the door in his face, but he stuck his arm out and kept it from closing.

"I'm not here to see Noah. I'm here to see you," he said, forcing me to back up as he pushed his way inside.

"You just don't take a hint, do you?" I asked, enraged by his relentlessness. "I don't want anything to do with you, asshole."

David kept advancing on me until my back was pressed to

the wall and he had cornered me. He caged me in with his body, his grotesque hand pushing a lock of hair out of my face while he smiled down at me.

"What do you want, David?"

"I want you."

"Well, I don't want you, so you can leave now."

"I think you might want to hear my proposal before you openly reject me, Lanie."

I bristled at his familiarity. "What did you just call me?"

He smirked, but he was clearly confused. "What? I called you Lanie."

I pushed my shoulders back and straightened to my full height as I took one purposeful step toward him followed by another. "I only allow those I consider my friends to call me by that name. And you, sir," I said, poking him in the chest as he backed up, "are no friend of mine."

He gave me a broad smile that was more creepy than friendly. "Babe," he crooned with his hands up in surrender, "why are we always making war when we could be making love?"

I shook my head. "Boy, you are really dumb, aren't you?"

"Hear me out," he said. "We don't have to be enemies. I know what you women really want, and I'm positive we can work out a deal where we both come out on top."

I crossed my arms and raised an eyebrow at him.

"Okay," he said with a shrug. "If you prefer to be on top, that's fine by me."

"You're disgusting."

"Can I finish?"

"I'm really not interested in hearing anything you have to say." I walked toward the door, but before I could open it to kick him out, David was there with his shoulder pressed against it. I looked at him like he was crazy because obviously he'd lost his mind, but he just flashed that toothy grin again.

"So here's the deal. You partner up with me, but stay here with Crawford for the time being as if nothing has changed. Let the sappy bastard fall in love with you, and then once you've snagged that magic lasso around your finger, you and I take everything. You help me get Scarlet Lotus, and I'll take care of you for the rest of your life. You'll never want for a damn thing again. Including the best cock in all fifty states."

I couldn't help myself. I laughed. Loudly. I don't think David appreciated the humor of the situation quite as much as I did because his face contorted into something that didn't look altogether human.

"What the fuck are you laughing about?" he asked.

"You," I said, pointing and still laughing at him. "You said that with such a straight face that it's almost like you actually believe I'd leave Noah for someone like you. But of course you couldn't really believe that."

His expression changed again, the angry furrow of his brow replaced with a knowing smirk on his lips. "Aw, I get it. You want your money up front. That's how my partner paid you, right?"

There was an abrupt halt to my giggling. I could feel all the blood in my face drain with his words, and I was suddenly paralyzed with fear.

"How much will it take? A thousand? Ten thousand? A hundred grand? Oh no, that's right. The going price is *two million dollars*, right? Damn, that pussy's gotta be lined in gold."

Oh, God. He knew.

"I don't know what you're talking about," I said, my voice sounding unconvincing even to my own ears.

"No?" Judging by the look on his face, it was safe to say he knew for sure that I knew what he was talking about. "Let's see if this rings a bell. Noah made a trip to a little club called Foreplay and then slipped in through the back door to attend a secret auction where he bought you for a cool two mill . . . to be his sex slave. Sound familiar?"

My whole body shook with trepidation.

"How did you know?"

David chuckled. "I might have access to a certain contract."

He found the contract? But how?

"What do you want?" I asked, ready to hear his demands.

He wrapped his arm around my waist and pulled me against his body. Then he leaned down and whispered into my ear. "I already told you. I want Scarlet Lotus. And I want to sample the golden pussy for myself."

"No!" I said, shoving at him, but he was too strong and I couldn't make him budge.

"Ah, why be so stingy? It's what you're paid to do, right? The difference is I'm offering you so much more than the measly amount my partner paid. You can have it all, including me. At least then you'll get to know what it's like to be with a real man," he said, and then he licked the length of my neck from my collarbone to my earlobe. "You do this or Noah's ship is sunk. I'll go to the board and the press about your little deal, and he'll lose everything; his company, his dignity, his standing in the public eye. Plus your folks will know their daughter is nothing but a common whore. So what's it going to be, Delaine?"

He palmed my breast and began to take liberties, squeezing it like it was a stress ball. I felt so completely vulnerable, and I was scared out of my wits. His hot breath fanned out over my skin, and he started to plant slimy kisses along the length of my neck.

My heart pounded furiously in its cage and I willed my mind to think of a way out of the predicament that I'd found myself in. Noah. I wanted my Noah. He'd be home shortly and then he'd . . .

And then it hit me. That was exactly what David was counting on. He wanted Noah to walk in and see him fucking me, just like when Noah had walked in and found him fucking Julie. David meant to destroy him completely.

So the decision I was left with was to either let him have what he wanted and break Noah's heart, or to refuse him and watch helplessly as Noah handed his company over to David Stone—a company his parents had built from scratch. Noah would be ruined, and my parents would know what I had done. But if he walked in and saw us together, it might do far more damage. Could Noah still love me after all that? Either way, it seemed there was no easy answer.

Images of Noah's face flashed across my mind: the anguished expression when he first told me he'd fallen in love with me, the light in his eyes when I finally got a chance to say it back, the desperation as he stood in the rain half naked and asked me to marry him. I couldn't rip his heart out. I refused to put him through the same thing Julie had.

Material things could be replaced. Noah was smart enough and had the talent to rebuild. As for his damnation in the public eye, people were bloodthirsty and ruthless when it came to celebrities, but as soon as the next star fell from the sky, his sin would be forgotten. And yeah, I would forever see the disappointment in my parents' eyes after they learned their daughter had sold her body for two million dollars, but the loss of their respect was a fair price to pay when I thought about the alternative. It was much more difficult to mend a broken heart, and Noah couldn't take much more heartache. It took a lot for him to finally trust someone else, and he'd put everything he had left in the palm of my hands. No way was I going to destroy a gift that precious.

"No," I answered David. "I belong to Noah, and Noah alone. I am his."

I felt every muscle in David's body tense as he registered my words. A low growl rumbled from his chest and he pulled back to glare down at me. "I *will* have you. Willingly, or not."

Before I had a chance to react, he grabbed my shirt and ripped it apart, sending buttons flying across the floor.

"No!" I screamed, and then I gathered every ounce of strength I had in my body and pushed against him.

It was enough force to make him stumble back, giving me room to get out of his clutches. I made a run for the door, but David was quick on my heels. Just as I reached for the door handle, he grabbed my arm and yanked me back, sending me sailing across the floor until I hit my head on the wall.

David stalked toward me, undoing his pants in the process. I scrambled, trying to get away, but he was on me in a nanosecond. So I did the only thing I could do: I fought. If he was going to take me, I wasn't about to make it easy for him. He hovered over me, and I kicked my foot out, nailing him in the balls.

"You bitch!" He doubled over, but the kick hadn't been enough to stop him. With renewed determination, he grabbed at my flailing arms and pinned me down to the floor. I was trapped under his weight, unable to move as he wedged his knees between my thighs and forced them apart while fumbling with my pants.

"Please! No!" I cried out. Tears streamed down my cheeks.

I squeezed my eyes shut to block out the horrific image of the disgusting man on top of me. He was a fucking animal; a panting, feral beast that was out of control with determined lust. The stench of his sweat burned my nostrils, and scalding tears ran freely down my face, their saltiness leaking past my trembling lips. At that moment I hated David Stone enough to want to kill him.

His hands went to the button on my jeans and I struggled to break free of his unyielding strength, determined not to let him touch me.

I was *not* a whore!

Just then, the front door flew open.

"Get the fuck off her!" It was Noah's voice, and he sounded demonic, as if he were possessed by Satan himself.

My bare skin felt an unexpected chill before I realized David was no longer on top of me. Instead, he was flying through the air, his body crashing into the side table with a sickening yet pleasing crack as its wood splintered under his weight.

Noah gave me a fleeting glance before he went after David, and I saw the rage that flamed behind his darkened eyes like red serpents licking a velvet sky. His shoulders heaved with angry breaths, his body tensed and ready to strike. I had never seen him look so fearsome.

He stalked toward the place where David lay among the debris trying to regain his bearings, but before he could get to his feet, Noah was there. Noah grabbed David's collar and drew his fist back, and then a loud crack echoed through the room when he landed the first blow to David's face.

David retaliated by grabbing Noah and throwing him back far enough to allow himself time to get to his feet. Blood spilled from his lip, and his face was swollen and discolored to an angry red. Then a battle cry clawed its way out of David's chest and he ran full force toward Noah, hooking him around the waist and driving him into the wall behind him.

"Noah!" I screamed as I got to my feet. I ran at them and jumped on David's back, wrapping my arms around his neck to put him in a choke hold. Admittedly, I probably didn't pose much of a threat. David proved that when he grabbed me and pulled me off his back to throw me back onto the floor.

It was the distraction Noah needed. He threw another punch, this one striking David's rib cage. David doubled over and Noah took the opportunity to land an uppercut to his chin, sending him flying back again.

When he crashed onto the floor, David's head lolled to the side and his body went limp. His face was bloodied and bruised, but that didn't keep Noah from continuing his attack. He straddled David and kept pummeling him over and over again. When he was satisfied David had no more fight left in him, he shook out his swollen hand and stood, looking down at his foe with disgust.

He turned toward me, his face quickly morphing from anger to heart-clenching concern, and then he knelt beside me. "Are you okay, kitten?"

Everything, the whole weight of the situation, finally hit home and I sobbed uncontrollably. David knew everything, and that still wasn't enough. No, he hated Noah so much, he was going to rape me just to destroy him. He was going to *rape* me.

I clutched Noah's shirt in my fists and pulled him to me so I could bury my head in his chest. "He wanted me to . . . And I couldn't do that to you, and he was going to . . ."

"Shh, shh, shh," Noah said, cradling me in his arms. "I know, kitten. It's okay. I'm here now, and I won't let anyone hurt you."

Oddly, it wasn't the fact that I had nearly been raped that had me so upset. Sure, that had a lot to do with it, but David hadn't gotten the opportunity to follow through on his threat. Noah had protected me, just like he had promised he would. What was most upsetting was the fact that David knew everything and would stop at nothing to see Noah a broken man.

It wasn't fear for my own well-being that had me so distraught; it was fear for Noah's.

I saw movement out of the corner of my eye just before heavy footsteps made a mad dash for the door. It was David, and he was running away. Noah turned me loose and made to go after him, but I pulled him back.

"No, you can't!" I yelled, holding on to him with all my might.

"He's getting away," Noah said, trying to pull my hands loose.

Grabbing his face, I forced him to look at me. "He knows, Noah. He knows everything."

And just like that, our perfect little bubble had popped.

9

i sort of like dez

Noah

Samuel had just dropped me off at the front of the house with my briefcase and a bouquet of flowers for my girl in hand. I stared in confusion when I noticed we had a visitor, and I knew for a fact it wasn't Dez. David Stone's Viper was parked in plain sight, and for just a moment, my mind flashed back to the day I had found him ass-fucking my would-be fiancée in my bathroom.

All I could think was, *Please, not her.*

My knuckles tightened around the bouquet in my hand until my senses brought me back to the fact that Lanie wasn't that slut Julie and she would never do anything of the sort to me.

Still, the fear was there. Had I let my guard down only to be fucked over again?

Haunted by the desolation that replayed like a wavy vinyl disc under the needle of an old phonograph, I found it hard to force my feet forward. It was as if they had been fastened down with cement blocks to the rocky bottom of a murky river, cutting off the freedom required to swim to the surface for a much-needed breath of air. My heart was giving me a pep talk like a motherfucker, but the agony over the possibility that Lanie could have fallen under David's mysterious spell overshadowed the trust I had given to her so easily. What the fuck did women see in him?

I was bitch-slapped out of my morbid thoughts when a bellow came from somewhere inside the house.

"You bitch!" It was David's voice, outraged and laced in venom.

The bouquet and my briefcase tumbled to the ground at the next sound, and the hair on the back of my neck stood at attention.

Lanie's scream was a desperate plea, and I took the front steps in giant leaps. Without a second thought, I threw myself against the door, my body numb to the pain I should've felt in my frantic attempt to get to her.

The violent scene was displayed before me; my girl had obviously been knocked to the ground by that piece of shit motherfucker. Her cheek had a huge bruise beginning to rise, and it was obvious that a heavy hand had landed there mere seconds before. Tears streamed down her cheeks and her eyes were squeezed shut.

He put his fucking hands on my girl!

My heart was seized by a myriad of emotions that seemed to take on a life of their own. As they took shape, a full spectrum of colors clouded my eyesight and rendered me helpless to the maniacal beast that lay dormant within. Horrific greens morphed into sodden blues of terror. Violent midnight shifted to an outraged orange consumed by disgust until my vision was inflamed with a demonic red that burned white-hot with the intensity of rage. And then finally everything went black with the vengeance every microscopic cell in my body needed to claim.

"Get the fuck off her!" I barely registered my own movement before I had David's clothes clenched in my fists and had thrown him across the room, away from my girl. Lanie looked up at me, and everything inside screamed for me to provide the comfort I knew she needed, but the driving force to make David pay for what he had done won the battle.

Fury consumed me until I was possessed with no control over my own body. Fists were thrown and connected, my back was slammed against a wall, and then Lanie leaped across the room and landed on David's back. It was when he swatted her away like she was nothing but an insignificant gnat that I snapped like a rubber band that had been stretched beyond its limit. I'd had enough of wrestling around with him like two scrawny boys grappling for dominance on a school playground. I was out for blood. I meant to beat him to a pulp until the very life force that kept the pathetic excuse for a human being alive was sucked out of him.

And I almost did. I was on him, hovering over him just as menacingly as he'd been hovering over my girl, punch after punch connecting with that slimeball's face. I could hear his bones cracking under my fists, a sound I found quite pleasing to the ear.

It was pure instinct that told me when I'd succeeded. David lay motionless on the floor, barely breathing. I shook out the sharp bolts of pain that shot from my hand and up my arm, not giving two shits about it, because it was worth it. Then, like a gravitational pull, I turned toward Lanie. Every trace of anger suddenly dissipated when I saw her face.

She needed me, and nothing would stop me from going to her.

"Are you okay, kitten?" I knelt beside her and looked her over for further injuries.

Her face had been blank and then suddenly, tears streamed unabated as the gravity of the situation came crashing down on her. She reached out and clutched my shirt in her hands, burying her face in my chest and sobbing uncontrollably.

"Shh, shh, shh." I did my damnedest to soothe her as I cradled her in my arms. "I know, kitten. It's okay. I'm here now, and I won't let anyone hurt you."

I meant it. With my dying breath, I fucking meant it.

We sat there like that for a little longer, Lanie crying and holding on to me like she was scared I might leave her at any moment, and me doing my best to console her. I had failed her. I'd promised to protect her and I'd failed. I should've been there, should've somehow sensed David's intentions. I knew he hated me, and I knew he would try to seduce her, but to try to rape her? It became evident that I'd never really known the man I used to call my best friend, and that made me even more disgusted.

I heard shuffling from behind me just before David made for the door like a bat out of hell. I'd be damned if I was going to let the motherfucker get away with an ounce of life still in him. I pushed Lanie away and tried to get to my feet, but she wouldn't let me go.

"No, you can't!" she yelled, desperately holding on to my shirt and preventing me from chasing after him.

"He's getting away." I tried to pull her hands loose, but she kept clinging to me.

It was her death grip on my face that forced me to look at

her. Black mascara streaked down her cheeks and her eyes were puffy, wide—like she was trying to get me to see something she knew, but I wasn't quite grasping. "He knows, Noah. He knows everything."

I froze, stiff as a twelve-point buck that had just heard a twig snap in an otherwise still forest.

"What . . ." My voice was caught in my throat and I had to clear it before I could go on. "What does he know? What are you saying, Lanie?"

"Everything. He knows about the auction, the contract, how much you paid for me, everything."

I clenched my teeth together and breathed deeply through my nose. "I don't care. He's not getting away with this shit." I pulled my cell phone from my pocket and started to dial.

"Who are you calling?"

"The police."

She shook her head back and forth frantically and put her hand over the phone. "No, Noah, please. You'll lose everything."

"Nothing is more important than you! Nothing!" I snapped, and she flinched at my words. I hadn't meant to take it out on her, but I was just so fucking irate.

I gathered her into my arms and held her to my chest, stroking her hair as I kissed her forehead over and over again. "I'm sorry, I'm sorry, I'm sorry," I said, rocking her back and forth. I pulled back and cupped her face in my hands, trying to get through to her. "Lanie, baby, he put his hands on you . . ."

Lanie pulled my hands from her face and held them in her lap. "I know what he did, but he didn't get to really hurt me because you stopped him, Noah. You stopped him."

Dear God, she was trying to comfort me. "He put his fuck-ing hands on you, and I can't . . . I just can't." I could feel the vise around my heart squeeze tighter. I dropped my gaze, no longer able to look into the innocent face of the woman I had failed.

Lanie pushed her fingers through the hair at my temples and lifted my chin so that I had to look at her again. "You lis-ten to me, Noah Crawford. This was not your fault. There was no way you could've known he would do that, so don't you dare start blaming yourself."

I started to protest, but she put her finger over my lips to silence me. "I'm fine. But if we call the police, everyone will know—and my parents can't deal with something like this, Noah. My mom just had a heart transplant. Do you really think she could handle knowing what almost happened to me? And my father would kill him. You'll lose your company, my father will be in prison, and that, along with knowing what I did, would probably make the heart transplant my mother re-ceived be all for nothing. I can't do that to them. No, we have to be smart about this."

Delaine Talbot never ceased to amaze me. In the face of the unspeakable evil that had befallen her, she was still thinking about everyone else. Never had a more selfless person existed in this fucked-up thing we called life. I didn't deserve her.

And of course, she was right. As much as it pained me to let David go, I knew we had to regroup and figure out what to do.

"Okay," I relented with a helpless sigh. "We'll do it your way."

I took her hand and pressed a kiss to her palm, content on

just having that. But when I tried to pull away, she climbed into my lap and wrapped her arms around my neck, her lips melting against mine. It wasn't a kiss that was meant to go further. It was simply a kiss that conveyed the love that we shared, the love that even that coward David Stone couldn't tarnish.

~$~

Later that evening, we were in the entertainment room, not really watching the outrageously expensive television that was playing *Lord of the Rings*. I was aware that knowing every line to the movie probably made me a geek, but so the fuck what? It calmed me down, even if it didn't take my mind off things entirely. That would be an impossible task.

I was wearing a pair of pajama bottoms that I happened to keep around the house in case I had visitors, and Lanie was perched in my lap, freshly showered, wearing nothing but another one of my white button-downs and smelling like the allure of sex. The actual deed itself couldn't have been further from my mind, though. Okay, to be honest, it was playing at the edge of my thoughts because that was what she did to me, but I would never act on it.

As much as she was trying to be a real trouper, acting like what had happened with that assfucker hadn't affected her, I knew that wasn't the truth. But I wasn't going to press her on the subject. She would talk about it if she wanted, and I would listen and offer as much support as I could. Until then, any contact we had of the sexual nature would be by her initiation alone.

"So he said he had access to the contract?" I asked. We were still trying to figure out what the fuck to do about the situation Stone had created for us.

"Yeah, but I don't get that," she said, lost in thought. "You ripped up your copy of the contract, and my copy is still in with my things. So where did he get it? Do you think he could've broken in here and made a copy or something?"

"Not likely," I answered, my fingers casually rubbing circles on her bare thigh.

The telephone rang beside us, interrupting our little brainstorming session, and I answered it. Dez was on the other end of the line, and she asked me to put her on speakerphone so she could talk to both me and Lanie at the same time. It was odd, but nothing seemed normal in our world anymore.

"You're on. What's up?"

"Hey, Lanes," she said in greeting to Lanie. The dull thump of bass music was in the background. She must have been at work. "So I finally figured out where I've seen that piece of man meat that was in your office today."

"Wait a minute, what?" I asked, confused.

"David," Lanie answered for her. "She saw David in your office earlier and thought she recognized him."

Well, wasn't that just an interesting tidbit of information?

"Where do you know him from?" Lanie asked.

"Right here at the club," Dez answered. "Every now and then he comes in after hours. I've seen him when I've stayed late to clean up or, um, meet that night's Mr. Perfect. But never mind that. Your boy sneaks right in the back entrance and disappears into Scott's office downstairs. It's usually a while before he leaves, but he's always toting a little white dust with him when he does."

"White dust, as in cocaine? Stone's snorting?" I shouldn't have been surprised. He'd always played around with recreational drugs when we were younger. I'd assumed that was all it ever had been.

Dez snorted. "That dude's so thick into it, a big, fluffy cloud probably pops out of his ass every time he farts."

Lanie rolled her eyes even though Dez couldn't see her. "Dez, I don't think it quite works that way."

"Whatever. I'm just saying. And I know you just rolled your eyes, bitch."

Lanie giggled, the sound like music to my ears.

And then it hit me like a fucking lightning bolt. "Scott."

"What?" Lanie asked, confused.

"Scott would have a copy of the contract as well. After all, he was the broker in the deal. Shit!" I pulled at my hair and let my head fall back with a frustrated growl. "I should've known that rat bastard would pull something like this. It's all about the bottom line for him. I'm sure that if David waved enough cash in front of his face, he'd turn over his copy of the contract in a heartbeat. I didn't have the slightest inkling they even knew of each other."

"I really hate him!" The words burst out of Lanie's mouth.

"Um, hello?" Dez said, reminding us she was still on the line. "What the hell are you two going on about?"

I looked at Lanie, searching her face to see if she wanted me to make something up. It hadn't dawned on me that she and I were still the only ones who knew about what had transpired earlier that day.

Without taking her eyes from mine, Lanie set her chin in quiet determination and spoke. "David Stone knows about the contract between Noah and me. He made that fact quite clear when he showed up here today and tried to get me to ride off into the sunset with him after helping him take Noah for everything he has."

Dez gasped on the other end of the line.

"Oh, it gets worse. When I turned down his advances and kneed him in the balls for calling me a whore, he decided getting heavy-handed with me would be a good idea."

"He did what?" Dez's voice was shrill with shock. "That son of a goat-cock-sucking whore! I swear to God, I'm going to rip his nuts off with my bare hands and shove them down his throat. And then I'm going to introduce him to my friend Chavez, a big, burly-ass Mexican who's done hard time at Oswald State, aka Oz, and has no qualms whatsoever about ass-raping another dude just for the fun of it. I hear Chavez has eaten so many Naga Viper peppers that his semen is literally liquid acid. He just might be the reincarnation of Beelzebub, but he's always been good to me, and I'm pretty sure I can get him to do me a favor. Of course that means I'll owe him one, but for you—"

"Dez, stop," Lanie said. I personally thought Dez was on to something and wanted her to set the wheels in motion, but Lanie apparently disagreed. "First of all, Oz isn't a real place. It was a television series. Second of all, we're not going to stoop to his level. We need to figure out what to do, so I need you to get serious and focus."

"You thought I was joking?" Dez asked, but Lanie ignored her.

"Wait a minute," I said, putting the facts together. "Stone said he had access to the contract, right? Not that he actually had it?"

"Right, and . . . ?"

The answer was simple enough. Money talked. "I'll pay Scott a visit and offer him more money than David was willing to pay for it. Then he wouldn't have any proof. We can sweep his legs out from under him."

"Hate to burst your bubble, but that's not going to work," Dez interjected.

"Why not?" I was a bit peeved at the halt order.

"Think what you want of Scott, but he's a shrewd business-man. You had him pegged when you said it's all about the bottom line for him, but think about it. Selling that contract to you doesn't make good business sense. He'd be getting rid of the only leverage he has to make sure you don't run off at the mouth about a business that thrives only because the discretion is so thick. There's no way he's going to hand that contract over to you. However, my gut tells me he won't hand it over to David, either."

"No offense, but I'm not sure I want to let the future of Scarlet Lotus be determined by a gut feeling," I told her.

"Noah, put yourself in Scott's shoes." Dez almost sounded condescending. "If word got around that he let a confidential contract like that leak out, not only would he lose his business in a massive raid, but no one would trust him with a deal of any sort again. Not to mention there's no telling how many hits would be put out on the man just because there would be the potential risk that he would leak identities in an attempt to bargain with the feds. You were there, Crawford. You saw the caliber of people he deals with. They're some ruthless mofos. Would you risk it?"

She had a point. Lots of points, really.

"So how do you think David is planning on getting a copy of the contract for himself, then?" Lanie asked.

"I'm not sure, but if I had to guess, I'd say he's planning on stealing it."

"Okay, then we just need to beat him to it," I said, squeezing Lanie's thigh triumphantly as she smiled down at me.

"Not you," Dez said. Seriously, she was getting on my nerves with the way she kept throwing up the red lights. "You walk in here and Scott is going to know something's up. I'll do it, but I can't do it alone. Lanie, get your shit together and meet me at Foreplay when it closes. I'll let you in."

"No way in hell is that going to happen!" I protested. "I'm not letting her do it, Dez. We'll have to figure out another way."

Lanie turned my head toward her and leaned forward. The first three buttons of the shirt she was wearing—my shirt— were open, and her breasts were looming like a carrot dangling in front of a horse's face. When she tilted my chin up, her lips hovered over mine, enticing me with the sweetness of her breath. "Noah, there's no other way. We have to do this. I'll slip in quietly, Dez and I will get the contract as soon as Scott leaves, and I'll be back in your bed before you even notice I'm gone."

"What if he tries to—" I started, but was interrupted when Lanie swept her tongue inside my mouth to lightly flick at my own before pulling back.

"He won't even be there. Besides, Dez will keep me safe."

I was under Lanie's spell and closed the fraction of the distance between our lips to tug on her bottom one with my teeth. "Safe and sound?" I asked, my voice sounding less and less like I was the dominant male in the equation.

She pressed even closer to me and shifted her ass over my cock. "Safe and sound. I promise."

Damn, but the woman knew how to weaken my resolve.

Lanie put her hand over mine on her thigh and slowly started to move it over her creamy skin until it was under the hem of her shirt. Somewhere in the back of my mind I knew I should stop her, but all that was shot to hell when she pushed my hand further until my fingertips skimmed the soft folds between her legs.

"I'll call you when I'm on my way, Dez," she said, and then leaned over and pushed the disconnect button to end the call. There was no further discussion. She'd won.

I nudged her hair back with my nose and nuzzled her neck, sucking and nipping at the skin there. Lanie spread her thighs and replaced her hand on mine, urging me even closer until my fingers slipped between her wet lips.

"We shouldn't do this," I said against her skin, but I didn't stop nuzzling or pull back my hand because I was a man and my genetic makeup wouldn't allow me to. Lanie was addictive.

"You would deny me what I want?" Her hand left mine and opened another button on the shirt until she could pull it to the side to reveal one of her perfect breasts. Then she nudged my head toward her chest.

"Never." I took the offering, my tongue flicking over the raised nipple before I sucked it into my mouth.

"Make me forget, Noah. Claim me as yours and erase the memory. I only want to remember *your* touch."

She needed this, needed me. And I would deny her nothing.

Lanie's hand moved back on top of mine, and she arched her back, simultaneously bringing her breast closer to my mouth while pushing both of our fingers inside her. She moaned, and I felt my cock twitch at the sound.

I firmly sucked on her succulent nipple, never able to get enough. The woman did things to me, made me lose every ounce of self-control that I fought to maintain. Her pussy was so wet and tight around our fingers—soft, like liquid silk. She pushed us deeper, maneuvering my finger so that it flicked back and forth inside her while the palm of my hand massaged her clit. Together, we were erasing the blasphemy. This was how it was supposed to be between a man and a woman.

"I want you inside me, Noah."

I released her nipple and softly kissed it once more before I mumbled against her skin, "Stand up for me, kitten."

She did, allowing both of our fingers to slide out of her, though she gave a disgruntled whimper. I smiled up at her, loving how cheated she felt. Lifting my hips, I pushed my pants down my legs before kicking them to the side.

When I sat back, I took my hardened cock in my hand. "Is this what you want?"

Her hair fell into her face as she looked at my lap and bit down on her bottom lip, eyeing my cock hungrily. She merely nodded, then straddled me, taking my cock and putting it at her entrance before sinking down on it.

It took some maneuvering and a couple of strokes to get all the way inside her, but I put my hands on her hips and we worked it out together. As she leaned down to kiss me, she moved her hand to the side and flipped a switch, turning on the massage mechanism in the chair. I moaned at the vibrating sensation under my nut sack. That feeling, mixed with the touch of Lanie's nipples ghosting along my chest, her seductive kiss, and her hot pussy clenched around my dick, was almost too much for one man to bear. But bear it I did. It was a delicious sort of torture.

"I love you, Noah," she whispered against my lips.

"Not half as much as I love you," I answered. I had no way of knowing if that was true, but I found it hard to believe any one person could love another as much as I fucking loved her.

She rolled her hips against me, seeking the friction against her clit. Her full breasts were right in front of me, teasing, so I pushed them together and took both of her nipples into my mouth at the same time. Pulling at my hair, she rode me hard, which was just the way I liked it. It was when I made a show of scraping my teeth along the hardened buds of her breasts that her head fell forward and her movements slowed.

"That looks so sexy. Feels so fucking good," she moaned, moving her hips with more purpose as she grabbed the back of the chair. Lanie only ever used the word "fuck" when she was pissed or when something I'd done to her felt particularly pleasant. Naturally, I loved hearing it.

Back and forth, she rocked over me, milking me for her own pleasure and giving it back to me tenfold. I was about to lose my damn mind, but managed to stave off my orgasm so that she could reach hers first.

I was rewarded for my efforts when I felt the walls of her pussy constrict even more around my cock and she began to move in a deliberate rhythm. Her lips were parted and her eyes were closed as she concentrated on the sensation. She was almost there, about to combust, but she needed more. I knew her body better than I knew my own, so I could read the signs. She needed the man she gave herself to willingly to take control and stake his claim.

"Give it to me, woman," I encouraged her. "Come on my cock."

I grabbed hold of each cheek of her perfectly round ass, lifting her and slamming her back down. I forced her hips to roll forward before doing it again and again and again. I could hear her fingers digging into the leather on either side of my head, and then her head fell back and her body seized as she cried out my motherfucking name with her orgasm.

I didn't waste a second. There was something I had wanted to do with her since that first day I found her in my entertainment room amidst the chaos she had provoked with the damn remote. I secured my arm around her waist and lifted us out of the chair before carrying her over to the pool table. She continued to roll her body in my arms unabashedly, still milking her orgasm, and the distraction nearly made it impossible for me to walk, but I managed to get her there.

With my other arm I swiped the billiard balls out of the way and laid her down, never leaving that sweet little slice of heaven in the process. Once she was safe, I pulled her hips to the edge, pushed her knees back, and spread her open with one leg in each hand. And then I thrust into her hard.

"Oh, fuck!" she cried out, and I stilled, mentally kicking myself in the ass for being so rough with her, especially after what she'd been through.

"Shit, I'm sorry, kitten. I . . . I didn't mean to." No apology was going to make up for what I'd done.

"No, it's a *good fuck*," she said, breathing heavily. "I promise, I'm okay. Better than okay, actually. That felt so incredible. It's what I need, Noah. Don't hold back on me. Please."

I was both stunned and relieved.

"Well, in that case, you might want to hold on to something because it's about to get so much better."

Lanie put her arms down at her sides and reached for the edge of the pool table, holding on for dear life. I grabbed her hips once she was secured and let her legs wrap around each of my arms. Then I pulled back before slamming into her again. The test drive proved everything was a go, so I let loose, driving into her furiously and with a quickness that left me panting.

Her breasts bounced to and fro with each thrust and my balls slapped against her ass with each unrelenting drive of my cock. Deeper and deeper I thrust inside her. Lanie got very vocal, her head thrashing back and forth. I could feel the sweat beading on my forehead, but still I continued to fuck her with reckless abandon.

And then I looked down at where we were joined, watching as my cock slid in and out of her tight pussy.

"Fuck, woman." I growled, unable to look away. "Your pussy is so . . . goddamn . . . *mine*."

My hips slammed into her over and over again, harder and harder, deeper and deeper. My thick cock stretched her tight opening and it was the most erotic thing I'd ever seen. The veins on my dick were supercharged with my pulsing blood, and the skin was coated in her wetness, the section that had been inside the firm grip of her pussy colored a deep pink from the friction.

Everything that had been building inside me snapped and I shut my eyes tightly to the unbelievable sensation of my orgasm. I growled, feeling my cock throb and pulsate inside her. Slamming my hips into her one final time, I came, spewing my seed inside the woman I would do any fucking thing for.

Once I'd given Lanie all I had to give, I pulled out of her

and loosened my grip on her hips. It was then that I noticed how hard I'd been holding on.

"Shit, I'm sorry. That's probably going to bruise." I leaned forward and placed lingering kisses on each red mark like I could actually kiss them and make them better.

Lanie's fingers went to my hair and I laid my head on her chest, listening to her heartbeat. To my surprise, I found that mine was synchronized with hers. As corny as it sounded, we'd become one. And I knew it was true: no matter what happened with David Stone or the whole fucked-up fiasco of the contract, nothing was going to come between us.

I meant it when I said I'd do any fucking thing for her. Even if I had to give up everything, be shamed in the public eye, and steal away with her to some deserted cabin in Alaska so she wouldn't have to endure the embarrassment of everyone knowing what she'd done to save her mother's life. I'd do it.

Because nothing was more important than her.

10

mission: impossible

David

Goddamnit.

I checked myself over in my bathroom mirror. My gorgeous face looked distorted, but at least I'd managed to clean off the blood and bandage the open wounds.

They wouldn't go to the cops. I was sure of it. They'd have to expose themselves in the process, and I was pretty damn sure prostitution and being involved in the human slave trade would carry a much higher penalty in the long run than what I'd almost done.

It wasn't supposed to have gone down like it had, though.

I'd planned it perfectly, or so I thought. Step one: make my proposition to the whore, threaten to expose their whole sordid affair, and bank on her natural gold-digging tendencies to seal the deal. Step two, my personal favorite: fuck her blind, let her know what she was missing by dissin' Big Daddy Dick, and leave her begging for more, all while waiting for Crawford to walk in and catch us in the act. And then the pièce de résistance: sit back and relax while I watched the bane of my existence go all self-destructo with the knowledge that I'd claimed yet another one of his prized possessions for my own.

But my shit had backfired on me. Delaine didn't accept my proposal, which meant Crawford wasn't going to see us bumping uglies. I hadn't figured on there being an actual physical altercation, not that I was sorry for knocking the bitch one. She needed to learn that this was a man's world and she'd do well to stay in her place. But then Noah had come in and busted my shit up.

"Fucking dick," I scoffed into the mirror before I walked into my office and poured myself a stiff one.

Swirling the dark amber liquid in my glass, I headed over to the window and looked out over the city. My city. I fucking owned it, or at least I would.

I winced when I took a drink and the glass made contact with my busted lip. A drop of alcohol landed right on the cut, stinging like hell and adding insult to injury.

"Goddamnit!" I roared, and threw the glass against the closest wall. It shattered, coloring the white paint with sprays of whiskey while tiny shards of glass rained down onto the floor.

I swore under my breath and decided to leave it there for the cleaning crew, then turned back to the window.

What had gone down earlier was the result of poor planning on my part. I should've allowed myself a little more time with her. Not that he wouldn't have wanted to kick my ass even if she had been a willing participant. It's just that if that had been the case, his fist wouldn't have packed quite as much punch. Wounded pride and a broken heart are a whole lot easier to deal with than a man with a superhero complex going on a Rambo rampage to defend his territory.

No matter—I still held all the power. Or at least I would before the night was through.

I didn't have to fuck his girl to destroy him. I already had that in the bag with the reveal I was planning for the board meeting on Monday. But I did have a point to prove. How many times had I tried to make the dumb fuck understand that women were only out for one thing? Money. Plain and simple. Gold-digging whores, each and every one of them.

Okay, maybe there was another thing they were out for as well: dick. They liked that shit, too.

When we were a couple of young punks, I'd tried to drill my theory on bitches into his thick skull, mostly because I wanted him to be available to hang with me on the weekends, or just whenever I needed a sidekick, but I believed what I said to be true. I'd seen my father change wives almost as often as he got a haircut. And every one of them left owning a little piece of his fortune—a fortune that should've rightfully belonged to me.

When we became adults, it was even more important for my partner to focus. I needed Crawford's head in the game if we were going to make our fathers' company soar to heights the old men couldn't even imagine. If he was all googly-eyed over a woman, a fucking cunt, he'd be too distracted to put his best foot forward, and I wasn't talking about the one attached to his third leg, either.

Chasing tail for the sake of getting laid was one thing. Allowing yourself to be pussy-whipped was something else entirely.

Crawford hadn't listened to me. Fresh out of college when his parents died, he had inherited his half of the company and had a gorgeous woman on his arm, and I was all but forgotten. And not just by my supposed best friend. My father had looked at Noah with so much pride and adoration it was almost palpable.

He'd never looked at me that way.

Noah Crawford was a rising star, had everything I didn't, and I was tired of living in his goddamn shadow.

Why can't you be more like Noah, David? My father's voice rang in my ears, a constant reminder that I would never live up to his expectations. I made mistakes; I was young, and I liked to party. But those mistakes were unacceptable to him.

My old man was weak, in my opinion. He shared his company with those fucking Crawfords when he could've claimed all of Scarlet Lotus's success for his own. The goody-goody Crawfords and their *Let's donate a sizable portion of our profits to charities, give back to the community, do something good with the blessings that have been bestowed upon us.*

Pfft. Those weren't blessings. It was hard work, my father's blood, sweat, and tears. But he never saw it that way. Truthfully, I think he was secretly in love with Elizabeth Crawford. I had seen the way his face lit up whenever she walked into the room. The bitch had him wrapped around her little pinky, and he'd have done anything she asked of him even though he could never have her.

Which just proved my point about the effect women have on men. And my dad wasn't even hittin' that.

Speaking of hittin' that . . . I had a date.

I opened another button on my shirt, showing more of my bronzed chest of iron—because that was the way I liked it—and then I grabbed my keys. It was getting late. Scott would be closing up shop soon, and he would be waiting for me with a fantastic piece of ass and a fuckload of pixie dust. Damn, but I needed a hit of that. Both of them.

And then afterward I was going to borrow that little nugget of gold I knew he was storing in his office. It was nothing but paper and ink to him, but for me, it was the future of Stone Enterprises.

Lanie

Warm water surrounded our naked bodies as we lounged in the outrageously massive bathtub. Noah's strong arms encased me and I closed my eyes to experience the sensation of the loofah he moved gently over my exposed breasts. My nipples had been in a constant state of arousal since I set foot in that house.

Funny, I had wanted to hate him so much back then. And there I was, hopelessly in love with the man who had purchased me with the sole purpose of having his wicked way with me whenever, wherever, and however he wanted.

The saying was true: sometimes it's when we stop looking for love that love finds us. And usually it's the person we least suspect who manages to lasso our heart and turn us inside out.

The Cooch was all for being turned inside out by the Wonder Peen at the moment. Or, for that matter, upside down and round and round. Insatiable hussy.

As if hearing her plea, Noah's free hand wandered down my side and over my abdomen until his long, thick fingers could delve between the swollen folds at the apex of my thighs to give her a proper greeting. His deliciously scented breath ghosted over my neck before it was replaced by his hot, wet mouth.

Noah's tongue was sinfully talented, his lips gifted with the ability to put all my senses on high alert. His teeth scraped my skin teasingly and I lifted my arm to wrap it around his neck. The loofah tumbled from his hand and he cupped my breast, his fingers gently rolling and tugging at the nipple. I could feel his hardness pressed to my lower back while the fingers between my legs explored every nerve ending within his reach. The delicious pressure of his lips, tongue, and teeth against the crook of my neck joined forces with the soft moans at my ear and drove me mad with need.

"Noah." My voice was more like a breathless plea.

He never faltered with his manipulations. "Tell me what you want, kitten."

The Cooch pulled out pen and paper and started making a list, but I ignored her. There would be so much more time for all the ways she could find for him to worship her later. I wanted to do something for him.

"You." I turned in his arms. "I want to taste you."

Noah groaned when I got on all fours between his legs and eyed him suggestively while licking my lips. The bathwater rocked with my movements, sloshing against the muscular plains of his abdomen. "Far be it from me to deny you anything you want."

He used the brute strength of his arms to lift himself until he was sitting on the ledge. Water cascaded down his body as he took his dick in one hand and began to stroke it teasingly. Another long arm stretched toward me in invitation. "Come, Lanie, suck my cock."

His words reminded me of my very first night there, the night he'd sat on his couch completely naked while smoking a cigarette. The skin on my arms pebbled from the memory and a pathetic, wanton mewl escaped my lips as I inched closer to him. When I was within reach, he buried his hand in the hair at the back of my head and guided me to the colossal append-age he had so graciously aimed toward my mouth.

Noah's hand squeezed the base of his cock and a sexy groan escaped his throat when I took him into my mouth. I circled his tip with my tongue before engulfing as much of his length as I could fit into my eager cavern. My lips stretched around him when he brought my head closer. His hand fisted my hair and he lightly pulled me back and forth, back and forth. When he propped his foot up on the side of the tub and leaned back against the wall to watch me suck him, I suddenly turned into quite the exhibitionist.

I released him momentarily and dipped my head between his legs. Keeping my eyes on his face, I licked his balls, taking them into my mouth one at a time to gently suckle him.

"Goddamnit," he moaned, and then his mouth dropped open and his chest began to rise and fall more rapidly.

My tongue made a path from the nook of his balls over his fingers and up his long shaft. Noah pushed my head down on him more forcefully and I could feel the crown of his cock at the back of my throat. My teeth lightly scraped against his smooth skin as he pulled me back and then pushed me forward again. His eyes were trained on my lips and I began to bob my head, sucking him deep. I swallowed and relaxed my throat to take more of him, moaning around the thickness in my mouth like it was the most delicious thing I'd ever tasted. Because it was.

"Fuck." His voice was almost a whisper—a rough, barely controlled whisper. "You have no idea how good you look sucking my cock. Harder, kitten. Suck me harder."

I sucked so hard my cheeks hollowed out. So hard you couldn't have convinced me his cock wouldn't be one giant hickey by the time I was done. Noah groaned and the muscles in his arms, chest, and abdomen clenched. Faster, harder, deeper I took him while he watched with rapt fascination.

I could've died a happy woman with his cock in my mouth. Death by cockstrangulation.

He moaned my name and then his face twisted up. "Stop, woman. Stop."

I kept going.

"No . . . fuck . . ." He growled and cupped my face in his hands, forcing me to release his cock. "I want to be inside you when I come." He was breathless, the veins in his neck taut and his eyes dilated, hungry, commanding. "Turn around and hold on to the ledge."

I mentally joined the Cooch in a cheer on the sidelines when we found out she was getting called in on the play.

I turned and spread my legs so he could fit between them comfortably, and I might have thrown in a back arch for good measure. When I felt his breath on the back of my neck, his chest pressed against my back, and his cock at my entrance, I nearly orgasmed on the spot.

His mouth was at my ear and I felt the tip of his cock slip between my folds, teasing me, never filling me with what I so desperately needed. I shifted my hips, trying to align my opening with his dick, but he pulled back, causing me to whimper at the loss of contact.

His breath caressed the shell of my ear with a voice that was deep and menacing, but I couldn't fear him. "Which entrance should I use, Lanie? This one?" he asked, moving the head of his cock over my opening. "Or this one?" He slid the tip over my asshole and applied a slight pressure.

"Whichever one you want. Just like you won't deny me, I won't deny you." My last experience with the backdoor entrance had been uncomfortable, even painful at first, but I still wanted to try it again. And I had indeed said I wanted to do something for him, so if he wanted to fuck my ass, then I was going to let him.

Noah chuckled in my ear, and even though I couldn't see his smirk, I knew it was there. "Is that so? So brave, Lanie. So giving. I love how willing your body is, how shamelessly you react to my touch. I can't wait to get my cock in your delectable little ass again, and I will. But this time, I think I'll go . . . here."

The thick head of his cock pushed into my pussy, stretching and filling me as he sheathed himself completely. I moaned and arched my back so I could rest my head on his shoulder. He cupped my breast in one hand while his other flattened on my stomach. Then he pushed on my abdomen, forcing me to bend ever so slightly, but changing the angle significantly enough that it caused me to gasp.

"Easy, kitten," he breathed into my ear. "Goddamn, you feel so good."

"You don't feel so bad yourself," I managed.

Noah moved inside me again, slowly rocking in and out while he lavished the back of my neck with openmouthed kisses. My head lolled to the side when the hand on my stomach moved further down and his fingertip began to massage my clit. I moaned again because it felt so incredible, and he pressed his chest even closer to my back.

I knew what he wanted. He wanted me to bend back over, so I did, holding on to the ledge so that he could have his wicked way with me.

And have his wicked way with me he did.

His lips moved over my bare shoulders sending a tingling feeling dancing across my skin. Removing the hand from my breast, he laced his fingers through mine at the ledge of the bathtub, the slight weight of his body on mine engulfing me so perfectly. The other hand moved back to my abdomen and held me there as he thrust in and out with greater purpose. His mouth was at my ear and I could hear every little grunt, feel every exhale of hot breath against my skin with each surge forward.

"I need to be deeper in you, Lanie. Deeper than I've ever gone before," he mumbled into my neck.

His hand slid down my body until he reached the inside of my left thigh. He pushed against it, urging me to lift my knee until it was perched on the side of the tub. Then he straightened and slowly thrust inside me.

"Ooh . . . ," I moaned at the sensation.

"That's it. Right there," he said as he rotated his hips against my ass, causing another moan to spill from my lips. "You like that?"

"God, yes." I could feel his cock swirling inside me, pushing against my walls, and I arched my back even more to give him better access. "I can feel you . . . your cock feels so . . . unngh."

"Yeah, I like that, too," he said as he pulled back a little and pushed back into me.

He made short, quick thrusts, each one more glorious than

the last. Everything inside my body bunched up. It was on high alert, threatening to explode with the glorious pleasure only he could give me.

"Harder, Noah. Fuck me harder," I said to spur him on.

He did just that. One hand wound itself in my hair and he pulled back on it, forcing me to lift my head while he fucked me like a madman. Long, hard, fast strokes brought his groin against my ass. Skin slapped against skin as his fingertips dug into my hip. My chest constricted, my abdomen coiled, my clit throbbed, my teeth clenched, and my fingers gripped the edge of the tub until my knuckles were white.

And then everything let loose all at once and I cried out with an orgasm that rocked my very foundation.

"Noah . . . ohhh . . . Noah," I moaned as my heart hammered in my chest.

"I know, kitten," he grunted, still thrusting ferociously from behind me. "Right there. I'm going to come. I'm going to . . ." He let out a growl as his hips slammed against my backside and he held them there for just a second or two before continuing his assault again with sporadic and irregular thrusts.

And then finally he stilled. It was like the calm after the storm clouds pushed away to reveal the sun once more. Blissful, peaceful. Contented.

His body slumped as he pulled from me, his forehead pressed against my back. "Woman . . . you're going to be . . . the death . . . of me," he panted.

Him? I was pretty sure I was in danger of suffering a massive heart attack, judging by the way my heart was trying to burst out of my chest. But boy, what a way to go. It ranked right up there with cockstrangulation.

~$~

Noah refused to let me go to Foreplay to meet Dez alone; I refused to let him go anywhere near the club and jeopardize the plan. I also turned down his suggestion that Mason or Samuel accompany me. However, I managed to get him to consent to my taking Polly instead.

I was pretty sure it was because of her mad driving skills. And by mad, I mean the chick was nuts behind the wheel of a car, and we'd be lucky to make it there in one piece. But, according to him, Polly was a force to be reckoned with when push came to shove. Maybe that was because she was pacing back and forth, throwing air punches in the general direction of all the internal organs in a man the height of David Stone. She was amazingly accurate, reeling off the name of each one as her fist found where it would be. It scared me just a little.

So there we were, parked across the street from Foreplay in the dark, waiting for Dez to call with the all-clear. The building looked deserted and lifeless, as far as I could tell. The parking lot was just about empty, and the neon sign had long been extinguished.

Polly was decked out all in black, including a pair of black combat boots. What the hell she was doing with combat boots in her wardrobe was a complete mystery to me. The thought crossed my mind that this might not have been the first secret mission she had been a party to, not that it would surprise me.

"Is your phone even on?" she asked for the cajillionth time.

"Yes, Polly, it's on."

Her leg bounced up and down like she'd had way too many cups of coffee. Also, I noticed she'd developed a serious case of shifty eyes. I swear, you would've thought we were casing the joint to rob it, knowing full well a whole SWAT team was wait-ing in the bushes.

"Check again," she said, because apparently she thought I was an idiot who didn't know how to work a stupid cell phone.

I rolled my eyes with an annoyed sigh and looked down at my phone, even holding it up for her inspection. Just then it vibrated in my hand, causing me to jump a little.

It was a text from Dez: *It's a negative on the EPT.*

Yeah, that would be the all-clear we were waiting for.

"Let's go," I told Polly.

We got out of the car, both of us being careful to shut the doors as soundlessly as we could. Hunched over, we made our way across the street and through the parking lot, all sorts of stealthy-like. The *Mission: Impossible* theme song kept playing over and over in my head, but I knew Tom Cruise didn't have jack squat on us. Once we reached the front of the club, we pressed our backs against the wall and I lightly tapped on the door. First two raps, a pause, and then three more.

"Is that the code you guys agreed on for the knock?" Polly asked in a whisper.

"No. We don't have one," I said with a shrug. "I just thought . . . Oh, shut it. I'm nervous, okay?"

Polly let out a squeak of a giggle and then hurriedly covered her mouth to stifle any more sounds. That was about the time Dez opened the door.

"What the fuck are you asshats doing?" she asked with a stern whisper, then turned her scowling face on Polly. "Are you trying to get us caught? This isn't a slumber party, Gidget."

Polly dropped her hand and did her best to keep a straight face. "Sorry."

"Cute outfit," she said as she looked Polly over, her tone of voice taking a sudden turn into Valley Girl land, which Dez *never* did. Polly was definitely rubbing off on her. I'd point it out later and watch her get all defensive because it would be funny.

Polly beamed at the compliment. "Thanks! You too," she said, looking her over in turn.

Dez was dressed in much the same way as Polly. In fact, it was the same outfit she'd had on when she'd shown up at Noah's to "kidnap" me. I was pretty sure it wasn't what she'd worn to work.

"Did you change?" I asked her, because that wasn't at all like Dez, either.

She gave me a well-duh look and stomped one foot lightly. "I couldn't exactly wear the same thing for both work and this, now could I?"

I rolled my eyes in Polly's direction. "Jeez, you are never allowed to talk to my friends again. You're like a damn disease."

Dez looked stunned. "What are you talking about?"

"You caught Polly's girly cooties. No worries—we'll get you fixed up with one quick visit to the prison on conjugal visit day."

Polly did the giggle-snort thing again, and then Dez moved aside to usher us inside.

"Is he gone?" I asked as the door closed behind us.

"I think so, but he always leaves out the back door, so I don't know."

"What do you mean you don't know? You didn't check?" The incredulous tone was evident in my voice even though I was still whispering. I held up my phone to show her the text she'd sent. "You said you're not pregnant!"

"Well, I might be a little bit knocked up. Those tests aren't always accurate."

I was going to kill her. I was sure the murderous glare in my eyes made that fact perfectly clear, but my death glare—which I'd practiced for years to get just right—never had any effect on my best friend.

Dez shrugged like it was no big deal. "Fuck it. If he's here, I figure we can knock him out."

I pulled her in close so she could hear me. "Um, Dez? These outfits might make us look like super-badass ninjas and all, but um, we're not."

"Now what are we supposed to do?" Polly's shoulders slumped in defeat. I knew it was killing her. Proper planning defined her life, so to have to wing it meant certain disaster in her book.

I threw my shoulders back and straightened to my full height. "We're going to go find out if he's here, and then we're going to get that damn contract," I said assertively, taking control of the situation. "Now let's get our ninja on."

The club was dark, though the emergency exit signs provided a minuscule amount of light. Of course Dez knew the layout like the back of her hand, and I knew the direction to the basement from my last trip there, so we were good to go.

As we descended the stairs, I almost expected the club's doorman to be waiting at the bottom with that damn clipboard that made him think he was a god or something. But he wasn't there. In fact, it was completely dark, so dark we had to trail our hands along the walls for some navigational guidance.

Before we got to the end of the hall, I could see light filtering out from under a door and hear music coming from inside the room.

Scott was still in his office. And then we heard voices coming from the back of the building, headed our way.

Polly grabbed the back of my shirt in her fist, and I did the same to Dez in turn, slightly yanking her back.

"Someone's coming! Now what?" I whispered, hurriedly.

Dez yanked my hand off her shirt and turned on me. "Don't get your thong in a twist, Lanes, and shush before they hear you. I've got this covered. Come on."

Polly and I followed her down the hall, and we managed to make it inside a little closet that was right beside Scott's office without making too much of a ruckus. No sooner had we gotten inside than the other voices stopped outside the door.

"Have fun, mate," a male voice said.

"That's Terrence," Dez whispered.

"Who's he talking to?" I strained my ears, but all I heard was the opening and closing of Scott's office door.

"So what? We're just going to wait here until they leave?" Polly asked.

We were packed in the tiny space like sardines, but it wasn't like we had any other options.

"Yeah, pretty much so," I said.

"Not necessarily." Dez maneuvered herself so that she could turn toward the wall that was on the opposite side of Scott's office.

"What are you doing?" I asked when she started fidgeting with something that looked like a sticker on the plaster.

She pulled at it and then a beam of light shot through a

hole. "I might have had a little safeguard placed in here in the event that some hottie was down for some kinky fuckery in the form of a closet quickie." She shrugged. "This way I could check to make sure the boss man wasn't looking for me."

"You're an evil genius, do you know that?" I asked, impressed with her ingenuity. "A total slut for gettin' down and dirty in a supply closet, but a genius all the same."

"I'll take that as a compliment," she said with a cheeky grin. "The best part is that these walls are paper thin, so the challenge to stay quiet while fireworks explode from my girly bits is particularly erotic."

I shook my head at her and leaned toward the hole. When I saw who was in the other room with Scott, I gasped and shot up straight, bonking Polly in the nose in the process. "Holy crap!"

Dez cupped her hand over my mouth because my whisper was definitely in danger of becoming a whole lot more than that.

"Christ!" Polly touched her nose gingerly. "You mind telling me why you're trying to break my nose?"

I pulled Dez's hand from my mouth. "It's David!"

Polly dropped her hand, her nose forgotten. "That asshole is here to steal the contract!"

I heard voices, so I leaned back over to look again, wanting to make sure I hadn't been seeing things. Sure enough, David was sitting on the leather couch next to Scott's desk. His face was puffy and bruised from his recent beating, courtesy of one Noah P. Crawford.

Scott's desk, by the way, was loaded down with blocks of what looked to be cocaine.

"Oh my, Jesus! Dez, give me your phone," I told her, reaching blindly behind me.

"What? Why?"

"Just put it on video and give it to me. Hurry!"

Dez slipped her phone into my hand and I put the lens over the hole, making sure to get a good view on the phone's screen. Dez wasn't kidding; those walls were paper thin. I could hear every word they were saying.

"What the hell happened to you?" Scott's voice had a bit of humor to it. I sort of wanted to laugh, too.

David put his fingers to the cut over his swollen eye. "Kick-boxing accident. I missed the bag."

"And what, kicked yourself in the face? A lot?"

"Shut up. You got another shipment of coke so soon? That's risky," David said, changing the subject. He sounded none too happy.

"It's not a new shipment. There's been an increase of in-house requests. Both from those little snot-nosed brats up-stairs and the gentlemen down here looking to score a whore and more."

"You're expanding to college kids? That's not something we've discussed. Last I checked, we're partners on this."

"We are. That's why I called you in." Scott stood and walked around to the front of his desk, leaning against it and crossing his legs at the ankles. "So let's talk about it."

"Nothing to talk about. It's too risky a move. Some punk kid rats and we're going down like the *Titanic*. Not smart. Call it off."

The right side of Scott's mouth drew up and he shrugged. "I suppose you've got a point, but it does make good business sense to offer the coke as a package deal with the girls. Those rich bastards aren't blabbing about shit, and you know it. They've got too much to lose. A two-for-one will help drive up the starting bid on the auctions."

"Now *that* I can get on board with," David said with a politician's smile. "Speaking of good business sense, my friend the senator will be coming to the next auction. I can't stress enough how important it is that we make him happy with the goods, both the flake and the ladies. How's the search for the twins going? Any luck?"

"Yep, that's reason number two for calling you in. Trust me, I am about to make your day, your week—hell, your whole year." Scott reached over to his phone and pushed a button, leaving the speaker on.

Terrence picked up on the other end. "Yeah, boss?"

"Show the ladies to my office, T," Scott told him, and then disconnected the call with another push of the button.

After a few moments, the office door opened again and two leggy redheads—twins—sauntered into the room. They had identical physical attributes from what I could tell, and wore identical short dresses in silver. Dang, even their saunters were identical.

"Be still, my beating heart," David said, adjusting the front of his pants. He flashed them that toothy grin he apparently thought was sexy but which was just creepy even without the Elephant Man mask he was sporting. "Hellooo, ladies."

Scott went over to the girls and stood between them. "Meet Izzy and Belle. They're perfect, right?"

"Hell, yeah. The senator is going to be very satisfied with this package deal. Gotta admit, I wouldn't mind sampling some of that for myself."

"I thought you might, and really, there isn't any reason why we can't. After all, I did say I was going to make your day."

David's lascivious gaze raked over the girl on the right. Down, up, and back down to her legs again, like he was doing his damnedest to undress her with his eyes. He didn't even bother to look away from her thighs when he said, "Why don't you come over here and wrap that pair of milky ways around my head, sweetheart?"

Oh, gag. Fortunately for him, his horrendous pickup line wouldn't stop him from getting laid. With a few bucks in their pocket those girls would be good to go, but I was pretty sure they were getting paid more than a few bucks.

"Izzy, I want you to be really nice to this gentleman. Really, really nice," Scott said, taking her hand and directing her toward David.

Izzy stopped in front of him and Belle walked up behind her sister to unzip her dress, letting it pool on the floor at her feet. Izzy was completely naked underneath. Judging by the look on David's face, I'd say he about lost his load in his pants right there.

"Goddamn, girl!" David took Izzy by the hips and buried his face at the apex of her thighs. She giggled and ran her hands through his hair, closing her eyes and letting her head fall back. I didn't blame her about the closing-her-eyes part. It'd be bad enough to have to feel it—I certainly wouldn't want to have to watch the man-beast as he ate her.

Scott laughed and walked over to his desk to pick up a couple of baggies of coke and returned to give one to David. "Here, Romeo. Let's party."

I should've turned away. What was about to go down in that room was disturbing on so many levels, but I couldn't look away. I was a very sick individual. It was like watching a freak show. I knew it was going to give me the heebie-jeebies, but I had to see it.

Belle was naked now, and both girls were sprawled out on the couch with David and Scott moving their slimy mouths and hands all over them. The girls didn't seem to be complaining, but . . . *gross!* I watched as David opened a baggie and shook the contents along the length of Izzy's abdomen. Then he took a straw and snorted the line-shaped powder. Izzy moaned at the same time, and that's when I saw David was pushing three fingers inside her while Scott looked on.

"Did I just hear what I think I heard?" Polly's nose scrunched up. "Ew! What the hell are they doing in there?"

"They're snorting coke," I whispered, almost more to myself than to Dez and Polly. I was completely in shock at that point. "And . . . and . . . getting their freak on."

"What? David and Scott?" Dez shoved me over so she could get a look at the screen on her phone.

"Damn, bonchickawahwah," she giggled. "Hey, I know those two chicks. They're the new girls. Guess now I know how they got promoted to assistant managers so quick."

"You've got to be joking," Polly said, but it came out as more of a question than a statement.

I shook my head. Polly squeezed in on my other side to have a look for herself.

I'd known David and Scott were a couple of sleazeballs whose behaviors were a special brand of unscrupulous at best, but I never imagined I would ever witness it for myself. For as long as I lived, I knew I would never be able to get that image out of my head. Not even if I bleached my brain, which was looking like a pretty good idea.

"Did Noah do that to his face?" Dez asked, and I nodded with a proud smile. "Damn, I think I'm in love with that man. Don't tell him, though, because then he'd want my body so bad, and that would be embarrassing for you and me both."

She went back to watching the show via the screen on her cell phone, which she'd taken from me, by the way. "Say what you want, but this is some sexy-ass shit. I'm saving this for later," she said, still recording.

That was disturbing to the *n*th degree, but so like Dez to want to add to her own personal porn collection. She liked the real stuff, none of that fake Smuttywood acting. I knew this because I'd stumbled upon her collection while looking for a decent movie to watch at her apartment one night.

We stood there for a few moments longer, because hell, what else were we supposed to do? I'd moved away from the phone because I couldn't stand to watch any longer. And then I thought I heard a sound from the other room. Curiosity got the best of me, so I pressed my ear against the wall and listened while Polly managed to nudge her way in between me and Dez until we were tits to tits to do the same.

Someone was moaning and groaning, and then, "Yeah, you love the Big Daddy Dick, don't you? Suck it harder, baby. I'm almost there." David's smug voice was disgustingly strained right before I heard another sort of distorted howling sound that could've been either one of the chicks or Scott for all I knew. Either way, it made my skin crawl.

Polly looked a little green in the gills. "Oh, that is just so wrong."

"What are they doing now, Dez?" I whispered across the space. Of course she was still watching, the hussy.

"Duh," Polly said. "They're coming."

I rolled my eyes. "Not that. I mean, now."

"No, she's right," Dez answered. "They are coming. At the same time. How'd they manage to sync that up?" What was worse was that her brows were furrowed like it was a math problem she was trying to solve. I'd bet good money she'd go home and work on the solution to that equation later. After a moment, she said, "Okay, so Sluts-R-Us just went into the back room, which happens to be Scott's personal bathroom. My guess is they're going to scour some of that spunk funk off each other. Tweedledick and Tweedlecum are firing up the puff-puff-pass."

I sank down onto the floor and let my head fall against the thin wall that stood between me and that stupid contract. "This is going to take forever. Noah's going to freak out and think something went wrong if I don't get back soon."

"Wait a minute, hon. Don't go getting all dramatic yet," Dez said, waving me over to see what was happening in the next room from her phone.

"We should probably take advantage of the time we have with them," Scott said, stroking his cock unabashedly until it started to harden again. As quick as that turnaround was, that coke must've been laced with a male enhancement drug. "Pussy like that doesn't come along every day, you know."

"Hell, yeah!" David crowed. He picked up his pants and fished his cell phone out of the pocket. "I'll be there in a minute. I'm expecting a call from the senator, so I should probably check my messages real quick."

As soon as Scott had joined the twins in the bathroom, David put his phone back in his pants and rushed over to Scott's desk. Taking another look over his shoulder, he opened one of the drawers and pulled out a manila folder. He grabbed the paper inside, placed it on the fax machine, and dialed some numbers.

"No, no, no . . . ," I chanted, knowing full well that piece of paper was the contract. *My* contract.

Polly growled. "That bastard!"

Said bastard stood there drumming his fingers impatiently while waiting for the machine to finish up. Once he got the receipt, he shredded it and then replaced the paper and file folder in the desk before practically skipping off into the bathroom to join the orgy no doubt already in full swing.

I hit my forehead against the wall. No way would I be able to keep him from using the contract as leverage against Noah now.

"Cheer up, Lanes," Dez said, a little too chipper. When I furrowed my brow at her crazy talk, she waved the phone in the air. "David Stone is in cahoots with Scott Christopher in both the drug *and* sex trade. It's all right here. I think that makes for a damn good bargaining chip, don't you?"

In that moment, Dez was the sexiest beast I'd ever seen. If she wasn't my best friend, I probably would've thrown her against the wall and shoved my tongue down her throat. She was right. We had all the proof we needed to bring David and Scott down. I wondered how well that would sit with Scott and all of his very influential clients. Not too well, I guessed.

"You should still get the original contract," Dez said. Since when had she become the voice of reason? "I know he's already faxed it, but one contract floating around out there is a hell of a lot better than two."

Good point.

"I'm going," I said, reaching for the door.

"Wait a minute!" Polly whispered harshly, putting her hand on my arm to stop me. "What if you get caught?"

"But if I don't go now, I might not get the chance to get the contract at all," I reasoned. "I'll go inside real quick, and if I don't hear the shower, I'll slip back out and we'll wait it out a little longer."

"Let her go," Dez told Polly. "We can watch from in here, and if she gets into trouble, we'll mount up and ride to the rescue."

"Um, okay." I could hear the reluctance in Polly's voice. "But if anything happens to you, Noah's going to go apeshit on me, so please be careful.".

"Of course." I nodded nervously and then turned the door-knob very slowly.

Once in the hallway, I tiptoed along the wall to the door to Scott's office. I checked the handle, finding it unlocked, and then pushed the door open slowly. My ears picked up the sound of the shower running and I could hear male and female voices from the other side of the bathroom door, though I couldn't tell which belonged to whom.

Hurrying over to Scott's desk, I opened the bottom drawer, where I'd seen David put the folder earlier. And there it was, filed under *T* for Talbot. I pulled it out and flipped it open to grab the contract.

A smile like the Cheshire cat's spread across my face once I had it in hand, then I replaced the folder and tiptoe-ran back across the room just as the shower shut off. I was careful not to make any noise when I slipped out of the door and pulled it closed behind me. Dez and Polly were already waiting for me in the hallway.

I held up the contract and Dez did the same with the phone. I swear, I was just about ready to kiss her on the mouth. With huge grins on our faces, Dez and I did our victory dance. It had been perfected over decades of friendship and really was just us shaking our butts from side to side in well-choreographed synchronization. Polly bounced up and down on her toes while giving us silent applause. And then we headed for the stairs to make our stealthy escape.

Mission accomplished. Maybe not the mission we'd set out with, but accomplished nonetheless.

11

dare to dream

Noah

All Hallows' Eve, better known as Halloween.

Cultures from all over the world celebrated the tradition in one form or another for a great many years. Although they each had their own history, no one really knew who had started the tradition or why, though it was most typically tied to pagan roots. Regardless, it remained a day annually celebrated throughout the world, one that allowed us to party with the dead on the one night they were permitted to cross over onto the living plane. It was all smoke and mirrors, fun at the expense of spooking someone else. Given its traditions and the situation at hand, it seemed apt that the all-important board meeting would fall on October thirty-first, a day where it was acceptable to dress up as someone you were not to play tricks on the gullible.

I was not gullible. But then again, neither was David Stone.

Monday morning came quicker than I thought it would. I was nervous, hoping like hell the plan we had concocted would be a success and not somehow backfire in our faces. Either way, by the time the day was through, the fool would definitely be determined.

And to the victor would go the spoils.

Win or lose, the whole masquerade would finally be over, and Lanie and I could live our lives without the fear of someone finding out about the secret we'd been keeping.

When Lanie had arrived home with the original contract in hand, we'd immediately taken it, along with her copy and my shredded version, and burned them in the same trash can she had used to torch the lingerie. Watching the proof of our arrangement disintegrate into ash was like a weight being lifted off our shoulders. Both of our bodies seemed to relax at the same time once the fire burned out, proof of how much stress it had taken on us physically in addition to the mental and emotional turmoil. Ashes to ashes, dust to dust. We had given ourselves a new beginning and we weren't going to take it for granted. Of course, there was still the issue of the copy David had sent by fax.

Dez had been only too happy to show me the prized video from their excursion. I hadn't known Scott was in the drug biz, but I wasn't surprised by the fact, either. What I was surprised by was David's involvement in the whole kit and caboodle. I'd never had an inkling, but then again, it was one of our investors who had turned me on to the auction. I supposed it made sense that David had introduced him to it in the first place. Still, David had been successful at keeping me in the dark. I was sure it had been a very lucrative business for him. Too bad he'd gotten sloppy.

And he was going to get sloppier still by attempting to expose to the board what Lanie and I had done. Talk about your double standards. Luckily for him, I was going for the mercy kill before it even got that far. He could thank the ghosts of my mother and father. They wouldn't want me to embarrass their friend and partner, David's father, Harrison.

And so there I was on Monday morning, moments away from the board meeting, and Lanie and I were riding my personal elevator up to my office. She had insisted on accompanying me for moral support and all that jazz, and truthfully, I was glad she was there. If, for whatever reason, shit backfired on us, we needed to be able to form a united front—or get the hell out of town in a hurry. I'd heard Alaska was really nice in the spring.

Lanie put her arms around my waist. "Nervous?"

I shrugged nonchalantly. "Nah, just another day at the office as far as I'm concerned. I'm really hoping the board approves of my newest charitable campaign, though."

Lanie turned me around and looked up at me. "I'm sure they will. You worked really hard on the presentation all weekend. That can't be all for nothing, right?"

She smiled, and the reassurance I saw in her eyes set my mind at ease. When she looked at me like that, it gave me a renewed confidence that couldn't be shaken. It was me and her against the world, and by God, I believed we had a damn good fighting chance.

The bell on the elevator dinged and the doors opened to show the hustle and bustle of the office before us. Employees were always on high alert when it came to board meeting days and tried to look even busier than normal. Everyone was decked out in their most professional attire, their expressions all business. A few looked up and gave me and Lanie a small smile in greeting and then went right back to work.

I let out a breath to steel my nerves. Lanie's left hand came to rest in the crook of my arm and I looked down at it, feeling like an ass because her ring finger was bare even though we were engaged. I'd have to fix that ASAP. She was still sporting the Crawford cuff bracelet I'd given her, but it wasn't enough. Marking her as my property back when she actually was, at least contractually, was one thing; symbolizing that she belonged to me by her own choice was something else entirely.

We stepped from the elevator and I escorted her to my office, where she would wait. Board meetings were always closed to the public, so she wouldn't be able to sit in. Plus there was no way I was going to have her anywhere near Stone. She was cool with waiting in the wings because Polly would be there to keep her company. As my assistant, Mason would be in attendance at the meeting, and he would have his phone dialed into Polly's so that she and Lanie could secretly overhear the entire meeting from my office.

"Everything in place?" I asked Mason when we walked inside.

I sat Lanie in the chair behind my desk, and Polly took the one on the opposite side. Like they were planning some undercover sting operation, Mason called Polly's phone and ran a check to make sure everything was a go.

"Yep. You ready, man?" Mason asked me.

I nodded and looked down at Lanie. "Here goes nothing. Can I get a kiss for luck?"

She rose to stand on the tips of her toes and tugged at the lapel on my suit jacket to pull me to her. Her lips found mine and she wrapped her arms around my neck. That kiss was chock full of words that didn't need to be spoken. When she pulled back, she pressed her forehead to mine and looked me in the eye with certainty. "You don't need luck," she told me, "but I'll take any opportunity I can to taste your lips"—as if she didn't have free access to them anytime she got a hankering.

"We're meant to be together," she continued. "So I have no doubt in my mind that everything will fall into place. Besides, you're Noah P. Crawford, and that name screams success."

"God, I love you," I told her, and I fucking meant it.

She smiled, triumphant. "I know, and I love you, too."

From the corner of my eye, I saw Mason lean over and kiss the top of Polly's head. "Let's go, man. Don't want Stone to get suspicious."

"Knock 'em dead!" Polly said with an encouraging smile. Our own personal cheerleader.

I kissed the tip of Lanie's nose and turned her loose so I could grab my briefcase. With a wink, I walked out of my office, Mason close behind.

Part of our master plan was to have Mason call Mandy Peters, David's secretary, to inform her that the meeting had been rescheduled for an hour earlier than originally planned. He'd done that this morning. David would have to rush around like a madman to get ready, but he'd do it, of course, because this was his big chance to bring me down. What he didn't know, however, was that the earlier meeting wouldn't include any of the actual Scarlet Lotus board members.

Mason and Polly had handled the setting up of the boardroom, instead of allowing the administrative assistant whose job it usually was to do it. It was essential to the plan that there be no interruptions. Plus we didn't want to run the risk of someone else overhearing all our personal junk.

Once we got to the boardroom, I saw my plan B sitting in the waiting area outside the door and gave her a nod.

"He's already inside," she told me.

"And our guest?"

"Waiting in the empty office down the hall."

"Good. Keep your ears on in case I need you."

"Will do," she said. As I started to go inside, she stopped me. "Hey, handle that shit in there, or I will. You feel me?"

Plan A was to confront David with all we knew and the proof that could ultimately destroy him. If that didn't work, plan B would go into effect. There was also a plan C, but it was a last-ditch effort, a desperate move that we didn't want to make unless it was absolutely necessary. I hoped like hell it wouldn't come to that.

A simple nod of my head in understanding was all the exchange we needed. Turning the handle on the door, I stepped inside.

I had to hide my snicker when I saw David's bruised and battered face, and I wondered what kind of story he'd made up to explain it away. He was already situated toward the front of the table, next to where his father, Harrison, used to—and sometimes still did—sit at its head.

Harrison had turned his control of Scarlet Lotus over to David, and although he sometimes showed up at the board meetings, it was on very rare occasions and only when something big was on the agenda. I had a sneaking suspicion David had insisted he be present for this one because he really thought he had some shit on me that might finally make him look better in his father's eyes.

I almost felt bad for him.

Almost.

I took my seat across the table from David with Mason at my side. David, the smug bastard, shot me an I-know-something-you-don't-know grin that looked mighty painful considering the split in his lip (courtesy of *moi*), but other than that, he kept his trap shut. It was probably the smartest thing he could've done. I, on the other hand, found it extremely difficult not to launch myself across the table and kill the fucker with my bare hands. In my mind, I kept seeing him hovering over my girl, trying to take something that didn't belong to him, something she had no intention of giving freely. But I kept myself in check. It was time to get this shit over with for good.

His assistant was there, of course, but she shouldn't have been. At least not for the purpose of this meeting. "Get out, Mandy."

She and David looked at each other and then at me before he guffawed. "Did you bump your head or something this morning, Crawford? Mandy is my assistant. She doesn't take orders from you."

I gave him a stone-cold stare. "You and I need to have ourselves a little chat. You like chatting, remember? Only I don't think you're going to want witnesses around for this one."

He laughed. "Have you been smoking crack?"

"Nope," I said, relaxing back in my chair. "Haven't been snorting anything, either."

He flinched, although it was barely perceptible.

"Fine, Mandy can stay. How's Izzy?" I asked with a smirk.

There it was. The slight widening of the eyes, the straightening of his posture, and then the look away. "The board meeting didn't get moved to an hour earlier, did it?"

"Nope."

David cleared his throat and turned to Mandy. "Give us a moment."

Confused wasn't even the word for the expression on Mandy's face. I'd say *clueless* fit it to a T, as that was what she was most of the time, but she got up and did as she was told, like a good little assistant.

"And what about your boy?" David asked, clearly indicating Mason's presence.

"Mason already knows everything. He stays."

"How about you tell me what this everything is?"

"Gladly. But first, do you have my contract with you?"

He grinned and sat back. "That's what this is all about?"

"Wasn't that exactly what you planned to make the board meeting all about?"

"If you pulled this stunt to try to talk me out of it, then you've wasted your time and mine," he said. "But if you're here to wave a little white flag and hand over your half of Scarlet Lotus in lieu of your total annihilation, I might be convinced to accept."

"Oh, I don't think it's going to go down like that at all. In fact, I think you'll be the one handing over your shares before we're done here."

"What do you know about Izzy? Better yet, *how* do you know about her? Have you been talking to Scott?" He couldn't have believed Scott Christopher would rat him out any more than I did. On the other hand, when a ship is sinking, rats tend to hop on board any flotation device they can find to save their own hide. Christopher wasn't plan A, though.

"Show me your hand and I'll show you mine," I challenged.

David sucked at his teeth as he met my stare. His fingers

drummed on the table before him until finally he slid his brief-case in front of him, popped it open, and took out a single sheet of paper. After closing the briefcase, he held up the contract for me to see.

"Here you go, Crawford. Proof that my dick really is bigger than yours," he said with a smug grin.

I'd seen his dick when it was ramming away into my slut of an ex-girlfriend's ass. Not even close.

"So what is it that you think you have on me?" he asked.

"I know you're using cocaine."

David chuckled, the relief in the sound revealing his nervousness about what I'd had to say. "Prove it."

"A mandatory drug test from the board will handle that."

He shrugged. "Fine, but it's nothing more than a slap on the wrist and my promise to get help for my addiction. I'm still sitting pretty, but nice try."

"You tried to rape Lanie."

Again he shrugged. "Her word against mine, and I have proof that she's a whore. Which means all I have to do is tell the police and the board that she told me she'd make that claim if I didn't pay her money. Simple case of blackmail. I'm the victim. What else do you have?"

I had plan B.

"Mason," I said without averting my attention from David.

Mason opened up his laptop, picked up the remote to the projector, and pushed a button. The white screen on the opposite wall lit up with the images of the video Lanie and the girls had recorded from the closet next to Scott's office at Foreplay.

David broke off our staring contest when he heard his own

voice claiming a kickboxing accident as the reason for his ugly mug. I chuckled because that shit was funny.

I looked at Mason and jerked my head toward the door. He nodded and went over to stick his head out into the waiting area. A couple of moments later he swung the door open wide, and in sauntered Dez with Scott Christopher in tow.

Scott came to an abrupt halt just inside the door, his attention immediately taken by the giant white screen playing an action-packed movie with all the right ingredients of a blockbuster: highly illegal business dealings mixed with very amateurish porno action.

Mason closed the door behind Dez because we were way past the line of inappropriate behavior in the workplace. Scarlet Lotus didn't need sexual harassment charges on top of the scandalous activities already well under way.

David bolted out of his chair when he saw Scott. "What the hell are you doing here?" I think it was safe to say he was surprised. And maybe even a little pissed.

If the flexing of his jaw muscles and the clenching of fists at his sides were any indication, I'd say Scott was just as stunned and every bit as pissed. The tension between the two of them was so thick it crowded in like the cramming of a dozen people into a phone booth.

Scott looked at David and then jabbed a finger in the air toward the Oscar-winning performance. "What the fuck, Stone?"

Plan B was looking very promising.

"You tell me! I thought you said your place was secure!"

Scott glowered at Dez, and I wasn't about to have that shit, so I stood up and pulled her behind me. Of course, Dez wasn't going for any of that damsel-in-distress stuff. I'd swear the chick was a dude under that skirt if it weren't for the fact that she clearly was not.

She stepped around me and lifted her chin in defiance. "I recorded that video. Did a pretty good job of it, if I do say so myself. Oh, and I quit. By the way, I'm not scared of you, so if you come after me, you better know I'll monkey-stomp your goddamn ass."

Scott waved her off like she was an annoying gnat. I was pretty sure he actually did consider her to be another inconvenience, one he didn't have time to worry about, which was a good thing. With any luck, he really would leave her alone. The same would not be true for Stone.

My guess was that Scott knew David's arrogance was what had gotten Scott into this predicament in the first place. Scott had to remedy that right here, right now, or else be prepared to go to war with the drug dealers and influential people he was involved with. It was a given that the suppliers of his cocaine were ruthless killers when it came to protecting their commerce, but he couldn't discount the high rollers to whom he sold not only cocaine but pussy as well. Their hands might have been baby soft and clean as a whistle, but their money allowed those same hands to stretch far and wide and hire another pair willing to get dirty for the right price.

"Do you have any idea what will happen to both of us if this gets out? Fuck that. I'm not going down with you. You better fix this shit. Pronto!" Scott turned toward me and put his hands on his hips. "What's he got that you want?"

"Half of my parents' company . . . and Delaine Talbot's contract."

I'd never seen a person's face turn that shade of red before.

Scott's head did this really slow turn toward David that sort of reminded me of Linda Blair in her most infamous role. "You stole the contract?" he yelled.

Naturally, I couldn't have all the yelling. "I'm going to need you to keep your voice down, Christopher. There are other employees here, and the walls aren't really all that thick. Speaking of which, I'm told yours are pretty thin as well. Might want to get that fixed," I said with a wink that went unnoticed because he was still glaring at David with murderous intent in his eyes.

"Oh, stop being so dramatic," David told him, smug as you please. "The contract is safe, and nobody is going to see it as long as Crawford hands over his half of the company. Relax."

I laughed. "Perhaps you missed the memo, David." I lifted my hand toward the screen. "Clearly, I'm in a better position than the chick getting cocaine snorted off her stomach while you stuff your clumsy fingers inside her sister's pussy like she's the Thanksgiving turkey at the crack house down the street."

David smirked. "I'm calling your bluff. We may not be best friends anymore, but we were once upon a time. I know you. You're too sweet on that little girl to let me make a fool of her publicly. Hand over the company and destroy all the copies of this goddamn video, or I'm exposing you *and* her."

He was right. I would do anything to keep the secret of our relationship from the public eye, even if it meant watching Scarlet Lotus be run into the ground by the likes of David Stone. But I still had one more trick up my sleeve.

Plan C it was, then.

"Mason," I said for a second time.

Again Mason got down to business with his laptop, and the

video from inside Scott's office stopped, only to be replaced with a different scene. This one did more than make my skin crawl. It made something not altogether human take shape inside me. I couldn't watch, but there was no escaping the sounds of the conversation that had taken place right before the assault. At first Lanie was pissed and David was smug. When she laughed at his proposal, he was the one who got pissed. And then he tried to force himself on her.

My body shook, fists clenching, jaw ticking, leg bouncing. I wanted to kill him. He was in my sights, a big fat-ass bull's-eye practically tattooed on his already battered face. The worst part about that moment was watching him sit there expressionless while taking it all in. There wasn't an ounce of remorse in his whole body. When Lanie screamed, I couldn't take it anymore.

"Turn it off," I told Mason, who did so as quickly as he could, but not before the scene where I burst through the door and grabbed David to throw him off my girl.

"Kickboxing accident, huh?" Scott asked. "Dude, you're sick. I can't believe you did that."

"Oh, don't act all self-righteous with me, you prick!"

"What the bloody hell have you done now?" A new voice entered the conversation, and we all whipped around toward the sound. Harrison Stone stood in the doorway with that authoritative look that said we were all in trouble.

In front of his iconic father, David gaped like a fish out of water. "Pop, it's not what it looks like."

Harrison waved his cane at his son. "Oh, save it. I already saw everything. Drugs, whores, attempted rape . . . Jesus, son. What do you do for an encore?"

"I, um . . ." David paused for several seconds then finally closed his mouth. No way was he going to be able to talk his way out of this one.

I wished I could've claimed Harrison's early arrival as part of my plan, but I couldn't. As Robert Burns said, the best-laid schemes of mice and men often go awry. Sometimes we just need to leave it all up to the universe to right the wrongs.

Just then Harrison turned toward me, a wide smile on his face, and took my hand in a firm grip. "Noah, my boy! How the hell are ya?"

I couldn't help the affection I felt for the man. He was my father's partner, his best friend, and he was family. How he had spawned someone as devilish as David was beyond me.

"I'm good, Harry," I answered, and because I just couldn't resist, I added, "Finally met the woman of my dreams and somehow managed to convince her to be my wife."

The look on David's face was priceless. He hadn't heard about our impending nuptials.

"Well, ain't that a kick in the pants! Congratulations, son!" Harrison clapped me on the back a couple of times, and his strength would've knocked me on my ass had he not had a death grip on my hand still. "I damn sure better be on that guest list," he warned.

Then he said more soberly, "It's no secret my boy's been trying to pry your parents' legacy from your hands. I haven't exactly been an avid supporter of that, but he's got a thick skull," he said, knocking on his own. "Can't get a lick of sense through to him."

David growled in frustration. "You founded this company. It's my legacy, too."

"Shut up, boy. Noah senior and I founded this company together. It was all *his* idea. And I can see you're busting at the seams wanting to tattle something on Noah, but I think I'll let him tell on himself." He turned back to me. "What's he got on you, kid?"

As embarrassed as I was to admit the truth, I knew it would eventually come out anyway. Better it be to Harrison than to the whole board, shaming the memory of my parents.

"I bought a virgin, and then I fell in love with her." The admission was quick, like yanking off a Band-Aid. And you know what? It didn't hurt nearly as much as I thought it would.

Harrison didn't look thrilled, but he didn't look disappointed, either. Kind of indifferent, in fact. He shrugged. "And?"

"And isn't that enough?"

"Let me ask you something, son. Is she worth all this?" He waved his cane around, indicating the shit I was having to put up with from his son.

"Yes, sir, she is," I said, meaning it. I'd endure David Stone on a daily basis for her if I had to. And then it clicked, as if I'd just put the last piece of the puzzle into place. I *didn't* have to. Lanie was all that mattered. My happiness was the only thing my parents ever wanted for me. And it was probably something David Stone would never have. With that realization fresh in my mind, I turned to David. "You can have—"

"Hold on, now," Harrison said, interrupting me. "Don't be so quick to throw in the towel, Noah."

"What are you doing, old man?" David asked, flabbergasted. "You don't have a say in any of this."

"The hell I don't. I still control those shares when you get right down to it. All it takes is an announcement from me to the board and you're out of here. You're an embarrassment to the company, and you're an embarrassment to me. I won't stand for your shenanigans any longer. Grow the hell up."

Harrison leaned over the table and took the contract from a stunned David, who couldn't react fast enough to stop him. He looked it over for only a second before handing it to me.

"Do you have any other copies?" he asked David, who did nothing but shake his head. "Good." Then he turned toward Scott. "Why the hell are you still here?"

"I have a stake in all this, it seems."

"And what would that be?"

Scott nodded toward Mason's laptop. "A video that can never see the light of day. If it does, me and your son are dead."

"If I can guarantee it won't, will you swear not to ever have anything to do with my son again?"

"I can do that. I don't want any trouble. I have my own business to tend to."

Harrison turned to me with his brows raised in a question. I nodded my acquiescence. I wasn't going to get everything I wanted out of the deal. As long as I had Lanie safe and sound, I'd let karma handle the rest.

"The video will be destroyed. Now get out of here, you're stinking up the place."

Scott wasted no time finding his way out. I didn't blame him. Harrison had this Clint Eastwood type of way about him that dared you to overstay your welcome.

"It seems the scales are now all tipped in your favor, Noah," he said, turning back to me. "What is it that you'd like to do now?"

"He bought a *whore*!" David yelled, clearly agitated by the turn of events.

Harrison lifted his cane to silence him. "One more word and I'll disown you." He turned back to me. "Noah?"

I looked up at the ceiling, seeing way past that to whatever great beyond was out there. This was for my parents. All of it. Because of the relationships they had forged in life, they were still looking out for me even in death. I would not allow their memory to be tainted, and that included their legacy.

I dropped my head to see David Stone in a whole new light. I almost felt sorry for him. Though his father was one of the greatest men I'd ever know, David had never seized the opportunity to learn from him. But he'd threatened everything I held most dear, so I couldn't pity him.

"Listen to me, David," I seethed quietly. "Not only do I have the ability to release your little personal porno to the public and destroy you, but that video shows evidence of drug *and* human trafficking, and let's not forget the other video of an attempted rape. You could spend a very long time in prison."

Dez leaned in and added, "And FYI, a big Mexican named Chavez already has you on reserve, bitch."

Harrison had apparently just noticed her for the first time, but judging by the look on his face, he was impressed. Dez had that effect on people. No doubt he'd be asking her out.

The expression on David's face reminded me of a cornered rat who had nowhere to run, no hole to dive into. "What do you want?" he spat through clenched teeth, clearly not liking the fact he had no other option than to admit defeat.

I gave him the same smug smile he had been wearing every

day since I'd found him in my bathroom with Julie. And then I metaphorically reached out and snatched the little bit of cheese his tiny paws had been clutching. "Not much, just your half of the company. Seems like a small price to pay for your freedom. Don't you think?"

"How do I know you won't expose the videos anyway?"

"You don't," I answered truthfully. "But as much as it pains me to do so, I give you my word. As long as you hold up your end of the bargain, I'll hold up mine. You can thank Delaine for that. She's far more forgiving than I could ever be."

"Or me," Dez interjected.

"What's it going to be, Stone?" I asked.

"Fine. It's yours. It's all yours," he conceded.

"Meeting adjourned," I mumbled triumphantly, and then led Dez and Mason out of the boardroom so I could go collect my winnings.

David's half of the company was only an added benefit. Delaine was the real prize—one I had every intention of savoring, and none whatsoever of squandering.

~$~

"I still can't believe it's really over," Lanie said from the passenger seat of my Lamborghini as we drove down I-55 toward Hillsboro.

It had been nearly a week since the board meeting, and with all the drama we'd survived, we needed a break. Hillsboro was quiet enough to afford us that break while also allowing Lanie a visit with her parents. She thought we were going to get a hotel room. I didn't make her think any differently.

"It's over, kitten." I brought our joined hands to my lips and kissed her bare left ring finger before giving her a crooked grin.

"Aw, there's the cottage," Lanie said when we came upon it.

When I released her hand so I could downshift and pull into the driveway, her brow furrowed—until she saw the expression on my face and knew I was remembering the last time we had been there.

"Noah, no. We're not about to do that again."

I said nothing as I opened my door and got out of the car. When I walked around to her side and opened the door, she had her arms crossed over her chest defiantly. "No, Noah. We can have all the sex you want at the hotel, but not here, not again. We almost got caught last time."

"We won't get caught," I assured her, then took her hand, pulling her from the passenger seat.

She came with me reluctantly. Linking my fingers through hers, I walked her around to the back of the house and kept going toward the pond and the gazebo.

"What are you doing? Are you insane?" She was frantically searching our surroundings for any evidence that the neighbors had seen us.

"Yes, as a matter of fact, I am." I pulled her up onto the gazebo step and walked over to the swing. "And it's your fault. You make me crazy."

I turned her so that her back was to the swing and lightly pushed down on her shoulders, encouraging her to sit. The sun was setting over the horizon and the orange and pink glow cast by its rays spilled over the perfect features of her face. The little family of ducks swam in an S-shaped pattern to the other side of the pond, their quiet quacks the only sound infiltrating our surroundings.

I kneeled in front of her, noting the confused look on her face. "I want to give you everything you desire, Lanie. Past, present, and future. And I will. I feel terrible for not doing this right in the first place," I said as I pulled the navy-blue velvet box from my pocket.

She gasped and put her fingertips to her mouth. "Oh, Noah."

"You know, for being the future Mrs. Noah Crawford, your ring finger sure does look bare." I smiled up at her and then opened the box to reveal her engagement ring.

It was a one-of-a-kind original, designed for one woman, but handed down to the next in what I hoped would be a very long line of tradition. Three carats of diamond clusters were set in platinum that was intricately woven in loops and swirls around a central emerald-cut sapphire. Nothing too extravagant; simplicity was its allure.

I took it from the box and reached for her shaking hand with a smile. "It was my mother's, and now I'd like for it to be yours."

I slipped it onto her finger and looked into her eyes. Tears gathered and spilled down her cheeks. Her smile was the most beautiful I'd ever seen, and I wished I'd hired a fucking artist to be there to capture the moment in all its infinite glory, forever immortalizing it in time.

I gave her a tender kiss. "I love you, Delaine Talbot."

"I know. I love you, too," she whispered, and then she looked down at the ring on her finger. "It's so beautiful. Thank you."

"You're welcome, but there's more," I told her with a devilish grin as I stood.

Her head snapped up. "More? What more?"

"Come on," I said, taking her hand and pulling her to stand as well.

I felt like I was dragging her along, and I probably should've slowed down some so that she could keep up better, but I was too damned excited to show her the next surprise. When we reached the Lamborghini, I turned and kept going toward the front door.

"Where are you going? Someone's going to call the police on us!" She tugged on my arm to get me to go back toward the car.

I pulled a little harder on her hand, forcing her to collide with my chest as I wrapped my arm around her. "Calm down, woman. Nobody's going to call the police on us," I said with a chuckle, and then I brought my hand from behind her so that she could see what I held: the key to the cottage.

It only took a second for that to register. She looked toward the front yard, finally noticing that the For Sale sign now had a Sold banner over it. "Noah, you didn't."

I could feel the smile tug at my cheeks, unable to not show how proud I was of myself for giving the woman I had fallen madly in love with the home of her childhood dreams. "Welcome home, Lanie." She stood there stunned while I put the key in the lock and opened the door.

As soon as I'd returned home from dropping Lanie off at her folks' house all those weeks ago, I'd made the deal on the cottage. It had been as good as sold, but when I offered four times the asking price, the owner had practically fallen over himself to accept my offer. Polly took over from there. I thought for sure she was going to spill the beans to Lanie, but I was damn proud of her for managing to keep her big mouth shut. And she didn't even go overboard on the decorating.

I took Lanie's hand and guided her over the threshold, closing the door behind me. Walking over to the mantle above the fireplace, I picked up the remote and pressed the button to set the gas logs ablaze.

"What do you think?" I asked when she still hadn't said anything.

She looked around. There had been some slight remodeling done, but I'd insisted that all the quaint nuances Lanie had gushed about were to be left intact. The floors had been stripped and polished and the furniture was all new, but earthy and plush. Every amenity she might ever want or need was there, complete with huge floor pillows that littered the space in front of the fireplace.

But Lanie still hadn't said anything, and that made me nervous.

"You don't have to keep it like this. I had Polly decorate it because I didn't want it to be empty when I showed it to you. You can redo everything if you don't like it."

She turned and closed the distance between us. "Shut up, Noah. You talk too much." She grabbed me by the shirt and yanked me toward her for a kiss that made my toes curl.

And she didn't stop there, either.

Her tongue—so soft, so pliant—moved against mine, sweet like cotton candy. I held her to me, taking all that she gave and giving more in return. Her body molded to mine, and the way she moved against me . . . Oh, God, the way the woman moved was maddening. She had come to me a virgin, with no sexual experience at all. And although my original intention had been to teach her everything I liked, her real teacher had been her own body. She knew what she wanted, and all inhibitions dissolved when it came to getting it. And by answering her own body's demands, she was answering mine.

Her nimble fingers drifted down the center of my shirt, freeing each button as she passed over them. She never broke the kiss, didn't come up for air. She didn't need to; every breath we took fed off the other's. Her hands slid inside the opening of my shirt and pressed against my bare chest. Every muscle in my body went taut at her touch. When she finally broke the kiss, I felt the loss instantly, but her attention went to the side of my neck, and that was pretty damn okay, too.

Supple lips pulled and sucked at the skin there as her tongue tasted me. I pressed Lanie closer, meeting her questing hips and rubbing the bulge in my pants against her center. She moved to my chest, her tongue swirling over one very hard nipple while cupping the flexed muscle on the other side. And then slowly she moved her hands over my shoulders, pushing my shirt free to slide down my arms and onto the floor.

When she turned her attention to my other nipple, I weaved my fingers through her hair. Chills ran down my spine when I felt her fingernails scrape against my abdominal muscles to the waist of my jeans. She pulled at them, forcing me even closer, and then I felt her hand stroking me through my pants with the perfect amount of pressure.

"Kitten . . ." It was all I could muster through my heavy breathing, as I was trying desperately not to lose my shit before my cock had even been freed from its prison.

She kicked her shoes off and I found my hands at the hem of her shirt. My thumb caressed the bare skin beneath, but it wasn't enough. So I lifted the shirt over her head to let it join mine on the floor. She was stunning in the frilly blue bra she wore underneath, the creamy mounds of her breasts spilling over the cups. I palmed them, squeezing and kneading through the thin material, the way I knew she liked it. My thumbs swept over her hardened nipples and she bit the skin on my chest in reaction. Yeah, she liked that. So much so that the button on my jeans popped open and her hand slipped inside for skin-to-skin contact.

I hissed when the heel of her palm swept over the head of my dick. "Christ, Lanie."

"You're so hard," she said in lust-filled amazement. She moved her hand against me as much as the tight confines of my jeans would allow.

I looked down so I could see her hand shoved down the front of my pants because I knew it would look fucking hot. I was right. The head of my dick was poking out of the top of my waistband, and apparently she saw it, too, because she quickly took her hand from my pants and knelt before me. Her hot little mouth was all over the tip, greedily devouring it. My balls tightened instantly and I had to grab the tops of her arms to pull her up before I shot my load right there.

"You gotta slow down, or I'm not going to last very long," I warned, holding her at arm's length.

A sultry gleam illuminated the baby blue of her eyes, and she pushed against my hold to tug on my pants. "I don't want to slow down, Noah. I want you. I want to feel you, thick and hard inside me. I want to taste your come sliding down my throat. I want to feel your lips and tongue on my pussy. I want it all, Noah. I need it all, and you promised you'd give me everything I wanted or needed."

"Fuck," I groaned at her dirty talk. It was a weakness, and she knew it. She had me wrapped around her little pinky, knew how to work me just the right way, how to twist my words to work in her favor. And far be it from me to go back on my word. It was as good as gold—and damn it all if I didn't want the same exact things she wanted. Except I had one more gift for her that was sure to make our evening together so much more pleasurable.

"Wait, Lanie. I have something for you," I told her as I reached into my pocket.

"More? But Noah, you've already given me a house and a diamond ring . . ."

I gave her a wickedly evil grin as I brought my hand to eye level and released my fist to let the string of pearls I was holding unfold. "Diamonds may be a girl's best friend, but pearls are a hell of a lot more fun," I told her with a waggle of my brows. She looked confused, but it didn't matter. It was merely a matter of minutes before she saw, or rather felt, for herself.

I grabbed Lanie and yanked her hard against my body, my mouth crashing onto hers as our lips met, our teeth clashed, and our tongues tangoed in a hard, hungry kiss. I sank to my knees on the floor pillows and she followed, never breaking the kiss. Her hands were everywhere, sweeping up my chest and over my shoulders to slowly drift along my biceps. I flexed them for her, knowing she loved it, and she moaned into my mouth.

While she was enjoying feeling me up, I made fast work of

her bra, snapping it free to push the straps down her arms and toss it to the side. Her round, firm breasts pressed against my naked chest and my lips found the spot where her neck met her shoulder. She moaned when I ran the pearls over her hardened nipples and sucked at the skin of her neck. Leaving the pearls for a moment, my fingers deftly released her jeans and pushed them over her curvaceous hips.

I kissed along the length of her neck to the spot below her ear and cupped her ass while taking the pearls and exploring her beautiful mound with my fingertips and the satiny smooth roundness of the pearls. The slightest of pressure from the beads teased her, made her beg for more until I pressed harder, rolling them around her swollen clit. She gasped and dug her nails into my back as she sucked and nipped at my shoulder. It drove me crazy.

I pulled back to look at her, my cock becoming impossibly harder as I watched the expression on her face tell me everything I needed to know but still wanted to hear. "Is this what you need, kitten?"

She confirmed my suspicion with a breath, "Yes, more."

"How about this?" Sliding my fingers and the pearls between her wet, silky folds, I coated them in her juices.

She moaned and nipped at my shoulder again while rolling her hips forward. "Mmm, more."

"So greedy, Delaine," I murmured against her ear, and then I took her lobe into my mouth, just as two of my fingers found her opening and pushed the pearls inside to give her exactly what she wanted.

She gasped and her head fell back, giving me ample access to her throat. I ran my tongue along her jugular and inhaled deeply. The scent of her arousal mixed with the light perfume she wore, and I licked my lips, suddenly feeling feral and starved.

"I can smell you, Delaine. Your arousal smells so sweet, so enticing." I pushed more of the strand of pearls inside her. She moaned, undulating and helping my progress until the task was complete. Moving my fingers back and forth at a slow pace, I used the pearls to stroke her G-spot while my thumb applied the right amount of pressure to her little bundle of nerves. She pressed her hips forward, begging for even more still.

"Feels good, doesn't it, kitten? You like it when I fuck you with my fingers?"

"Yes. Oh, God, yes." She spread her thighs as wide as her pants would let her and moved against my hand. "Give me more."

"More? Like this?" I pumped my fingers inside her with the pearls. She made this sexy little sound that made me want to rip those pearls out and shove my dick deep inside her. She was slick and silky soft, and I thought I was going to lose my mind. "Fuck, kitten. You're so goddamn wet. I need you to lie back. I want to see."

Lanie held on to my shoulders and I slowly lowered us until she was lying on the floor pillows. She protested with a pouty groan when I removed my fingers from her to pull her pants the rest of the way off. I needed to see all of her, watch as I worked my fingers inside her. She spread her legs for me, an eager invitation to do as I pleased with her. And I would.

Her wetness glistened in the light of the fire, the string of pearls hanging from her opening to entice me even more. I licked my lips in anticipation of tasting her, but I pushed my fingers back inside her to stir the pearls again. "Fuck, that's a beautiful pussy, Delaine. And it's all mine."

Without warning, I hooked the strand of pearls and slowly pulled on them. A low groan came from my girl, growing louder still with the roll of her body. I nipped at her hip, entranced by the sight, but no longer able to help myself. So I ripped the strand out of her all at once.

"Oh, God!" Lanie came, her body arcing off the floor. For a moment I thought maybe I'd hurt her, but she bit down on her lip hard to stifle a keening moan.

My fingers found their mark, plunging inside her to stroke the slightly rough patch of her G-spot, pushing her orgasm to extend beyond measure. She moaned and arched her back, and I leaned over and took one pebbled nipple into my mouth. My tongue flicked over it, back and forth, my teeth grazing it, oh so tenderly.

"Harder, Noah," she pleaded breathlessly.

I complied, on both ends. Thrusting my fingers in and out of her, sheathing them all the way up to the knuckles, I sucked and pulled at her nipple with my teeth. Her answer was a hard tug on my hair. I fucking loved the rough stuff, and she knew it.

"I need you inside me now." She rolled her hips against my hand. "Please?"

Yeah, I felt her pain. I needed to be inside her, too, couldn't stand not being there any longer. And that kind of pissed me off because there was so much more I wanted to do with her, but I figured, fuck it, we had the rest of our lives, so I pulled my fingers out of her.

Holding my weight up on one arm, I unzipped my pants and pulled my cock out. My lovely assistant swept her hands over my ass, pushing my jeans down enough to allow me movement. I should've taken the time to take them off, but the moment was there and I wasn't about to press the pause button.

Lanie was eager, lifting her hips, but then I decided a little teasing would be fun. So I rubbed the head of my dick along her slit and then pressed it to her clit while rotating my hips. She moaned loudly when she looked between us to watch the head of my cock rubbing against her. I loved to torture her, build up the anticipation, so I slid it back down, pressed forward at her entrance, and then pulled away again to repeat the cycle.

"Please, Noah . . ."

Yeah, I liked to hear her beg for my cock.

I smirked down at her. "Please what? You want me to fuck that beautiful pussy?"

She nodded and bit down on her lip, her chest rising and falling. To further drive home her point, she brought her knees up and held on to my ass with both hands to undulate beneath me. Yeah, that was enough of that shit. My woman wanted cock, she was getting cock. I looked between us and pressed the head of my dick to her entrance, slowly pushing into her. We both moaned out our pleasure at finally being joined, and I couldn't help myself—I wanted more of that feeling.

"Goddamn, that feels good, doesn't it?" I asked her. "There's just nothing quite like the first time I push into you. The way your pussy grips my cock—so hot, so soft, so wet. That feeling . . . it's second to none. Let's try that again, shall we?"

I watched when I pulled out of her. Her juices coated my cock, and her opening, having stretched to accommodate my girth, melted back to the tiny hole it had been before I'd infiltrated it. It was an amazing sight to behold.

The glint of wetness on the pearls to my side caught my eye and a wicked idea formed in my head. I picked them up and wrapped them in a single layer around my cock, making it ribbed, for her pleasure. Lanie grinned at me when she saw what I'd done, the look in her eye reminding me once again of the night we'd traded tit for tat and I'd taken her virginity. She was game. And I was horny as fuck.

I pushed forward again, watching the head of my dick disappear as she stretched to take me in. My eyes rolled to the back of my head when I felt the pearls shimmy along my shaft. If the sound Lanie made at the same time was any indication, I'd say it was as good for her as it was for me. Knowing that, I couldn't stop my hips from surging forward as I buried my entire length inside her. She squeezed my ass in her hands, holding me there while she undulated beneath me, rubbing her clit against my groin.

I encouraged her, wanted her to do what came naturally, because that was what got me off. "That's it, kitten. Do what feels good to you. Use my body for your pleasure."

"You're so thick, so hard," she moaned. "I love the way your cock feels inside me. And those *pearls* . . ." She growled the last word, her eyes closing in total bliss.

Fucking A. My million-dollar baby had turned pro on me.

I pulled back and slammed back into her. "Like that?"

She dug her nails into the cheeks of my ass. "God, yes! Faster."

Moving inside her with five quick thrusts, I gave her what she wanted, and then I stilled, completely sheathed. I rotated my hips to give her the friction she needed against her clit. Plus it did some pretty amazing things to my cock when those pearls rolled around like that.

She moaned. "Oh, Christ . . . just like that. Don't stop."

I pulled back and rolled my body, pushing back into her over and over again. I managed to find a steady pace that was neither too fast nor too slow. She rocked against me, meeting each push and pull of my hips with her own. The pearls worked me, she worked me. The way her hands gripped my ass and her walls tightened around me as I moved back and forth inside her was indescribable.

"Noah, I'm going to—"

"Do it," I moaned, still moving inside her. "Let me feel that pussy squeezing my dick." My cock grew impossibly harder with each thrust, my own orgasm building and building until I thought my balls were going to explode.

"Right there, kitten. Right there," she keened, and then I felt the familiar pulsing of her walls around my cock as she cried out my name with her orgasm.

I quickened my pace, thrusting harder, deeper, helping her to achieve every single plateau of her climax. I couldn't take my eyes off her. She was beautiful in the soft glow of the fire. A light sheen of sweat coated her creamy flesh, her lips were bee-stung and cherry red, and her eyes were closed with their thick lashes caressing the soft skin beneath as she let it take over and carry her away.

"I'm the luckiest man in the world," I whispered, and then I leaned forward to taste those luscious lips.

Once, twice, three times I nipped at her mouth. My cock

slid in and out of her, the pearls rolling along my length. Her breasts pressed against my chest, her lips licked at mine, her fingers clung to my ass. It was too much.

"You feel so good, Lanie. I can't hold on much longer," I warned her. "I'm going to come all over that beautiful pussy of yours."

Lanie shook her head and then looked me in the eye. "You've denied me too many times. I won't let you deny me again. Come in my mouth, Noah. I want to taste you."

"Shit . . . I don't know if I can hold out . . . feels . . . so good," I warned, doing my best not to come.

"Give it to me, Noah. Fuck my mouth," she demanded.

I pulled out of her, reluctantly, but like I'd said so many times before, I wouldn't deny her anything she wanted. She may have started out as my sex slave, but I had become hers.

I made quick work of removing the pearls and then straddled her chest, my cock bobbing and soaked in her juices when I brought it to her mouth. Running the tip across her lips, I coated them in her own come. "Taste me, Delaine. See what my cock tastes like with your juices all over it."

She opened her mouth and I pushed my cock inside. Her lips closed around my girth and she hummed in appreciation, savoring our joint flavors. I held the back of her head and thrust my dick in and out of her mouth.

"Do we taste good, Lanie? Do you like the way you taste on my cock?"

She answered with a moan and then grabbed my ass, pulling me deeper inside her mouth. I could feel the back of her throat pressed against the head of my dick, and she swallowed, constricting my cock. That was all I could take.

"Fuck, kitten! Fuck, fuck, fuck!" I called out as I pushed

even deeper still and my cock pulsed with each spurt of come that shot down the back of her throat. With each gulp she took, I could feel more constriction. She slowly bobbed her head back and forth, milking me until I went flaccid in her mouth.

"Goddamn, woman, that's enough," I chuckled, forcing her to let go of my dick. "You keep that up and I'll be hard all over again."

"And what's so bad about that?" she asked.

Swear to God, I fucking loved her.

I dismounted her chest and lay next to her, pulling her body over mine like a blanket so she could rest her head on my chest. Her left hand was on my stomach and I looked down at it. The stones of my mother's engagement ring caught the light of the fire and reflected a rainbow of colors. It had finally found a home.

I had finally found a home. Which reminded me . . .

"So you never did say," I started. "Do you like the house?"

Lanie lifted her head and looked at me. A slow smile crept across her face. "You know I do."

Yeah, I did.

"But I'm just not sure how all this is going to work," she continued, drawing patterns on my chest.

"How what is going to work?"

"Well, you have the house in Oak Brook and now we have the cottage as well. Where exactly do you plan for us to live?"

"Yeah, about that," I started, suddenly feeling like an ass for not having discussed any of this with her beforehand. In my defense, I had planned to talk to her about it after showing her the house, but then one thing led to another and . . . well, there we were. "You know how David is signing over his half of the company to me?"

"Yes . . ."

"Well, Mason has been so loyal to me over the years, and knows the ins and outs of the company so well, that I thought I'd make him my partner."

"Noah, that's wonderful!" she said, her eyes alight with joy. "Polly is going to absolutely flip her shit!"

I laughed, knowing she in fact would.

"Wait a minute, though," she said, settling back down. "What does that have to do with where we're going to live?"

"Oh, right," I said, getting back on track. "It really doesn't have anything to do with where we live, but eventually Mason's going to be controlling most of the things that will require a constant presence at the office. So that means we can live wherever you want. If you want to live here on a permanent basis so that you're closer to your folks, I can set up an office here and work from home."

"But Noah, your parents' home . . . that's all you have left of your family," she said, her voice sounding heavy.

I hugged her to me and kissed her forehead because I wanted to, and because she was still being selfless. "You're my family now, Lanie. And I plan on us having lots and lots of beautiful little Lanies in the future. And maybe at least one Noah to carry on the Crawford name."

Her brows shot up, her eyes widened, and a broad smile spread across her face. "Babies? You want babies?"

"Mmm-hmm. Lots and lots of babies."

"Well then," she said thoughtfully, "we're going to need an awfully big house to accommodate all those babies, don't you think?"

I shrugged. "I suppose so."

"And Polly is going to need someone around to keep her

busy while Mason is working long hours at the office. Otherwise, she's just going to be all over his ass for not being around as much."

"Probably," I agreed.

"My mom's better and Dad's back to work. And Dez has been looking for a place to stay in the city as well . . ."

I knew what she was getting at. "Kitten, are you trying to tell me that you want to live at the Crawford estate?"

She got a guilty look on her face. "Is that terrible of me? To not be jumping at the chance to live so close to my parents?"

"Not at all. You can visit them anytime you'd like. After all, we have a quaint little home here as well. Christmas, Easter, a little summer vacation, whatever. We don't need a reason to drop everything and come for a visit."

"Plus, we don't have a nosy neighbor guy back in Chicago. And you don't have to shirk your responsibilities at Scarlet Lotus, either," she said.

"Hey! I take offense at that," I teased playfully, tickling her side.

"I'm kidding! I'm kidding!" she laughed.

"So, Chicago?" I asked, wanting her to make the final call.

She nodded. "Chicago it is."

"Good," I said, satisfied with her decision. I forced her to roll over so that I could rise up on one elbow and hover over her with a devious grin. "Now, let's get started on making those babies."

I leaned down to kiss her, but she placed her fingers between our lips. "I had that contraceptive shot, remember? I can't get pregnant right now."

I shrugged. "Doesn't hurt to practice."

She giggled and finally relented, letting me kiss her long and hard as the fire crackled in the background. That was the way I wanted it to always be between the two of us: carefree laughs, erotic lovemaking, happy and free. Free of cheating exes, free of backstabbing friends determined to see us ruined, free of feeling like you're the only one who can save the life of someone you love and taking drastic measures to do so. Free of that isolated feeling of living alone.

It wasn't exactly the same dream that every other red-blooded American had, but the foundation was the same: someone to love, someone to care for, someone who wanted nothing more than to do the same for you in return—someone who had your back come hell or high water.

And we would have that dream. I'd make damn sure of it. I wasn't so naïve that I thought everything would be perfect. We'd have our own small battles to fight, but in the long run, we'd win the fucking war.

We would have our happily ever after.

epilogue
bringing sexy back

Lanie

It was the eve of the second anniversary of the day my life had been turned upside down, inside out, and spun round and round, sending me in a new direction. Two years since the day I had put myself up for auction in a nightclub called Foreplay that traded women to men of wealth and power in exchange for a hefty payment.

The other women in my group had done it for their own reasons. I had done it to save a life. My mother's life, to be specific.

Two million dollars was what I'd gone for. Auctioned off to the highest bidder, Noah Patrick Crawford, CEO of Scarlet Lotus. He would own me for two years, use me to satisfy his every sexual need as he saw fit.

That man would teach me how to suck a cock properly. That man would give me the first of many orgasms, introduce me to my inner Cooch—and she to the King of Fingerfuck, the Ridonkabutt, the Assterpiece, the Wonder Peen. That man would pop my cherry, turn me into a wanton hussy, and rock my ever-loving world. That man would infuriate me to no end—in and out of the bedroom—and then ride in on his white horse to save the day.

That man was now my husband.

And the father to our daughter, Scarlett Faye Crawford.

Scarlett was the apple of her daddy's eye. She'd been born less than a year after we married. In fact, I had been pregnant with her at our wedding ceremony and hadn't even known it. I was certain I had conceived our daughter the night Noah gave me my engagement ring.

His mother's ring.

That night will be forever etched in my mind, its perfection so blindingly glorious in every way. He had offered the precious diamond to me as well as his heart, his everything. He belonged to me, and I belonged to him.

Surrounded by the walls of my dream cottage—the house I'd secretly coveted as a child—our life had begun anew. We'd whispered our desires and our dreams, and yeah, we'd made love like there was no tomorrow. It was hot. It was magical. It was perfect.

He had told me that night that he wanted lots and lots of babies. And I was more than happy to oblige. Scarlett was the first of many more to come.

Yes, she was spoiled. She had everything imaginable—clothes, toys, books—and lacked for nothing. But more important than all of those materialistic things, she was loved. Loved by people who doted on her every whim, every fancy.

She had almond-shaped eyes the color of precious sapphires framed by lush dark eyelashes. Creamy soft skin to sprinkle our kisses on, thick chocolate ringlets that begged to be brushed and adorned with bows and ribbons, and a smile that could make the masses bow at her feet. We were all under her spell from the moment she took her very first breath.

But Scarlett was a daddy's girl through and through.

Don't get me wrong—she loved her mommy, but Daddy was the hero in her book. She was wrapped around his little finger, and he was wrapped equally as tight around hers. So was my father, Mack. I couldn't even begin to tell you about the jealousy that raged between those two over her attentions. Mack was her Pappy and threatened to sue for grandparent visitation rights one weekend when Noah had "thoughtlessly" planned to take Scarlett to the same toy store that he wanted to take her to without first checking with him to see if he ever had any intentions of doing so.

Confusing? Yeah, I thought so, too.

It was ridiculous how they fought over the child. Always trying to one-up each other in the gifts they bestowed upon her or places they took her. I was pretty sure Mack would even have taken out a second mortgage on my childhood home in an attempt to keep up with Noah's abundant wealth.

Eventually the rest of our family and I had decided an intervention was in order. That had been a week ago. I mean, seriously, Scarlett had enough love in her tiny, fist-sized heart to go around, and it wasn't fair for them to constantly put her in the middle. Auntie Dez, Gammy, Aunt Polly, and I had left with her for the week to go visit Aunt Lexi and Uncle Brad in New York, leaving Daddy and Pappy to stew at home by themselves. They'd needed the time-out.

The week we'd spent in New York was fun, but I'd missed my husband. And, okay, I'd missed his many assets as well. I wasn't talking about his ridiculous fortune, either. Loaded down with yet more goodies for Scarlett and a new wardrobe for myself—Polly, Dez, and Lexi; need I say more?—we headed home.

By the time we returned, Noah and my father had bonded through their mutual misery over Scarlett's absence. As for me, what was I? Chopped liver?

But my pique lasted just a few moments. After a brief greeting and many repetitions of *Daddy missed you so much*, Mack swiped Scarlett from my arms and ushered my mother out the door. She was theirs for the weekend.

And I was Noah's.

No sooner had the door closed than I found my back pinned against it and a very eager husband pressed against the length of my body with his hands flattened out next to my head. His face was only inches from mine and I could feel the warmth of his breath as it fanned out over my face. Slowly his lips came closer to mine.

"Don't ever fucking do that to me again," he said, and then his lips were on mine, fierce and demanding.

He wasn't angry, not in the least bit. Just really, really horny and desperate for some release.

Um, yeah. Me too.

"I missed you so fucking much," he mumbled into my skin as he directed his attention to my neck.

The Cooch agreed. She'd missed him as well. In fact, I distinctly heard the sounds of some sort of bonchickawahwah music playing in the recesses of my mind. She was blowing the dust off her knee-high red leather boots and blue unitard, stopping momentarily to contemplate Noah's black tie and those black wraparound heels we knew he was particularly fond of.

As if it mattered in the least.

His hand was under my skirt, cupping my already drenched center. His fingers stroked and probed as only those of a skilled King of Fingerfuck could. The other hand was kneading my breast, rolling the hardened nipple between his thumb and finger. And that colossal cock was grinding against my hip.

The Cooch gave him a finger curl and a sultry whisper: *Hey there, big boy. Why don't you come on over here and we can talk about the first thing that pops up?*

Double Agent Coochie was most definitely a hoochie.

As for me, on the other hand, I decided to play hard to get. During my pregnancy with Scarlett, our sex life had become somewhat vanilla. All because Noah was worried he'd hurt the baby or me somehow.

Anyway, once she was born, it just sort of remained that way out of habit, only there was less of it. Sure, we had stolen quickies and rushed releases in the shower, and none of which was any less mind-blowing, but that raging inferno of lust that we had shared at the beginning of our relationship had dimmed to a slow burn. I wasn't complaining, but I missed the tit for tat, the challenge, the part where one of us said, *Let me get you real good and pissed off and then fuck the shit out of you so that you remember who owns you.*

And I was going to get it back.

With as much conviction as I could muster, I shoved him in the chest, pushing him away. He looked up at me, confused and a little wounded. But I gave him a wink and what I hoped was a sexy smirk to clue him in on my game.

"Screw you, Noah! Do you know what tomorrow is?" I snapped.

Again with that confounded look.

"I can see you don't, ass!" I said, lifting my chin indignantly as I stalked toward him. "It just so happens to be the two-year anniversary of the day we met. The day you bought me for two million dollars to be your sex slave so you could do whatever you wanted to me, however and wherever you wanted to do it, because you're a sick bastard who gets off on dominating me for your own pleasure. You've loved forcing me to bow to your will, lording me into submission just because you had enough money to do it."

I stood nose to nose with him—so to speak, since he was taller than me and all. My girls were pressed against his hard chest and the heat rolled off him in waves.

"Lanie, I—" he started, but I cut him off.

"My name is Delaine! You don't get to call me Lanie!" I snapped.

And there it was, the lightbulb. I could see that he had gotten it at last, and judging by the arrogant smirk that spread across his face, he was game to play.

He grabbed a fistful of my hair and yanked my head back while cupping my ass and pulling me against him roughly.

"Well, if our little contract expires tomorrow, I guess I'd better make the most of my last night of ownership," he said. My nipples strained against my shirt at the reemergence of Noah the sex god. "I must warn you, this won't be nice. It'll be hard and rough, but you will love every minute of it. And you will do as I say because I own every inch of your body. Your fuckable mouth, your tight little pussy, your forbidden ass—they all belong to me, and I will fuck them how I see fit, if I see fit to do so. You are here for my pleasure, just as I am here for yours. Have I made myself clear?"

"Quite," I snarled back at him. "Let go of me! I hate you."

"Yes, but you love the way I fuck, don't you?" It wasn't a question. More like a statement of fact.

He released the hold he had on my hair and took a step back. "On your knees, Delaine." He tugged on his belt buckle. "I've had a very trying day and I'm in need of the stress management that I know you give all too well."

"Here? In the foyer?" I asked.

He shot a hard look at me, lifting his eyebrow as if to say I had some nerve to question him. "Did I stutter?"

The Cooch gave me a mental high-five, and then she pulled out her mini DVD recorder and started filming, yelling, "Quiet on the set! Action!"

In one swift movement, Noah had shoved me to my knees and the colossal cock was sprung from its prison and waving a long-time-no-sucky-sucky at me. And I was pretty sure that was a tear on the slit of his head.

By all means, let me kiss that tear away, Your Colossalness. After all, big boys aren't supposed to cry, and my oh my, you are big.

Noah let out a hiss when my tongue came out and swept up the drop of pre-come on his tip. The corners of my mouth twitched triumphantly, and I proceeded with my torture. I gave him an openmouthed kiss, and then let out a greedy little moan as my lips wrapped around his head and I sucked hard.

"Fucking shit, goddamnit," he growled, yanking my head away by my hair.

I would be lucky if I wasn't bald by the time he was done with me.

He looked down at me, his voice deep and husky. "Oh, you want to play dirty, do you? I can do dirty." His words slithered through the air and lapped at the sensitive spot between my thighs like a serpent's tongue. "Seems you need a little reminder of who's in control here, Delaine."

He grabbed the base of his dick with his free hand and bent at the knees to push the head past my lips. "Stay just like that," he ordered. "I'm doing the fucking here. You do the sucking."

Holding on to my head with both hands, he started thrusting in and out of my mouth, showing no mercy and pushing in as deep as the confines of my mouth would allow, which meant he was hitting the back of my throat. Truthfully, I was struggling to keep up. Noah's cock hadn't exactly shrunken over the last couple of years. My mouth was stretched open as far as it could go, but I still managed to apply some pressure with my lips, curling them in around my teeth to keep from shredding his glorious cock.

"Harder, Delaine. Suck me *harder*," he ordered in a growl that shot straight to my girly bits and caused them to start doing a little tearing up of their own. Seriously, I needed a drip pan or something for all the basting the Cooch was doing.

His hips surged forward, hitting the back of my throat and giving me a little more than what I could comfortably take. I gagged, the motion causing my throat to tighten around the head of his dick. Noah shouted a string of profanities and pulled out of my mouth, yanking me up to my feet. His mouth came crashing down on mine in a ferocious kiss.

With the strength and speed of a superhuman, he threw me over his shoulder and took the stairs two at a time. He didn't stop until he'd reached our bedroom, kicked the door open, and thrown me on the bed. Shoes and clothes went flying across the room as he undressed us both with urgency. And then my hips were lifted off the bed, my legs thrown over his shoulders, and my neck bent at an awkward angle as Noah's face plunged between my thighs—right where I wanted it.

"Oh, God!" I cried out at the feel of his lips, tongue, teeth. He was eating me alive, and it was the most delicious feeling in the world.

His fingers spread my folds open, the fleshy pink of my hidden treasures exposed as the pads of his fingers worked my clit in circular motions. It was an erotic performance of his extreme capabilities, and I had a front-row seat to the show. I saw and felt his tongue push into my opening, long and thick as he stroked me from the inside out. Then his fingers smacked at my pleasure nub, spanking it in quick succession with the perfect amount of force.

"Noah . . . please," I begged, squirming as much as I could given his crushing hold. I bucked my hips forward, wanting more, even though his face was completely buried in my pussy. He held my lips open and sucked at my clit, his tongue making quick flicking motions over the hardened bud. Then he sucked my clit into his mouth again, hard, pulled back on it, and let it go with a pop. Once again he sucked it in and pulled back excruciatingly slowly before letting it go and eyeing it while licking his lips.

"Your pussy is the sweetest in the world, Delaine. And it's mine!"

I loved his possessive nature, but keeping in character, I felt it necessary to remind him of one thing. "Just until tomorrow, asshole," I said, my voice dripping of defiance.

Noah bared his teeth and growled at me, his face contorted in anger—he was an exceptional actor. None too gently, he lifted me from the bed and pinned me against the wall with his body.

His lips were at my ear, hot breath panting heavily. "You'll be banging down my door within two days, begging for my cock," he said while gripping my ass and lifting me off the floor.

"Not bloody likely," I seethed back even as I wrapped my legs around him.

In retaliation, Noah sank his teeth into the tender flesh where my neck met my shoulder. Hard and unforgiving, he thrust his hips forward and entered me.

I cried out in pleasure, throwing my head back against the wall. My face scrunched up and I clenched my teeth, welcoming the raw, primal feeling. It was exactly what I wanted, what I needed.

"Yeah, you like that, don't you?" he said with a smirk as he wound my hair around one hand and held me with the other. He pulled out and slammed back into me, the force of his thrust pushing me up the wall with a jerk.

"You fucking love my cock," he snarled, punctuating each word with a rigid plunge that went deeper and deeper inside me. "You can try to deny it all you want, but you and I both know I own that pussy, Delaine."

I dug my nails into his back, holding him to me as the power from his thrusts drove me up the wall and back down again. I buried my lips into the crook of his neck, sucking and tasting the salty sweat of his passion mixed with fury.

This was my Noah. This was the man who could drive me to the brink of insanity and then yank me back before I had a chance to fall over the edge. And then he'd do it all over again until finally he let me go and I plunged into the stormy sea of orgasms that raged below the jagged cliff.

Fucking Noah was an extreme sport. And oh, what a rush it was.

I came, calling out his name as he grunted with each surge of his hips. And then my body was a wet noodle in his arms.

"I'm not done with you yet." His voice was demanding, assertive. He pushed our entangled bodies from the wall and carried me over to the couch. That couch was where he'd first fucked my mouth, and a montage of frames from that encounter flooded my thoughts: Noah standing over me, dominating, with one foot propped up on the couch while he pushed and pulled his cock in and out of my mouth.

The Cooch hit rewind and showed it to me all over again with a devilish smirk on her face.

He pulled out of me and flipped me over onto my stomach, his hand pressing down on the center of my lower back while the fingers of his other hand dipped inside me and curled in and out. Then he pulled them free, sliding the slick evidence of my orgasm through the valley that extended to my ass, entering and coating my other opening with the natural lubrication my own body secreted.

I was one hundred percent game, but I was also still very much in character. I shot death glares at him from over my shoulder and sneered, "Don't you fucking dare!" The shameless shift of my hips toward him was a complete contradiction to my words, so he knew what I really wanted.

"I told you, Delaine. I own every inch of your body, and I will have what I want," he said as he moved his fingers in and out of the forbidden entrance. "And what I want right now"—he leaned forward until his lips were once again at my ear—"is to fuck this tight ass."

His voice softened a bit and he kissed my cheek. "Are you ready, kitten?" No amount of role play in the world would prevent him from making sure I was okay. My comfort level was always most important to him.

I nodded and arched my back, offering up what we both wanted.

"Good girl." Slipping back into character, Noah rose back into his previous position and sank to one knee behind me while propping the other on the couch.

I felt the pressure of the head of his cock at my entrance and then he was inside me, pushing ever so carefully as he sheathed himself and moaned at the pleasure. Noah and I had done this many times since our first, usually only on special occasions, so it wasn't nearly as painful as it had been the first time. In fact, it was really quite pleasurable.

I lifted myself up on one elbow and pushed back into him, but the pressure of his hand on my back stopped me from going any further. "Easy, woman. Always so eager." I could hear the smirk in his voice, and his insistence of treating me like a fragile piece of china was grating on my nerves.

"Are you going to fuck me, or are we going to stay here all day like two dogs knotted up?"

His hand came down hard on my ass with a loud smack and a tinge of pain. If he hadn't been holding me in place, it could have been disastrous, considering the precarious position we were in.

"That was a warning, Delaine. Now hold still or I might decide not to be so easy with you."

I turned my face into the armrest of the couch to hide my grin, because yeah, that was hot as sin.

Going back to his business, Noah spread the cheeks of my ass and I imagined the look of concentration that must have been on his face as he ogled the sight, trying for all his worth not to let his control slip. He pulled back a little bit only to roll his hips forward a fraction further than where he had been before. His groans and my moans intermingled in the air between us and had a little make-out party of their own. He repeated the movements until the muscles in my body, rigid at first, relaxed, giving him the cue he was waiting for before moving more freely.

"Goddamnit, that feels so good." His voice was breathless, tightly controlled, as he moved in and out of my ass.

With one hand on my hip and the other slipping around to manipulate my clit, his pace quickened. Deep, throaty grunts echoed throughout the room and his thrusts became more insistent. The sound of skin slapping skin joined in on the party, making an orgy out of our sexcapade, even though we were the only two invited. I was moaning and keening like a seasoned porn star, and the Cooch was getting it all on tape.

"Right there, kitten," he groaned when he found an angle that was preferable.

But I was on the edge again, and even though I'd already come once, it just wasn't right for him to dangle the proverbial carrot in front of my face without letting me have a little nip of it. "Don't you dare stop," I said, and Noah kept going, pinching my clit between his fingers even as the telltale moans of his impending orgasm built in his chest.

"Don't stop. Don't stop. Don't . . . stop . . . ," I called out as I came yet again.

I should have known he wouldn't leave me hanging. That was not Noah Crawford's style at all. He *always* satisfied.

I hadn't even reached the peak of my orgasm before the rumble that had been percolating to the surface within Noah's chest reached its boiling point, forced its way up his throat, and exploded from his lips in a string of profanities. His thrusts were uneven, jerky, and insistent as he held me immobile and used my body to milk himself dry of his semen.

My body, numb and devoid of energy, collapsed onto the couch. I struggled to catch my breath. Every muscle coiled in preparation when I felt Noah's movement behind me and I knew he was about to pull out, which I never found to be all that pleasant. He made fast work of it, though, and then his body was covering mine. Always the attentive lover, he showered every inch of skin within the vicinity of his lips with chaste kisses.

"I really fucking love you," Noah said between gulps of air. "I'm so glad I didn't bail out on that auction and leave you to Jabba the Hutt."

I giggled and smacked at his bare thigh. He laughed at my halfhearted attempt.

"You were worth every penny I spent for you and more. Happy anniversary, Delaine."

"Yeah, right back atcha," I managed to say playfully between labored breaths.

Double Agent Coochie and the rest of her filming crew— the Assterpiece, Ridonkabutt, and the Wonder Peen—gave us a standing ovation. No, the film wasn't real, but what Noah and I had just done was yet another memory reel to add to the collection that made up our lives together. I was lucky enough to be able to cue them up for instant replay anytime I wanted, and I did so often.

What started out as a woman's desperate attempt to save her dying mother had turned into a love story for the ages. Hollywood wasn't likely to buy the rights to our story, and we would never find our names in lights, but we were a smash hit in our own world. And that was all that mattered.

acknowledgments

My decision to publish the *Million Dollar Duet* did not come quickly or easily, but I'm glad I did it. Obviously, this page is dedicated to acknowledging those people who gave a little bit of their blood, sweat, and tears to help me make that happen. So let's get on with it, shall we?

First and foremost, I simply must thank my incredibly talented friend and mentor, Darynda Jones. If it hadn't been for you, this adventure would have taken an entirely different direction. I am convinced people are put into our lives for a reason. Lady, you were put in mine to help make my dreams come true. I love your luscious face.

I still can't believe how lucky I am to have scored my very remarkable agent, Alexandra Machinist, and my extraordinary editor, Shauna Summers. You are two of my most favorite people in the world. Thank you for taking a chance on me.

Huge thanks to my prereaders: Patricia Dechant, Melanie Edwards, Maureen Morgan, and Janell Ramos. You are my anchors, my sounding boards, and my biggest cheerleaders. Love you. Mean it.

A special shout-out to my street team, Parker's Pimpin' Posse, and most important, my loyal readers, thank you. I wish

I could call you all out by name because it is your support that keeps me doing what I'm doing.

Last, but not least, I must thank Abyrne Mostyn, because diamonds may be a girl's best friend, but pearls are so much more fun.

Thank you all. FLYAS!

C. L. PARKER is a romance author who writes stories that sizzle. She's a small-town girl with big-city dreams and enough tenacity to see them come to fruition. Having been the outgoing sort all her life—which translates to "she just wouldn't shut the hell up"—it's no wonder Parker eventually turned to writing as a way to let her voice, and those of the people living inside her head, be heard. She loves hard, laughs until it hurts, and lives like there's no tomorrow. In her world, everything truly does happen for a reason.